THE IRONY OF BEING

By
Emily Kunz

ISBN: 978-1-7358575-1-0

For my mom, who has read everything I've written with pride in her eyes.

PREFACE

⁓

The one lesson of substantiating value that my mother taught me when I was young was this: The only ones who ever win in life are the ones who have tried every possible method to achieve their goals.

As with every limited occasion when my mother offered her words of wisdom, I soaked in that piece of advice like a sponge and have stuck to it ever since. To me, the woman who raised me was incomprehensibly powerful, an indomitable force of nature.

Now, I suppose that many children feel this way about their parental figures, regardless of who they are as people. But at that time in my life, amidst blessedly untouched innocence, those words were the only things I had to teach me anything about rising to the top. So I've done it: tried everything to achieve the various goals throughout my life.

And the funny thing is, as I sit here now, I can finally see the barriers I have built and the destruction I have created. I have succeeded, yes. Succeeded brilliantly. I think I must believe, in the end, that this is all that matters. All I have accomplished must be worth the consequences. At least, this is what I tell myself. For if I didn't, I truly would lose all the sanity I have left.

1
MADELINE

The most important thing to know about us Blairs is that we find success with just about everything, no matter what gets in our way. When any of us have goals, we find a way to accomplish them. That is, after all, the sole purpose of our lives.

I, Madeline Blair, have probably accomplished more and lived a grander lifestyle by the age of seventeen than most people have in twice that time. My life has accelerated at a rapid rate since I was young—much like a rapidly escalating roller coaster. I simply have yet to see the downfall of that roller coaster.

My father taught me how to read when I was eighteen months old, and now I have a 4.2 GPA because of my high grade in AP English.

My mother ingrained in me a fiercely competitive spirit, starting with my first lacrosse game when I was four. Now, I'm at the top of my class and in the close running to be valedictorian next year.

Jenavieve, my older sister, taught me all the keys to charm and popularity. As she is five years older than me, she had me wearing clothes and makeup by the time I was ten that none of my peers had yet, but would in time.

Basically, my life was set up by those around me to be successful in every way possible: Academics, appearance, and social life have all been smooth sailing. And while I'm extraordinarily grateful for my family's assistance in my accomplishments, a strong part of me wishes I'd done some of those things on my own.

Jenavieve's life, too, was shaped by those most involved in it. For instance, I think she could have made it as a makeup artist.

But it's no wonder that she is graduating from Harvard this year and then continuing with law school. Prestigious education and law school run in the family. And besides, my father has always said that it is of utmost importance to not mask your potential with unattainable and unrealistic personal desires (like, I don't know, being a makeup artist).

Thus, my sisters and I have received the best education in Malibu and have been drilled since a young age to work as hard as possible—all so that we can live up to our full potential of being overwhelmingly wealthy, prominent public figures like our parents.

My dad: Big-time lawyer, often traveling for cases, does a lot of work for celebrities. My mother: CEO of Detail, an immensely popular social media-based company dedicated to exploiting celebrities' personal lives—with an uncanny knack for unwavering accuracy. She once single-handedly exposed Leslie Banks, a famous actress, for fraud, robbery (I mean, really, what sort of multi-millionaire steals?), *and* an affair, all making the same headline. My mother is ruthless, and also badass.

Together, my parents are a force of nature, an inherently wealthy and socially elite pair. They go to the best parties, know the most sophisticated people, frequently dine with the hottest celebrities. They maintain a perfect public presence and practice impeccable social etiquette. As their children, this means that Jenavieve, Ashley and I must, too, be perfect by default.

Jenavieve has always been natural at it all. She can laugh at the right moments, make comments both innocent and wise beyond her years, stand with straight posture and flit breezily from one socialite to another at parties. Because of that, I suspect she has always been my parents' deep-down favorite. She appears in the public eye to be nothing less than perfect, and she's a natural at it.

I myself am fairly good at not being a family embarrassment, I suppose. Mostly, I try to be obedient and do as my parents say. For years, I tried imitating Jenavieve, but I eventually realized that I am substantially more awkward than she is and will never have the uninhibited social ease she projects.

It takes more effort for me to be the upper-class social princess. I think it's because it doesn't appeal to me. As much as I appreciate all the privileges I've had growing up, the idea of following in my parents' structured, money-making, methodically precise way of life doesn't attract me. But I do know that, as a representative of James and Evelyn Blair, I must keep up the act. So I manage.

Ashley, on the other hand … well. She has a mind completely her own.

2
ASHLEY

It is not that I dislike my family. Although my repeated disordinance and lack of family values may state otherwise, I do love them all. The unfortunate truth is, however, that I can find no way to relate to them.

I am the third and final Blair child. When I came into the world, my parents were at the height of their careers and working exceedingly long hours. Maybe I lash out so much now because my mother was too busy with work when I was an infant to hold me and calm me down when I was upset.

Not only were my parents thriving with their careers, but they already had two other young daughters. Honestly, I don't know why they had me. I figure it was a mistake, and that doesn't bother me. In fact, I hope I wasn't planned, because if they seriously wanted to bring me into an environment of such little attention, my opinions of them as people would significantly drop.

Of course, I'm glad we have money. But that's about the only thing I can say I've really liked about how my parents have raised us. And not even what they do with the money. Just the money itself.

Because what they do … oh, what they do with the money. It's all about using their wealth to project an elegantly elite social dominance over everyone else.

The multi-million-dollar Malibu pad with sleek surfaces and an infinity pool. It may sound like every kid's dream, but it's not so fun when you're not allowed to touch anything in the living rooms, must maintain your own bedroom's spotless white interior, and can't add a splash of color or personality to any visible surface.

"Impairs the welcoming nature of our home," is my mother's response whenever I ask her if I can hang up some of my artwork on the wall or, God forbid, put some family pictures on top of the baby grand.

I guess the sharp edges and spotlessly sleek interior of our home are welcoming to all the judgemental and money-oriented snobs that my parents invite over constantly. But ask any of my friends, and I think they would all prefer board games strewn about and the smell of home-baked cookies as opposed to 24-karat-gold chandeliers and mahogany hardwood floors.

I figure that Jenavieve and Madeline adapted to my parents' ways because they realized it would be the easiest way to live a secure lifestyle. After all, the voracious appetite of human nature normally craves stability and security. Something about how my mind works just lacks that craving.

Of the three of us, Jenavieve best embodies the Blair legacy. She is the epitome of social grace and family obedience. She had a 4.0 GPA all through high school. Pre-law at Harvard, somehow graduating a few months early. Impeccable appearance and attendance at every social event. Easy smile, the right questions and comments. She lacks all awkwardness, all streaks of rebellion. She is the perfect poster child.

And the most peculiar thing about her—to all of us, I think—is that there is nothing wrong with her. You take a real look into people, and you can always find something dark within, some deep imperfection. But not with Jenavieve. She is completely, undeniably perfect.

3
JENAVIEVE

"My name is Jenavieve, and I am *not* perfect." Four years later, and I can still remember saying those exact words to him.

It was a crisp Friday night, early in my freshman year at Harvard. My friend Harper was throwing a party that most freshmen would inevitably be kicked out of. She was two years older and had an older brother who lived in a house off campus. He was conveniently gone for the weekend. Thus, she wanted to limit the number of freshmen spilling alcohol and leaving a mess all over her brother's house.

I, however, knew Harper. She had been my group leader during Orientation Weekend, and we had immediately clicked. If it hadn't been for that random assignment of leaders to incoming freshmen, I wouldn't have met Harper, so I wouldn't have been invited to that party in the first place.

So many people think my life is this blessed, glamorous sea of connections and popularity. In reality, the glamour of my life has merely been attributed to fortunate outcomes of randomness.

Of course, I was slightly nervous to go to Harper's party. Being surrounded by a bunch of older, more confident students was an intimidating concept. Harper, however, was convinced that everyone would love me and that this was the perfect time for me to make my "debut."

"Jenny, hon'," she sighed, "my friends are all going to love you. You're smart, gorgeous and mature. I've been telling them all about you all week, and they can't *wait* to meet you. You'll fit right in with us, I promise."

Having a group of friends, people here at this big new school who could take me under their wing ... it was an opportunity that I couldn't pass up. So I dressed up, put on makeup, did my hair and went to the party.

With the aid of a slightly drunk Harper, I made my way through the rooms of her brother's house, being introduced to everyone as "Jenny, the cool freshman I've been telling you about." It took me some time to feel comfortable among them all, but eventually I realized that they could accept me as one of them, so I started acting like one of them.

They liked me. They, like Harper, thought I was charming and fun and full of life. For maybe the first time, I felt valued for more than my biological link to two highly successful figures in Malibu.

It must have been around two o'clock in the morning, and I was a bit buzzed, more from the energy of the night than the effects of the drinks. I found myself outside, alone on the second-floor balcony. The night air was crisp and refreshing, and I felt satisfied and invigorated by the success of my night.

Leaning against the railing, I glanced contentedly around the neighborhood. Most of the lights in the houses around me were out, shutters drawn. But not here. This place was still filled with light and that kind of rare energy created by youthful human connection.

I was so content, so lost in it all, that I didn't hear him open the sliding glass door and step onto the balcony. It was only when he spoke that I knew I wasn't alone in my observations of the little universe around me.

"Pretty quiet out there, huh?" The sound of his voice made me startle momentarily, but I quickly regained my composure and turned my head to see him.

Tall, muscled, quiet and observing. Close-cropped curly hair, dark skin, dark eyes. He was the sort of intensely attractive person you usually only conjure in your own mind. Except he was standing right in front of me.

"I'm Max," he said, ambling over and leaning against the railing next to me.

"I don't think Harper introduced us, but I'm—"

"Jenny, yes, I know," he interrupted with a slight chuckle. Out of the corner of my eye, I could see his mouth slightly upturned, his impossibly long eyelashes.

"Harper's been telling all of us about you," he continued. "Saying how perfectly you'd fit in here with us despite being a freshman. Gotta say, I didn't really believe it. The whole perfect thing."

He paused for a moment and glanced over at me. I looked back, just watched him watching me with a look of genuine fascination on his face.

"But I stand corrected," Max shrugged. "The way you just owned it in there. They all respect your confidence, and because they respect you, they like you. So. I just wanted to say, congratulations, Jenny." With a slightly amused expression, he slowly turned and sauntered back to the door. "Harper was right. You fit in just perfectly, which makes you, well, pretty damn perfect."

There was something irritating about his tone of voice, the amused cadence of his comment, his assumption that I was the perfect poster girl everywhere I went. I couldn't let him get away with it.

"Actually," I said loudly enough to make him pause. "My name is Jenavieve, and I am *not* perfect."

For a moment, he just stood there in the doorway, back turned to me, not moving. And then he laughed. Of all of the things, he started laughing. A deep chuckle that made his whole body shake.

"Really? What's so funny now?" I glowered, nostrils flared.

Finally, he turned to face me, and on his face was a grin that made my heart skip a beat, and still does.

"Oh, nothing," he continued with that smile of his. "Just that you said, you know, that you're not perfect? With just enough conviction that I might actually believe you."

4
EVELYN

Creating Detail and marrying James Blair are tied as the pinnacles of my life. Unlike my husband, I didn't come from a family of extravagant wealth. Or really, any wealth at all.

I grew up on the outskirts of Los Angeles, geographically close to the center of media and moguls, but nowhere close to all of the fame and fortune. My mom raised me alone, which is what kindled in me a deep desire to never raise my children alone.

Never letting up, always doing schoolwork, I did what I had to do to create the glamorous future I desired. Secretly, I always wanted to be well-known and financially successful because I lacked both of those things as a child.

Because I enjoyed school and knew from a young age that my mother couldn't afford to send me to college, I worked hard to earn scholarship money.

After hours upon hours of applications, standardized testing and interviews, I opened my mailbox one humid day in the spring of my senior year to find an acceptance letter from Pepperdine. Full-ride scholarship.

I wish I could say it was more difficult for me to leave my one family member behind, but in all honesty, my deep desire to escape my life of lower-class mediocrity won out against my emotional ties to my mother.

Once I found myself living in Malibu, a cesspool of beauty and money, I was driven to work that much harder to build a life for myself. I had found a place I admired and didn't want to leave or feel distanced from. I almost immediately loved Malibu, and I wanted Malibu to love me back.

By the time I was twenty-three, Detail had been created and was running off the meager amount of money and experience I had. It was a small, print publication at the time, but it was something. It was a start.

I knew that in order to grasp a wide audience's attention, I had to give them content they wanted to know about. And, like me, the majority of people wanted to know about those they both envied and admired.

I had a few strong connections—mostly within the world of the spoiled celebrity children I pretended to enjoy at Pepperdine—which I used to feed me information about famous figures. I then published the information, only using what no other major publishing company or magazine had revealed yet.

Gradually, I got better and better at uncovering celebrities' secrets, and I learned how to find people who were deep on the inside and could be hired for a sizable profit.

I also got better at becoming ruthless. Some friends had to be fired, some very personal information about people's lives had to be shared on Detail. I finally realized that to succeed, I couldn't hold back in any aspect.

From there, my company grew rapidly in the public eye, as my employees and I seemed to come up with fresh and accurate new content day after day.

Thus, by the time I was twenty-four—one year after Detail was launched—the cheap publication I had started just out of college was worth $10 million.

Finally, my life had taken off the way I had wanted it to since I was a young and yearning adolescent for whom fame and fortune was an illusory vision. I was constantly being interviewed and was a guest at several high-end parties before realizing I could throw my own.

It was during one of my parties in Malibu that I met James. He was a year older and had just graduated from law school at Harvard. Having grown up in Malibu, he had wanted to "return to his roots" and was employed at a firm near my apartment.

After talking to James for less than ten minutes, I was smitten. He was tall, dark-haired, handsome and endlessly charming. And he seemed to think everything I said was interesting and fully fascinating.

His attentiveness touched something deep inside me that had not been breached before that point. Someone was finally taking me, and all the work I had done, seriously.

It didn't take long for us to fall in love. We were two young, successful, bright people who fed off each other's energy and devotion to both our work and each other.

In the winter after I turned twenty-five, we were married in a beautiful sunset service on Zuma Beach in Malibu, the place that had captured my heart before even James had.

A year later, I gave birth to our first daughter, Jenavieve. She, unlike me, was born into a life of comfortable wealth and security, and nothing brought me more satisfaction than that.

And now, I have my three beautiful, brilliant, independent children. Detail has long since made the move to the internet and is worth ten times more than it was when I was twenty-four. The parties and events are more frequent in number and greater in extravagance.

My life is exactly the way I had always wanted it to be. Most people have at least some quiet discontent about *something*, but I don't. My only wish is that I could say the same about my husband.

5
JAMES

I used to believe that Evelyn was the one person who would make me the happiest I could be. When I married her, she felt like the final piece in the puzzle of my developing life, and I felt sure that my wife was everything I didn't already have but desperately wanted in my life.

And then I held Jenavieve for the first time, and I saw just how easy it is for love to expand beyond your wildest expectations and imaginings.

After experiencing the overwhelming surge of love and emotion that only arises after holding your first baby for the first time, I think something in me changed. I saw that there was room for expansion in my life. There was room for more.

Of course, my family's life is probably the most "more" anything can be. When Jenavieve was two, we bought our beachside home filled with windows and accessorized with an infinity pool. People are over all the time now, and the parties Evelyn throws are teeming with people and luxuries.

My job as a lawyer has escalated to primarily working for prominent celebrities, which means Evelyn has that many more people to invite over, and that many more people to expose on Detail. These people are smart enough to know who she is and the depths she'll go to to expose them, but being invited to Evelyn Blair's parties apparently means more to them than getting exposed all over the internet the next day.

The downside to working for so many celebrities is that it means I'm often in Los Angeles, where the majority of them live.

Missing out on a substantial part of my kids' lives is difficult, but I'm confident that they can continue to thrive without me.

My wife has grown even more beautiful with age. Her company is flourishing, her home is beautiful, her friends are plentiful ... and the kids. The best thing we ever did was raise such fiercely confident, uninhibitedly motivated and independent children.

Jenavieve is graduating from Harvard this year and continuing with law school. Madeline is excelling in high school, and universities are already reaching out to her. Ashley, too, is exceedingly intelligent, and has a fierce and independent spirit that can't be tamed.

Finally, there's Elizabeth. She may be different from the rest of the Blair family, but she is just as important to all our lives, including my own. And she is something else entirely.

6
ELIZABETH

I may not be a biological member of the Blair family, but they are mine as I am theirs.

When I was a newborn, I was left on the porch of the Blairs' home in a pink onesie and a wicker bassinet. Slightly unconventional for our modern times, I know. But I figure my mom was young and scared, and she thought a glamorous couple with a huge house and stable careers would make for great parents.

It would have been so easy for Evelyn and James to just take me to CPS, which would have moved me around varying foster homes indefinitely. But they didn't do that. Instead, they brought me inside, set up a nursery, and let me live as one of them.

Well, not *exactly* one of them, but that is completely understandable. In exchange for my education, the big bedroom overlooking the ocean, and all the other privileges I have, I just have to work a bit.

The work isn't strenuous in the slightest, and I enjoy doing it. It's the least I could do for the family who accepted me as practically one of their own. Really, I just cater the parties, cook meals, and drive Madeline and Ashley around when they need a ride.

And in return, I get a safe and beautiful home with safe and beautiful people. I'm not even a year older than Madeline, so the two of us have been very close since we were infants. Madeline's first word was even "Lissie," and the nickname has stuck between the two of us.

We used to pretend we were twins, dressing alike and insisting that I wasn't actually many months older. In our fantasy, Evelyn and James were just keeping our twin status a secret.

The game lasted for most of our childhood, until I started working more and it became clear that I wasn't Madeline's twin sister. But it didn't stop us from being best friends, and Madeline still treats me like her twin.

Jenavieve was always like my older sister, giving me advice and looking out for me. So we were close in a different way than I was with Madeline, and it was hard for me when she left for Harvard. But it's such a great place for her, and she deserves all the happiness and success that school can give her.

Ashley and I have had a harder time connecting. Despite all my efforts to talk to her, she doesn't reciprocate, and it's clear she's not my biggest fan. Madeline insists that it's just a side effect of Ashley's rebellious nature, but I sense it's something deeper.

I've always tried my best to be there for her, though, and I think she sees that. I hope she knows she can come to me for anything, and I'll always be waiting with open arms.

Evelyn and James have been great to me, and they're incredible role models. But they're both not around very much. With James usually traveling and Evelyn usually working, the only time I really spend with them is when we're planning events or parties.

All in all, though, it's a beautiful life. When I consider the many bad paths I could've been sent down had the Blairs not accepted me into their home, I'm filled with an overwhelming wave of gratitude.

No matter how much I ever do for that family, I will never be able to repay them for the kindness they've shown me.

So, the most I figure I can do is show them that I love them and appreciate them endlessly. No matter what, they're my people. And I will do absolutely anything for them.

7

Another therapy session. I don't particularly like these. The therapist tries to wring all the emotions out of me, which I'm not keen on.

She sits in front of me now. Deep-set eyes peering over her glasses at me. Waiting for me to answer her question. We've already been through all the pleasantries. How are you feeling today. What has your day been like. Isn't the weather nice.

And now, she expects me to actually start talking. After everything I've done, I should be able to answer any question this woman throws at me. But I'm so closed off from everything and everyone that this task, this task of really talking to someone, feels more than I can bear

Then again, I've already borne much more than I ever would've imagined.

She says my name. Tries unsuccessfully to awaken me from my nostalgic and deprecating stupor.

I twirl the bracelet on my wrist. Fidget my feet. Tap my fingers idly on the table.

"Why are you here?" she asks.

I answer only because I know she won't let me leave until I do. And I answer honestly. I promised myself I would always be honest. Out of all the failures of my life, I won't let this be one of them.

I sigh. Raise my head and look her straight in the eye. "I am here," I say, surprised by the assuredness in my voice, "because I am an absolutely terrible human being."

8
MADELINE

∽

"Madeline, people are going to be here in five minutes! Please come down!"

Over the sound of my mother calling me from downstairs, I can hear her stilettos clicking furiously about as she perfects every last detail before the guests arrive.

I take one last look in my vanity mirror. Center my silver necklace, tuck a strand of honey-brown hair behind my ear. Adjust the straps of my purple dress. There's really only one person I care about at any of these parties, so there's no reason to spend hours upon hours perfecting my appearance.

Leaving my room, I poke my head in next door. Of course, Ashley is lying on her bed with her headphones in, seeming oblivious to the fact that she's expected to start socializing with all of Malibu and beyond in four minutes.

Sighing, I cross the room and pull a headphone out of her ear.

"Hey!" she shrieks.

"Ashley, c'mon. People are about to be here. We've gotta go downstairs." I'm about to throw in the fact that these events mean more to our mom than most other things, but then I figure that will only further Ashley's desire to *not* join the party.

21

Descending the stairs, I meet, as always, the once-over my mother gives me before each public appearance. She must be satisfied today, because she smiles quickly and pauses her running about to say, "You look great hon'!" She then resumes whatever it was she was doing before I came down.

I find Elizabeth at the kitchen counter, arranging cheese and crackers on a platter. "Mind if I steal one?" I ask her.

"Oh no, go ahead! I doubt anyone will care, considering this display is already bad. Hopefully the guests don't notice."

I laugh and pop a piece of cheese into my mouth. "Lissie," I say, disobeying the no-talking-with-food-in-your-mouth-ever rule, "it looks great. And you know they'll all be paying much more attention to the bar than the cheese."

She laughs knowingly and goes back to arranging her cheese. It's a little disheartening to me how many people get wasted at these parties. The guests may act "sophisticated" at first, but after the real dancing begins at around eleven o'lock, everyone loses inhibition and reaches for the alcohol with little else in mind.

A steady stream of guests begins to pool inside, and I go and talk to each one of them, joined by Ashley about a half hour in. It feels like work to smile at all of them, laugh at all their relatively humorous and unimportant stories.

I smile for real only when Noah walks in. Tall, dark-haired, gray-eyed Noah, endlessly sweet and the only person I've ever enjoyed hanging out with at my mom's parties. His own mom is the chief financial officer of Detail, which means the two of them have been coming to my mom's parties since forever.

Just a year older than me, Noah was the only person other than my sisters who was around my age at all these events when we were young. As the years have gone by, we've bonded further over our shared distaste for the parties.

The funny thing is, though, that the parties aren't so bad anymore. Because I get to see him.

Seeing me across the room now, he smiles and lifts a hand to wave at me. Grinning, I cross the room to say hi and give his mom a hug.

Sherri Smith, like Noah, is endlessly kind and happy and sweet. A single mom, she raised Noah alone, and she clearly did a great job of it. I've always admired and respected her for that.

After talking to me for a few minutes, she heads off to find my mother, leaving Noah and me to go socialize for a few more hours. If it were up to us, we would go down to the beach and just stay there the whole night. But that's not how these things work, and we both know that.

So we make our rounds, exchanging pleasantries and engaging in polite conversation with everyone:

"Yes, I'm seventeen."

"I know, college is right around the corner!"

"I do miss Jenavieve, but she'll be home soon for her college graduation party."

By the time it's eleven, I'm exhausted from the repetitive questions and scripted, perfunctory answers. Across from me, Noah's face reads the same. He nods his head toward the door, and I immediately walk over. I slip out onto the patio, Noah holding the door for me on my way out.

No one is actually in the pool, but lots of people are standing around it, talking loudly and beginning to dance to the bass-filled music playing over the speakers. Noah and I take a left, go out the gate, and walk along the side of the house to our spot.

Lining the infinity pool is a long row of these big, pink bougainvillea bushes. They overlook the beach and are propped up by a ledge my parents built for the flowers when they bought the house.

Down at the far side of the house, there's a small niche of sand between two flower bushes, just big enough for two people. Concealed from the watchful eyes of everyone, Noah and I have spent countless hours in that place, watching the water and the stars and having real, non-scripted conversations.

For a while now, we've stolen away at eleven each time because that's when the heavy drinking and chaos start to kick in. Ashley likes this part because she gets to sneak in a martini or two, but Noah and I aren't into the whole drinking thing. We'd rather be away from it all, in our little hideaway in the flowers on the beach.

We settle into our burrow now, me kicking off my shoes and lying back in the sand, Noah lying next to me. I glance over at him. The flower bush above us makes a shadowy, crisscrossed pattern on his face, and there are grains of sand in his hair.

"Look at that one, Maddy," he says softly, pointing up. He has this little thing for stars. Not the sort of obsession where you know every name and constellation, but he enjoys looking at them.

Staring up at the sky, I try to find the star Noah's looking at. The sky is freckled with them tonight, cloudless and covered with pin-pricks of light.

I'm not seeing anything special; they all look the same to me. I tell him so. He laughs and gently takes my hand, guiding it to the spot where his star is. My heart quickens a bit, and I tell myself to stop. It's Noah. It isn't like that with us. It would be too complicated if it were.

"See?" he says, pointing my finger to the far left, where, sure enough, there is a star seemingly bigger and brighter than the rest.

"Yes, I see it now." I smile and try not to show my disappointment when he lets go of my hand.

A loud laugh reverberates from somewhere in the party above us—a drunken, obnoxious laugh.

"I always wonder if they actually *enjoy* getting drunk, or if they think they're just obligated to do it," I say to Noah, my eyes still on his star.

"Neither," he answers, and I'm surprised by the self-assured quickness of his response. "I think they just do it to escape."

"Escape? Escape what?" I snort. "Look at them. They have unlimited luxuries and opportunities. What could they possibly be running from?"

"What do *we* always run from when we come down here?"

Noah and I stop watching the star and look at each other. I thought it was a rhetorical question, but he seems to be waiting for my answer.

"Well, we don't like it," I insist. "We're not into the drinking and partying and superficial conversation. You and I just aren't meant to be socialites. But that's us. If you're saying they all drink to escape, then why? They *choose* the parties. We're just here because our parents make us."

There's a pause as Noah takes this in, absorbing my words and formulating a response in his mind.

"What I think," he says thoughtfully, "is that they all start off thinking this'll make them happy. I mean, you watch the movies and see in the magazines these people who have so many *things*, and I think a lot of people feel that if they had all those things, they could be happy too.

"But the thing is," he continues, "they don't realize that the movies and magazines that show all these happy people with their cool things? Aren't really real. They're fake. Their job is to make the rich people look happy. But who knows if they actually are."

"And since we're around it," I say, "we know it's not real. We see first-hand that they all *pretend* they have these great lives, but there's nothing wholesome and real about them."

"Exactly," Noah nods. "If everything is so expensive and luxurious, then what stands out? What is there to truly care about?"

"I don't know," I say softly, and I'm thinking about all the people getting drunk right now to make themselves feel like their lives are more joyfully enriching than they actually are.

"Hey, at least we've avoided it," Noah says, interrupting my thoughts. He looks at me and half smiles. "I like to think that we have more important things to live for than money. You know? Things, real things, that we really care about."

There's a charged silence now, and we're both staring at each other, neither of us saying a word.

I don't want to ruin this moment, but I also know that I don't want to ruin the friendship we've had for so many years.

So I look away. These little moments, they can't happen with us. No matter what I may want deep inside, I couldn't handle losing the boy beside me.

"Well, I should, uh, probably go." Noah breaks the silence and rises to a sitting position, brushing the sand off of his shirt. He gives me that half-smile again and stands, slowly turning his back to me and walking back toward the house.

"Wait, Noah," I find myself calling. I can't just let him leave in this awkward way. He turns, locking those gray eyes on mine.

Stop, I tell myself, because I know my face is flushed. Hopefully he doesn't see it in the dark. "I'll see you in a few weeks, right?" I ask. The parties never really end. They're a constant stream of gatherings and celebrations—any cause to come together, even if in the most superficial ways.

"Yeah," he responds, "see you then, Maddy."

"See you then," I say softly. And even though it's probably vacuous and futile, I find myself lying there, watching his star shining steadily, for a very long time.

9
JENAVIEVE

After that first exchange, Max and I quickly became attached. I think that a few times in your life, you meet someone who you know will always stick with you. And you can't really explain it, but you just know that this particular person will always be in your life, in one way or another.

That, for me, was Max. In the one simple conversation we had at Harper's party, I had let on more to him than most people knew after years of knowing me. Because, to be truthful, I mostly just let people believe I'm perfect.

It's easier than explaining the alternative. That beneath the layers of what people see on the surface—good grades, beauty, social ease—is a girl who contains more darkness than anyone would ever believe.

So even *telling* Max that I was not, in fact, a perfect human being was sign enough to me that he meant something special. He was different, and I felt I could trust him and maybe, just maybe, he could actually understand me someday.

But after that first night, our relationship didn't rapidly escalate into deep talks about the meaning of life or our fears from childhood that we were never quite able to shake. I think we both wanted to take that part slow. At least I know I did. Letting people into the deeper

27

recesses of my mind isn't something that is easy or preferable for me, and it would take time for even Max to go there.

We went out every weekend and explored Boston with the ease and spontaneity of two carefree college students trying to have fun. Max and I had a wholesome and real connection. Our times together were an endless stream of laughter and conversation. And both occurred with an ease and contentedness seen only between two people who are so comfortable with each other that all words can be unfiltered, and for whom "fresh out of bed" is a perfectly normal and accepted look.

And when he kissed me … when we connected in those ways, there was nothing but the feeling, in all its purest forms, of *right*ness. I knew that there was no one else's arms I'd rather have hold me, no one else's lips that I wanted on mine.

Elizabeth was the first one from home to know about him. When I came home for Christmas that year, I stole down to the kitchen one night after everyone was upstairs in bed. Everyone except Elizabeth, of course. She was always doing something for us, even if she didn't have to.

At the time, she was making cookies. Humming softly, contentedly cutting holiday-themed shapes in the sugar cookie dough. Curly blonde hair up in a short ponytail, a few locks spilling over and framing her face. The same old Liz.

I sat at the barstool and told her about Max, all the way back to the night I met him, not leaving out a detail. I described how we sat in the chairs on the balcony afterwards, talking until three in the morning. How his eyelashes tangled when he blinked. How his dimples deepened when he laughed hard. How he watched me with the deepest attentiveness and sincerity whenever I spoke.

The whole time, she continued working, putting trays in the oven and wiping down the countertops, all while wearing a quiet smile and listening to my whole story.

Afterwards, when she knew I was finally finished, she met my eyes and grinned, her eyes twinkling.

"Wow, Jenavieve," she said, sounding a little mystified and amazed. "It sounds a lot to me like you're in love."

I could feel my face burning. "Psh, no," I tried to play it off smoothly. "I don't *love* him. I mean, I've only known him for like three months. He is special and everything, don't get me wrong. But I think saying I'm *in love* is a bit premature."

For a moment, she didn't say anything, regarding me thoughtfully. Then she shrugged and went back to washing the cookie pans.

"Okay," she said nonchalantly, facing away from me. "I just think that you shouldn't turn your back on your feelings. If you're in love with this guy, you should tell him. Life's too short, Jen."

This, coming from a fourteen-year-old girl. And still, her words struck something within me. A deep, impenetrable something safe-guarding all of the emotions I kept blocked off, day after day.

This, I realized, was now one of them. Whenever my feelings got too strong about anything, I pushed them down and refused to confront them. Over the years, I found that this strategy was easier than feeling the extremes. More specifically, extreme sadness or pain.

But the catch was, this method of holding myself back from my emotions also meant I couldn't feel extreme joy. Which meant I couldn't feel as impossibly good as I knew I could feel with Max if I just let myself.

Of course, I didn't say all of this out loud. I couldn't. In fact, all that passed my lips was a whispered, "I can't."

I can't what? Feel? Allow myself to reach beyond the more basic emotions out of fear I might feel anything close to what I had felt a few years ago? Or can't tell Max I loved him? I still don't know what was going through my mind at the time.

"Look, Jeanvieve?" Elizabeth said tentatively. She put down her rag, leaned against the counter across from me and peered, a little sadly, into my eyes. "We both know that your feelings have a way of transforming you. And I know it wasn't good, in the past. But maybe it is now. Maybe these feelings are the type that can transform your life for the better, not the worse. And you deserve that. Thoughts filled with *light*, not darkness. At least I definitely think you deserve it."

I still remember the aftermath of that comment. I hadn't really cried in so long, but after what Elizabeth said, I felt the old familiar pressure in the back of my head and experienced that blurry vision you get when you're trying to hold the tears in.

Because she was right. And of course, she was right—she was the only person, up until that point, who knew anything about what had starved me of my emotions and more.

10
ELIZABETH

～∞〇～

When I began doing actual work for the Blairs, I quickly picked up on the importance of recognizing people's feelings so that I could help them with whatever they needed.

They were a family of steadfast and independent individuals, so it wasn't always easy to see what they were thinking. Besides getting annoyed at the little things, none of them let on to the true struggles of their personal lives.

Over time, I came to recognize all their tells. I've always joked with my friends at school that I would be a great poker player, because I know how to read people at an expert level. Truly, it takes expertise to get inside the head of any Blair.

James' tell is that he looks away. As a lawyer, it's a crucial part of his job to make eye contact and engage with whomever he's talking to. These mannerisms carry over at home when he's talking to the girls about their days, or at parties when he's listening to people's stories. So when he can't make eye contact, there's something seriously troubling him.

Evelyn's giveaway is that she moves. Not that she's not already a very active person—she always seems to be running around frantically, perfecting one detail or another. But it's when she's doing something idle or pointless, like wiping down counters I just cleaned, that it's clear something is wrong. No one could improve my pristine countertops.

Madeline mumbles when she's really upset about something. She's a clear speaker and good conversationalist, so it confused me for the longest time when she would start randomly mumbling incomprehensibly. It finally hit me that her incoherent speaking was the sign that something was going on, and my mystery was solved

Ashley's tell is a little more obvious: giving up. Whenever she isn't arguing about something, it's clear she's not herself. That's because she is the single most overtly argumentative person I know. So when she ceases to fight, that means she's lost all hope.

Jenavieve was the one I couldn't figure out. Unlike the rest of her family, nothing about her characteristics or mannerisms stood out; she was just kind of the same, day after day. She, like everyone else, got mad at little things, but she was open about them. Annoyance with a friend. Upset about the B+ on her chemistry exam.

These sorts of things didn't need to be hidden. As far as we all knew, what made Jenavieve upset were small, everyday troubles. But I just knew it couldn't be that simple. There had to be more complexity to her feelings. I just had to figure out her tell.

I came to notice it gradually. Unlike with the others, it wasn't as easy to see. In fact, it was very difficult to see. One would only notice something was wrong if they were truly looking for it.

It was her eyes. In nine out of ten scenarios, Jenavieve Blair's eyes were filled with the sort of light that signified only pure and innocent happiness. But when she wasn't surrounded by others, her eyes took on a blank, vacant and darkly troubled look.

The thing was, this look was frequent. Almost every night, when everyone was leaving the dinner table and not focused on the others around them, that look appeared in her eyes. I saw it as I cleaned up the kitchen or ironed one of her shirts as she sat waiting.

With anyone else, those moments of unsettlement were relatively fleeting. They went away fairly quickly, as do most problems.

So that's why I knew there was something seriously wrong with Jenavieve. No one okay was so troubled for so long.

At that time seven years ago, when I noticed something was going on with Jenavieve, I was only eleven. Pretty young to try and delve into the possible reasons of upset for someone four years older than myself.

But my instinct to watch out for all of the Blairs prevailed, and I decided I would have a mini intervention of sorts. In other words, I would ask her what was wrong when nobody else was around. Maybe that way, she would admit to being troubled by something a little deeper than her "bad" test scores.

About a week later, Jenavieve was helping me clean up after dinner, something she occasionally did just to help me out, I guess. Everything was quiet, and everyone else was upstairs. It was my opportunity.

"Jenavieve?" I broke the silence timidly, a little cautiously. She glanced up at me and raised her eyebrows. "Are you okay?"

I mentally kicked myself for being so forward so fast. "I mean," I continued, trying to soften my question, "you just seem a little off. Like all the time. It just feels like there's something bugging you, and maybe it's nothing because it's not like you ever talk about it, but I don't know. I just think something's going on with you, maybe."

Her response was quick. Almost as soon as the word "maybe" exited my mouth, she said, "Oh no! I'm fine." Her eyes softened then, looked a little tired and a little sad as they watched mine.

Maybe I looked scared or confused. Not just because I thought something was wrong in Jenavieve's life. But because I realized then that I had been noticing for some time the dark hollows under her eyes.

I knew then that she must not have been sleeping, or at least not sleeping regularly. Something was bothering her enough to throw off her normal teenage sleeping cycle.

"Really, Elizabeth," she added, that slightly sad expression still on her face. "I'm okay. You shouldn't have to worry about me, anyways. It's all good. You just worry about school or clothes or whatever it is eleven-year-olds worry about."

She smiled and turned around to put something in a cupboard. Maybe her little speech would've thrown off a normal eleven-year-old, but not me. Because I wasn't a normal kid. My whole world revolved around the Blair family. I knew them probably better than I knew myself.

So I knew that Jenavieve was hiding something for my benefit. She had always protected me and helped me out in all aspects of life—which was why I wanted to turn the tables for once. She was the oldest, so who was there for *her*? It had to be me.

But for the time being, I played it off. "Okay," I responded hesitantly. "But I'll always be here if you want to talk about anything."

The kitchen was clean by that point. I walked up to my room, closed the door and lay down on my bed.

I sighed, my eyes on the ceiling. But my mind elsewhere. If Jenavieve wasn't going to tell me what was wrong, that meant I was going to have to do some searching of my own. One way or another, I would get to the bottom of it—and I intended to do so quickly.

11
EVELYN

My mother, Beatrice Anderson, was the Los Angeles, outer-boroughs version of Superwoman when I was young. I even believed that my father was Superman, and my mom played along with it.

I was big into the idea of some heroic, powerful man swooping in and saving everyone from harm, so I chose to believe that was what my father was doing. In my innocent mind, my dad was flying around the world, saving people from all things bad.

What my mom knew, but I of course didn't, was the reality. My dad was a participant in the gang rape that created me, and is now probably off somewhere strung out on heroin, scaring people more than helping them.

"When is Daddy coming back?" I would ask as I perched on my mom's lap, watching her brush out my blonde hair in the tiny bathroom mirror.

"Well, Evvy," she would respond in the most lovingly kind way, "he's really busy being Superman. He's sacrificed a lot by being away from you, but he knows you're proud of him."

To this, I would nod and envision the superhero I recognized from TV because I had no idea what my father actually looked like. Still don't. I have no interest in seeing the man who hurt my mom.

She really was a good mother, and she took care of me to the best of her ability. We didn't have much, and she couldn't make much money because she had never graduated from high school. She was only sixteen when I was born, and she dropped out to raise me. After she spent time focusing on caring for me as a newborn, she found work at the grocery store in our neighborhood and made do with that.

Her own parents were alcoholics, so they weren't present much in her life. When I was born, they constantly complained about my crying, which motivated my mom to make enough money to move us out.

It took her two years, but she finally saved enough to move us into the tiny house I grew up in, two blocks down from my grandparents' house.

Our bungalow was not glamorous. Two rooms, small living room and kitchen. One tiny bathroom. There were 746 total square feet.

What we had didn't constitute much, and I know my mother was aware of that. But it was the best she could do, and she took pride in our home and our life there.

The house was always clean, my clothes were always washed, and there was always something to eat. My life was maintained efficiently. Maybe to the barest minimum, but I was still a fairly safe and healthy child.

When I was little, my mother wrapped all of her interactions with me in complete tenderness. She told me that my father was Superman, read stories to me in the most soothing tone as I fell asleep. Used up her month's savings to surprise me with a pink tricycle, which I rode around the neighborhood with glee until the ribbons fell off the handles and the pedals creaked. Played hide-and-go-seek with me every night when she got home from work and old Mrs. Wilson next door left after watching me all day.

In those days, Beatrice Anderson was kind and loving and endearing, raising her toddler with utmost care. I have fond childhood memories because of her, and I never forgot that.

But as I grew older, the softness faded and the sharp edges appeared. I believe my mom wanted a different life for me, the life she would've strived for had she not become unwillingly pregnant with me.

So she became harsh. Strict, a little condescending even, militantly drilling me to do my schoolwork and do well on tests.

She stopped playing hide-and-go-seek somewhere around my seventh year, and instead greeted me by pulling a beer from the fridge and asking me if all my homework was done.

I wouldn't consider her an alcoholic, but she did have a drink every night after work. She must've hated her job, because I can still picture her clearly as she looked night after night: head in her hands, dark curls framing her face wildly. Cheap gas-station beer sitting on the table next to her.

I saw this dejection over work and her life in general, and I grew to strongly dislike and fear it. If this house, this neighborhood, this job, and this lifestyle made my mother so miserable, I wanted nothing like them in my future.

So I made school my top priority. I knew it was my only way out. What I had to do was stand out in my academics enough to get a good scholarship to a college far away from Los Angeles. Somewhere I could do something different.

The thing was, I didn't really know what other sorts of lives existed. All I knew was my little bungalow on the outskirts of Los Angeles. That is, until my mom started auditioning for movies when I was about ten.

I hadn't known she was into acting until she told me about her high school drama class one night while we were eating dinner.

"I really loved it," she said nostalgically, a wistful smile on her face. "School in general was a bit difficult for me, but when I went into that drama room for fifth period every day during my sophomore year … It was my favorite place in the world."

She told me about the plays she had been in, the singing and dancing lessons, the improv and awkward scenes and many lines she had memorized.

"It was the only place where I didn't feel judged when I was pregnant," she said softly. By this time, I knew that my mom had been young when she had me and had to leave high school because of it.

"People in that room didn't care about my huge belly. They didn't whisper or anything. They just cared about how good I was at acting, and I was thankful for that. "

My mother would be gone for auditions for a few days at a time, at first rarely, and then increasingly as I got older. When I expected her to come home, I always had the table set and the house cleaned. I would wait anxiously, wringing my hands and watching the clock.

At first, she faced the rejections calmly, playing them off as if they weren't a big deal, for my sake. But as her gentle nature faded away as I got older, so too did her efforts to hide her disappointment over her Hollywood rejections.

I came to dread the days when she arrived home, bringing with her the contagious despair of rejection.

It finally became too much for her. I still remember the day. I was fourteen, and I knew how bad it was when my mom walked through the door and threw her overnight bags violently on the floor.

"Ahhh!" she wailed, slapping the table, throwing the pillow from the couch, making everything but me a physical outlet for her anger.

"Goddamn it," she groaned, muffled, head in her hands. Then, "I'm sorry."

Her voice was so small, so childlike, so helpless in that moment. I sighed and sat next to her at the table, placing a hand softly on her back.

"It's okay, Mom," I said quietly. "You don't have to be sorry. You're trying your best. You'll get it someday, I know you will. It just takes time."

"You don't understand," she said angrily. "I will never 'get it.' The only ones who ever get the parts are those Beverly bitches. The ones living in their nice mansions in the heart of Beverly Hills, with lots of money and *lots* of connections.

"They're not even good," she cried, a tear marking a stained pathway on her dollar-store foundation. "But of course, their nice designer clothes and special, high-up friends helped them beat out the poor single mom. It isn't fair. It isn't *fucking* fair."

And then I felt angry. Not at my mother or her anger. Instead, I was seething at the circumstances that blocked her from what she so desperately wanted. It wasn't about her talent, or even her charm. It was about how much money she didn't have and how luxurious a life she didn't lead.

"You're right, Mom," I said, the fire rapidly igniting inside me. "It's not fair. And you know what? Someday, you'll be right beside them. I'll work so hard in school that I'll go to a good university and find a good job, with lots of money. And I'll use that money to buy you a nice house, right next door to those Beverly bitches. Okay?"

I meant it, too. My mother looked up at me then and laughed a little. Smiled sadly. "Alright, Evvy," she whispered. "That's good. You work hard. You get somewhere, further than I could. You deserve so much more."

"So do you," I said, and I was surprised by the shakiness in my voice. My face burned with shame. Because I knew, deep inside, that everything was my fault. Well, and my dad's. If he hadn't raped my mom, I wouldn't have been born, and my mom would've had a much better and more stable life.

"I'm sorry," I whispered. "I'm sorry I was born, and that you have to look at me every day and think about what happened."

What she said next may have been the best thing my mother ever said to me, and it remains one of the most comforting memories I return to in times of despair.

"Honey, no," she said, brushing the tears from my cheeks. "You look at me."

I did, meeting her dark eyes through still-blurred vision.

"You remember when you were little, how you thought your dad was Superman?"

I nodded, feeling ashamed at having made my mom play along with that stupid game.

"I played along with it because it's true," she said firmly, as if reading my mind. "Your father, despite everything, gave me the best gift in the whole world. Maybe not invisibility or flying." She smiled, and in her eyes I saw the soft, warm mother from years ago.

"He gave me *you*, Evelyn. And for that, I am grateful. Every single day, I'm so grateful to that man."

I will never understand how my mother had so much grace.

12
ASHLEY

All I'm aware of is that it's the last event before Jenavieve's huge Harvard graduation party. Other than that, I don't know the occasion, and don't really care to find out.

Our house is the go-to for every occurrence. Any wedding, birthday, baby shower, welcoming a new resident, hiring a new employee for Detail … the list of things people can think of to celebrate is endless.

We even once threw my dad's cousin's daughter a princess party for her fifth birthday. Needless to say, everyone showed up, and everyone got wasted.

A long while back, the parties were actually bearable because I had Madeline and Jenavieve to hang out with. And then Jenavieve got too old and popular, and Madeline and Noah became inseparable.

So then it was just me. I grew to hate the parties because of how alone I was. In fact, I grew to despise my life in general, because all anyone around me seemed to care about was money, gossip and booze. The only good ones, my sisters, had found other people to spend time with. So, I was left to my own devices.

It was endlessly boring for a few years, but only because I was young and dumb enough to not notice the two things right in front of me that I finally discovered last year, when I was fourteen.

Those two things are alcohol and Dashton Little. When it comes to alcohol, it's not like I can get flat-out wasted at my parents' parties, in my own house in front of everyone. I wouldn't really mind embarrassing my parents. But I care enough about my reputation to not completely blow it and ruin all chances of getting out of here after high school. Preferably out of the country. As far as I can get.

Anyway, I get a little bit tipsy. When the drinks come out, everyone and everything blurs together, and all anyone cares about is their glass of chardonnay. Which means it's easy for me to slip in a drink or two. I just have to avoid getting too close to my mom or dad.

It was when I was a little tipsy at a party sometime last year that I met Dashton. A famous and very attractive young actor, he had befriended my mom when he did a commercial for her a few years back. He's been coming to the parties quite frequently ever since.

Every girl within a few years of his twenty was star-struck. Wavy blondish hair, golden skin, green eyes. He was beautiful in the way that normally only Photoshop can achieve. And he was entirely out of my league, so I didn't even try. Six years older seemed like too big of a gap back then.

He didn't talk to any of those girls who bent over backward trying to get his attention. Instead, he walked around quietly, observantly, talking to the adults rather than anyone his own age.

People gossiped that he was gay, but I knew better. He just wasn't interested in any of the shallow model girls who were so in love with him.

The prime similarity I saw with him was that we both weren't interested in anybody or anything at the parties. Dashton was there to be seen by people who could help his acting career, and I showed up because I was the daughter of the hostess.

Enforced attendance. That was all it was for both of us. He, however, was seemingly content with meandering slowly about the house, taking some samples of Elizabeth's food here, eavesdropping on dull conversations there.

Meanwhile, I spent my time at every party drinking. By the time I was almost fifteen, it had become a more constant and enjoyable way to pass the time. I still had no one to hang out with, so I usually just took my bottle of chardonnay out to the front porch around eleven, when everyone else was inside or out back.

Once on the porch, I drank as much or as little of the wine as I wanted, lay down and maybe closed my eyes for a little while, and then went upstairs to bed. By that time, everyone else was too drunk to notice my absence, and my parents were too busy entertaining to care.

Not that they cared much anyways, as long as I maintained a reasonably polite persona.

On the night I met Dashton Little, I was wearing one of the only dresses I've ever actually enjoyed. Shimmering silver Dior cutting off just above my knees, skirt billowing when I moved. Sequins shimmering in the changing evening light. My hair was pulled up in a bun that my mother proclaimed to be stylish, a few strands of loose hair framing my face.

You remember these little things about how you looked when you met your person.

Childishly, I loved the way my skirt billowed when I moved, so I was twirling. Bottle in hand, I hummed softly and pretended I was dancing. I was a little drunk, a little less inhibited, a little less annoyed at the party and the people and the lack of them around me.

When Dashton pushed open the front door, taking a break from the party I supposed, I didn't even stop dancing. I wasn't much fazed by him. Any other girl would probably freak out upon being alone with Dashton Little. But he didn't impress me.

"Aren't you a little young to be drinking?" he inquired, and I realized that was the first time I had ever heard him speak. Deep voice, fringed with a bit of genuine concern but also with a hint of amusement.

Drunkenly, I deadpanned, "Aren't *you* a little young to be *famous?*" and went back to my twirling.

He chuckled a bit, walked over and deftly snatched the bottle from my hand.

"Hey!" I shrieked, laughing a bit but also a little panicked at the prospect of losing my only company. "Give that back!"

"Talk to me," he said simply. And that's all it took. One look into those piercing green eyes and I saw the care behind them. He actually wanted to talk to me. Me, of all people. A drunk, lonely fourteen-year-old.

"Fine," I tried to say nonchalantly, but I could feel my face heating as I spoke. I dropped to the porch step, my skirt ballooning around me as I sat down. "And what is it you'd like to know?"

He sat casually beside me, leaning his back on the step behind us, lazily stretching his designer-clad feet in front of him.

"Well," he sighed and shrugged lightly. "Why you're out here alone, for one thing."

Perfect. Time to explain to the hot boy beside me that I was a lonely, antisocial loser with a complete disconnection from my family.

"Um." I considered how honest I felt like being. Then I figured, if he cared enough to ask, he should get the truth. "I just don't really *have* anyone."

Dashton lifted his eyebrows but refrained from commenting. He just watched me carefully and more curiously now.

"I mean," I filled in, "when I was little, these parties were okay because I had my older sisters. We would hang out, play games and stuff, you know? And then my oldest sister, Jenavieve, got all pretty and popular, so she went off to do her own thing with, like, everyone, because everyone loves her.

"And then," I sighed, "my sister Madeline just got closer and closer with this guy Noah. His mom works with my mom, so the two of them are at all these things. And Noah's a nice guy, but, well. Apparently nicer than me."

I shrugged, chuckled a bit to ease the pain I was surprised to still feel.

"So that left me with no one. But I still have to show up, because I'm a Blair and these parties are what we do, ya know? It's just boring as hell. And it just always pisses me off, too. I mean, I'm expected to devote my damn life to these dumb parties for the sake of the family, but no one in my family cares about my life. Kind of a one-way street there. But yeah. That's why I'm drinking alone."

I remember looking up at him then, trying to gauge his reaction to my story. And I was surprised to see genuine emotion in his eyes. What I liked about that emotion, though, was that it wasn't pity I was seeing. It was just pure empathy. Like he felt bad for me, but for the right reasons. If that makes any sense.

"Wow," he remarked quietly, his eyes still on me. "That sounds lonely. And, uh, I know a thing or two about feeling alone," he smiled slightly. "You're about the only girl I have talked to in the, what, five years I've been going to your parents' parties."

I couldn't stop myself from falling for him—this beautiful, mature, older man who chose *me* to take a genuine interest in. He wasn't even flirting much or trying to hook up with me on the spot. He just *cared*, and that is what I've always loved most about Dashton Little.

My whole life up until that point, I had just been waiting for someone to genuinely care about me. So that night I met Dashton will always remain clear in my memory as the night I found the attention

I had been looking for. And, at the same time, found the great love of my life.

***

Now, it's a year later, and we're holding the last event before Jenavieve's graduation. I am wearing a tight, black, strapless dress and black velvet heels. Silver diamond stud earrings with matching bangles. My bright blonde hair is down and curled. I have to look good because Dashton will be here tonight, and I haven't seen him in three months.

He's been in Taiwan shooting his new movie. His career has been skyrocketing and I swear his acting gets better with every part he plays. I tell him so, but he always laughs and denies his greatness.

The night I met Dashton, we exchanged numbers and immediately started texting. It was simple and innocent conversation, but I still got caught up in talking to him all the time, whether during class or at the dinner table.

We hung out at the parties too, sneaking away to the front of the house to talk and, eventually, make out. It was a mutual want, a mutual need. We fell in love fast, and no amount of closeness to each other ever felt close enough. It still doesn't.

I stand at the side of the garage now, leaning against the wall in what I hope to be a seductive way. He should be here any minute.

Right on cue, he materializes from around the other side of the house. Taller and more muscled, golden-skinned, wavy-haired and green-eyed than before. He immediately breaks out in a huge, gleaming, teeth-revealing smile upon seeing me, and my heart drops straight to the driveway.

My own smile spreads across my whole being, and I shriek with joy. Unable to hold back, I run to him, and for a minute we are exposed to all as we crash into each other, holding on tightly.

I feel the physical and emotional jolt of electricity as I hold onto him, as he buries his face into my neck, pulling me even closer. My skin tingles at the spot on my neck where his warm lips connect.

Breaking free at last, I grab his hand and pull him over to the wall where I'd been waiting and we immediately begin kissing. In these moments, we are almost one person. So fiercely devoted to each other, so fiercely hungry for *more* of each other.

It both intimidates me and excites me how much I want him. And I know he feels the same way.

And I know, even now while kissing him, that our love has broken and will continue to break limits. Our age gap, his fame … they are all excuses set in place by mindless beings to further separate people from loving each other as beautifully and desperately as I love the man beside me.

Luckily for us, for some time now I have accepted that rules and regulations are meant to be broken. If we don't consider them real, then they aren't.

So I kiss Dashton Little with the assurance that nothing will ever stand in the way of our love if we don't want it to. Which means there's nothing but clear skies and smooth sailing ahead.

13
ELIZABETH

I prepare the food and other accommodations with a little more excitement than usual today, because I work with the knowledge that in less than a month, our family will be complete again. Jenavieve will be back for her grand graduation party, which will be the event of the year.

Humming spiritedly, I bounce between chopping cucumbers and dicing tomatoes for my salsa dip, which is a favorite appetizer. In truth, though, it's not just Jenavieve's return that has me feeling so happy.

Not only will she be home for a little while before she goes back to law school, but the rest of the family will be happy for her to be here. Not to mention, it's the April of my senior year of high school, which means I have about two months left.

And, best of all, I've been accepted to Pepperdine. I sent in my formal acceptance today.

Evelyn told me she could help pull some strings if needed, as she is a Pepperdine grad, but I did it all on my own. I worked hard for years to get the best grades I could, which has paid off. Because now I get what has always been my goal: to attend a top-notch, dream school only ten minutes away from the Blairs.

It's the best possible scenario for me. I'll get my education and this family, too. I'll be able to visit constantly and still help with events. My life will continue along the path I have always intended, and nothing makes me feel more self-assured and relaxed than that.

I watch as the guests filter in. I smile at some, wave at others, compliment more still. When Noah walks in, the distress on his face is evident. I smile a little sadly at him, remembering our conversation from earlier this morning.

Because we both are seniors and go to the same small private school, Noah and I have been in classes together since we were five. I'm nothing close to what Madeline is to him, but he and I are good friends and have been since we were young.

Which is why this morning I knew, just by seeing his expression as he leaned against my locker before AP psych, that something was off with him.

"Hey Elizabeth," he tried to say cheerfully, smiling without his teeth. "You decide on college yet?"

"Actually, yes," I said, and couldn't stop myself from beaming. "Pepperdine for me, and I'm officially committing right after school."

"Wow, congratulations. That's fantastic," Noah smiled encouragingly, and I knew his enthusiasm was genuine. He'd known this was my dream school for some time, just as I knew Stanford was his.

"And what about you?" I inquired, although a part of me felt I already knew the answer. He looked too troubled for someone who had gotten into his dream school.

"I, um. Well, I got in," he said a bit quietly, and the way he said it indicated just how awestruck he still felt. "I got into Stanford."

"Noah, that's … that's amazing!" I shrieked a bit. "I mean, do you realize how few people get into that school? And you did it!"

No response. Just his close-lipped smile, nodding humbly, but still a lot less happily than someone whose dreams had just been fulfilled.

"I don't understand why you aren't, like, jumping for joy right now!" I added, trying to get him to feel a bit more of the excitement I knew he should be feeling.

"No, it's ... it's not *Stanford* that's bad, or anything," he said emphatically, shaking his head. "I mean, that whole thing is ... you're right. It's incredible. Beyond incredible. And I'm going, and I'm so excited about it. It's just that I didn't really think it would actually happen, you know? In the back of my mind, I always thought it would be Pepperdine, so now, making this bigger move is a bit more unexpected."

I noticed the slight, but still perceptible, reddening of his skin, and I knew exactly what was going on.

"Let me guess. You're telling Madeline tonight," I said quietly. "And you also really don't want to leave her."

Noah sighed, exhaling through his nose and rubbing his face with the palm of his hand defeatedly. "Yeah," he answered softly. "I do have to talk to her about it. And I don't want to leave her."

And there was nothing really for me to say back to that. So our conversation ended on that note, with both of us feeling dejected, me by the knowledge that this boy cared about my best friend more than she probably knew.

***

As I watch them now, Noah and Madeline going out back as they do all the time, I can't help but marvel at the complexity of humans and their relationships, at the ways in which people love each other without even saying so.

I don't know what Noah and Madeline are, in their eyes. But I do know that the two of them care deeply for each other. I just don't know if that care will ever turn into something more than it is.

Maybe it shouldn't turn into anything, I tell myself as I pour champagne into flute glasses. Maybe it will save both of them from hurt and separation in the long run.

But maybe, the flicker in my consciousness whispers back, maybe, it is all worth it. Telling the ones you love that you love them, even though you're afraid of what might happen next.

Because you always must consider that perhaps, what will happen if you take the risk is simply worth whatever comes after.

14
MADELINE

~❧~

Noah and I are settled into our alcove, watching the stars like usual, but there is a tension surrounding us that usually isn't there. Something is clearly bothering him, but I don't have any idea what it could be.

Finally, he breaks the silence and fills in the gaps for me. Taking a deep breath, he says, "So, I have some news."

"What?" I ask quietly. I and cannot tell by his tone if this is to be wonderful or terrible news.

"I, um. Well," he starts again, and I can feel his body shift and tense beside me. The starched sleeve of his button-down barely evades my arm's touch. "I got into Stanford, and I sent in my acceptance yesterday," he says, a bit quickly and all in one breath.

The first thing I feel is relief. He isn't hurt, or sick, or something bad like that. But then, the implication of what he is saying sinks into my consciousness, and I am aware of a heaviness descending upon my chest.

He'll be gone. In about four months, Noah Smith will no longer be by my side at these parties, or anywhere else for that matter. He'll be gone.

Suck it up, I tell myself harshly, before my voice wavers. Because if he heard the waver, then he would know something is wrong, and I don't want him to worry about me. That's the last thing he needs. He should be happy, and I tell him so.

"Noah, that's incredible," I say in the most enthusiastic voice I can muster. "That's so great. You're going to be so happy there, and the things you're going to do ... it's going to be beyond your wildest dreams. Really."

And I'm smiling for real now, with the most genuine sincerity one could feel. Noah will have a great life, in a beautiful place with beautiful people and the sorts of academics that will guarantee him a fulfilling future.

So how can I possibly be sad, knowing that he will be more than okay? I can't, and I repeat this to myself over and over, like a silent mantra: *Can't be sad, can't be sad.*

"Thanks," Noah responds quietly, and I can't stop myself from looking over at him. He's still tense, still has his eyes on the sky. He must feel my eyes on him, but it's like he can't look over at me right now.

The next thing he says makes me understand why.

"I'll really miss you, Maddy," he says softly, and with so much sincerity I can feel my heart melting.

"I mean, really," he adds, and I'm taken aback by the almost shaky quality of the normally calm, self-assured tenor of his voice. "It's going to be really hard, to not—"

"I know," I interrupt before he can go further. Instinctively, I reach out and rest my hand on top of his.

Stupid. What a dumb thing to do, I scold myself, and can feel my heart beating rapidly. I don't know what I should do now, so I just keep my hand as it is.

Then, something curious happens. He freezes, stiffens for just a moment before I feel his hand relax beneath mine. And then, smoothly, almost as if rehearsed, Noah flips his hand over and interlocks his fingers with mine.

Every muscle in my body ceases to move, as if any movement I make will ruin this moment forever.

In all our years together, nothing even close to this has ever occurred. I find myself thinking about how he will be gone before I know it, how it isn't wise to feel this way about someone who will soon be out of my life forever.

But there is still something unbreakable anchoring our hands in place, and neither of us makes any effort to disturb it.

So we lie here, hands interlocked, the sides of our bodies pressed together. Not speaking, just breathing and watching the stars, sharing space with the contentment and ease we always have.

I wordlessly and almost unconsciously nestle my head into his shoulder, finding a comfortable spot there. He rests his head on top of mine, and I can sense his eyes closing at the precise moment mine do.

This would be a nice way to live, I think to myself, the world around me nothing but Noah holding me and the sound of the waves in the night.

I doze off, and am awakened later by the vague realization that he has slipped off silently, without a word.

15

~∞~

"**B**eing a terrible human being is a subjective concept," the therapist says thoughtfully, evenly. "I mean, no one on this Earth is perfect."

"But they aren't like me, trust me," I grunt. And it's true. There are very few others on this planet who would be so wholly and darkly destructive as I have been.

No matter what she's about to say, I tell myself, nothing will erase the fact that my existence is a waste. I'm a waste of energy, a grand failure as a part of the human species.

Nothing can undo that, and all of my actions only support my intrinsic awfulness of being.

"So why do you consider yourself so terrible?" she asks softly, pushing her glasses up a bit farther on her nose so that she can peer at me with even more attentiveness than she already is.

"What I mean," she continues, "is, what is the biggest reason you believe you're such a terrible person? There must be a pinnacle to it all, something that triggers these dark emotions of yours."

She's right. There is a pinnacle. It may not mask all the other horrible outcomes of my actions, all the destruction I have created in my life and in the others around me. But there is something that is, by far, the worst of everything.

"Someone died," I whisper hoarsely. And one flashback to that horrific day blinds me with the sort of pain that nothing can soothe except for the substances one can't get their hands on in a mental institution.

"Because of me," I elaborate, because I must keep my promise to be fully honest, "someone is dead."

The therapist looks a little taken aback, I notice with the slightest sliver of contentment. She is finally fazed by me a bit. She can finally start to grasp how awful her patient is and how hopeless her efforts to treat me will be.

"So yes, I am terrible, and someone innocent died because of it," I say assertively. "Tell me, is there anything fundamentally worse than that?"

Her lack of response assures me I am right.

16
JAMES

Sip, comment, laugh, move on. Sip, comment, laugh, move on. I rotely perform the duties of a host despite feeling on the edges myself. I may be in a constant state of discomfort here, but Evelyn knows how to speak to them all, and she genuinely enjoys it.

Which is why I retain the polite and socially acceptable cadence of the rhythm in perfect beat. I smile and pretend to care about people's perfect children and perfect homes and perfect lives. Evelyn is content, filled with the ease and stability of someone who has full control over their life. She is happy, and I constantly tell myself that this has to be enough for me.

And yet the discomfort masks everything else like a thin, ill-fitting cloak—the discomfort of knowing the truth about what my wife holds dear.

She thinks her world is beautiful because she is in the very center of it all. There isn't anything she is missing out on because she undoubtedly has everything. Evelyn is the epitome of social grace, success, prosperity.

But it isn't enough. I watch her now, in her dark-blue dress, swirling her little clear glass of champagne. I see her laugh and how the laugh stretches across her face with joy. I wonder how long the laugh will remain genuine.

Because it will not last forever. The glamor and sophistication of a life lived fully on the inside offers its comfort and stability for a time, until you recognize that you're living within the confines of boundaries. Boundaries that, once breached, declare you the outcast you were trying so hard to avoid being in the first place.

I would know, considering I followed the exact path I'm afraid Evelyn is going to hurtle down. Inside, mistake. Outside, pretend to be inside to dull the pain of not fitting in.

It truly is a cruelly vicious cycle, I think to myself as I raise my glass in a solitary toast to my great expectations. The silent tormentor of any dreamer's life.

***

November 11, 1993. The day I introduced Evelyn to my parents.

It was a warm day, fringed with a hint of crisp autumn wind. I remember all this because I also recall thinking that day that she looked like an angel in a beautiful, peach-colored dress that fluttered with her every move.

The idea of introducing her to my parents didn't particularly interest me because the artificiality and supposed superiority of their lifestyles didn't appeal to me then. I would like to say they don't appeal to me now, but I believe that would make me a hypocrite.

The thing was, I knew by then that I wanted to marry her. Why would I not? Here was a beautiful, independent woman who strived to succeed in all areas of life.

Evelyn Anderson was the sort of person I could easily have a wonderful life with, and I knew that from the moment I met her. She would be a good wife, a good worker, a good socialite, a good mother someday.

Never did I doubt that. Never did I doubt that my life would become wonderfully and thoroughly perfect upon marrying the beautiful girl beside me, the beautiful girl in her beautiful dress with her beautifully intense aspirations.

I knew that when I introduced Evelyn to my parents that day they would approve. She was polite, financially successful, an easy conversationalist. The sort of person who fit into the world of socialites and wealth I had been raised in.

What I didn't expect, however, was just how much they would enjoy Evelyn. My father especially.

"Son, let's step inside for a moment. Fix ourselves a drink," my father said to me after a spell of conversation on the terrace with Evelyn and my mother.

I joined him in the kitchen, where he poured some scotch in a crystal glass and slid it amicably across the marble countertop to me. As I took a sip, I contentedly watched the women through the window.

Evelyn in her peach dress. Laughing that tinkling laugh of hers at something my mother was saying. Both women smiling, silhouetted against a setting Malibu sun.

"Ahem," my father interrupted my reverie. "James," he continued, "I just wanted to have a private moment to tell you how very impressed I am with your choice."

Your choice. As if it had been I and I alone who initiated this relationship, I who blessed Evelyn with my presence.

"The girl is lovely," he said with a hint of surprise in his voice. No shocker. Since I was a child, my father had expected the worst from me. So, he always found himself surprised when I actually did something that exceeded his limited expectations.

"She has grace and intelligence and a steady disposition. And just enough fire to ensure her success," he added with a chuckle. "Really. There's no doubt in my mind that Evelyn will always be at the top of the pyramid with Detail."

"Well, Father, I'm glad you approve," I said, with the utmost effort to mask all traces of sarcasm with sincerity.

"Oh, I don't just approve," he responded. To this day I can see the glint of satisfaction in his eye and the way the setting sun illuminated his contentedness.

"I like her, Son, and fully support your relationship with her. In fact, I strongly hope this continues. I think it's very good for you. Good for all of us, quite frankly."

"So," he smiled with genuine approval at me, then lifted his sparkling crystal glass. "A toast. To new beginnings, maybe even a new Blair."

"To new beginnings," I replied cheerily, but inside, I couldn't stop the spread of uneasiness coursing through my body.

There was no way for me to halt the darkly unsettling notion that if my father loved Evelyn so much, there must be something wrong with her.

***

September 15, 1984. I was fifteen years old, running to be sophomore class president. It was the day of elections, the day I would find out the results.

Everyone was required to drop their ballot in the box by the end of the day, and I was almost sure I was going to lose to the other candidate, Ben Hatching.

Ben was a nice, outgoing guy, and when it came down to it, he had more friends and more connections than I did. Even though he was only a sophomore, he was the starting quarterback on our football team. That alone guaranteed him lots of votes.

The thing was, I wouldn't have cared so much about losing to Ben had it not been for my father. Being the president of my class sounded like a lot of work, and I was already busy with school and friends and everything else I would rather be doing.

But it was one of those few things that I knew would win my dad over. Only excellence would make him truly proud of me, and I guess in his mind, being class president qualified as excellence.

So I had to win. It was either that or go home and face the humiliation and disapproval over yet another failure.

And after fifteen years of going home and recognizing the disappointment over my every move, feeling it settle into me, I didn't think I could do it one more time.

Unfortunately, I was running out of time. I had campaigned well, to the best of my ability at least. I'd delivered a good speech, practiced so many times that I memorized it.

Everything about my performance up until that point had been clean and fair. Ben's, too. As I said, he was a nice guy, an even-keeled kid who seemed to genuinely care about our class.

Everyone liked him. Which is what, I realized, I needed to change in order to win. If people didn't like Ben anymore, they wouldn't vote for him. It was that simple. All I had to do was find something wrong with him.

I decided this was going to be difficult, as I tried desperately to dig up some last-minute way to slander him. Until I saw him talking to Angela Shelling.

Angela was a year older than us and had created the biggest scandal of the year when everyone realized she was pregnant.

The thing that caused everyone to talk, though, was that no one knew who the dad was. People were obsessed with this drama and it still had not let up. I still constantly heard the rumors, the whispered accusations behind locker doors.

And now, here he was, leaning against Angela's locker and talking quietly to her. So simple: Ben was the father of Angela's baby.

Except I was sure it wasn't true, and I was even more sure that Ben was comforting Angela, trying to be a good friend to her when everyone else was whispering behind her back. Not brainstorming baby names.

But it was easy, so easy, to grasp hold of, and just believable enough that people might fall for it.

I immediately began spreading the word. Voting closed at one o'clock that afternoon, and it was eight o'clock in the morning. Five hours for a rumor to take hold.

It only took one. I showed a few of my friends the grand spectacle of Ben with Angela at her locker. They were appalled enough and trusted my word enough to tell everyone in their vicinity that Angela had been knocked up by none other than Ben Hatching, sophomore class presidential candidate.

My friends believed me because up until that point, I had always been nothing but honest. There was no reason not to be because nothing in my life ever posed a threat other than my own inadequacy. My dad may not have approved of the vast majority of my life, but that was mainly because of imperfect grades, which was something only I could control.

So when Ben came along, he was a whole other entity who was more than internal competition. I had to do whatever it took to win because losing to someone else would be the ultimate embarrassment.

By nine, my paternity scandal had ignited and was spreading like wildfire. Everyone was talking, and everyone was disgusted with Ben, the former perfect boy. After all, my private school was tiny, and it didn't take long for word to spread.

It wasn't much of a surprise when they announced my name as sophomore class president later that day. When my name was announced over the intercom, my friends in class applauded and patted me on the back, congratulating me. Said they were glad that loser Ben didn't win.

I remember how I felt. In retrospect, I should have been happy. My goal had been achieved, and I was going to make my father proud. But even still, I can conjure up that old familiar lump in my throat, the need to avert my gaze from anyone congratulating me.

I wasn't proud when I heard I'd won. I was disappointed, which was ironic. In trying not to disappoint my father, I disappointed myself.

And was he ever proud. When I came home from school and told him the news that day, it was like a whole other man was standing in front of me. The next time I would see him like that would be when I was accepted into Harvard, and I swear even then he wasn't as proud as when I won sophomore class president.

He took me out to my favorite restaurant that night, just the two of us, which almost never happened. Throughout the meal, he treated me like an adult for the first time, and for a fleeting moment my guilt faded and I erased Ben's confusion and disappointment—and my immoral actions—from my mind.

But it couldn't last, and my guilt overcame me during dessert. It was probably because spreading the rumor about Ben was the first time I had lied, and I didn't know how to handle it. So I came clean. I told my father everything as he ate his lemon meringue pie, then nervously waited for his disappointment or even anger.

But he was neither angry nor disappointed.

For a long moment, he didn't even respond. He calmly scooped up a piece of pie, chewed it thoughtfully, and chased it with a sip of Muscat.

"Well, Son," he finally said, and I was unnerved by the quality of unwavering calm in his tone. "You used your resources, is what you did. Hell, exposing the competition is something politicians have done for years," he chuckled.

"But Father," I said, confused. "Ben didn't ... he's not—"

"You don't know that," he interrupted before I could continue. "And even if you do, what's done is done. This whole thing shows me that you care," he said with a note of approval.

"You care enough to have done the most you could to ensure your success, and for that I am proud, James."

But for the wrong reasons, the voice in my head said back, and beneath the internal disappointment lay the growing layer of disgust for and distrust of the man who had raised me.

***

October 20, 1999. It had been a long day at work, and I needed to just relax, clear my head for a bit. Too late to golf, too dark to walk the beach. I wasn't much of a drinker, but the newly opened bar down the block wasn't a bad place to be.

There was my beer, and it was cold and crisp and refreshing, and the service was nice, and the place had this dim lighting that made everyone kind of blend together into a sea of darkness.

Except that darkness made the beautiful people stand out like pinpricks of light, and the beautiful people in that bar consisted of one person, and one person only.

She was overwhelmingly pretty, and whenever I looked up at her, I was struck by the notion that there was no one else on earth who had a more joyful laugh, a smile that glistened brighter, bluer eyes.

So I lifted my drink, then finished it off and ordered a vodka on the rocks.

Because what else do you do, really, when the beautiful woman capturing your attention isn't your wife?

17
JENAVIEVE

"Are you sure it's a good idea?" I can't stop myself from asking again. We are in Max's apartment—which I practically live in—and I'm sitting on the bed, packing more and more of my clothes into the looming moving boxes.

"Jen, we've been over this," Max says patiently, but I can hear the tinge of exasperation in his tone. "This is what *you* want to do, and that's what matters. Everything else is just not as important, you know? Your happiness is the most important thing."

I look up at him and am struck again by how perfect he is. Max Grayson, at once handsome and intelligent and kind and caring, so very caring, of me.

"Are you sure it's what *you* want?" I inquire nervously, but I mean it. Because if he's not okay with it, then I'm not okay with it. When you love someone as much as I love Max, their feelings inevitably become as powerful as your own.

Max comes over to the bed, leans over me and kisses my forehead. "Yes, it's absolutely what I want," he says with confidence. "You know how much I love Malibu whenever we visit your family. It'll be a good place for us."

We really are doing it, and I must remind myself that it truly is happening. Never did I think I would return to Malibu after leaving for Boston four years ago, and yet here I am. Returning to my roots.

"I think it will be, too," I say quietly, thinking of my family and the beach and the job opportunities I can pursue through my well-connected parents.

Of course, they don't know what Max knows: that I'm not studying law anymore. Instead, I'm going to Pepperdine to get a master's degree in Clinical Psychology .

Because I've seen what passionless work does to people. Growing up attending social event after social event with my parents' high-society friends, I observed the way the vast majority of them drank without hesitation. The way the women unsuccessfully tried to cover up the bags under their eyes with makeup, the way the men would rub their faces with their hands in frustration when they thought no one else was looking.

And after seeing what that passionless void did to their states of minds, the way they faltered through life with only inadvertent and fleeting pleasures to soothe them, I decided I would not turn into one of them.

So I'm not. I'm following what I want to do. Deciding to put my energy toward what keeps me up at night: the human brain, and all that can go wrong with it. And Max is on board, which means my life will be okay. I will have Max, and I will study psychology, and I will create my own life in the place that I know will never stop calling me until I return.

We already have a condo ready for us when we arrive tomorrow. However, my family is expecting only a brief visit for my graduation party. Max and I will stay with them as planned for a few days until I find the right time to tell them that I'm breaking family tradition while simultaneously moving closer to the family.

Of course, Max sees I'm overwhelmed, because before I know it he is opening his arms to me. I immediately walk into them and bury my face in his soft gray shirt that I like so well, the one that smells like his cologne mixed with a bit of my perfume and that distinct, vaguely minty personal scent belonging to him alone.

"Have I ever told you how much I love you?" I say to him. I feel his chest move as he chuckles.

"Once or twice," he teases. "And I think you know how I feel about you."

"Hmm," I pretend to consider his words, pretend to wrack my brain for the feelings he knows I don't need said aloud to make true.

"I don't know, Grayson." I grin, peering up at him. "You might have to remind me."

"Oh, really?" he laughs, and pulls away from our hug to look at me. "Well, I can think of a couple ways to do that," he smirks, then pulls me over to the bed.

***

I wake up the next morning in Max's arms and filled with the sense of excitement surrounding the prospect of seeing my family after a long time without them. Today I will get to see Madeline's smile, hear Elizabeth's laugh, listen to the oddly comforting sound of Ashley arguing with our parents.

After eating breakfast, Max and I pack up our final things. The moving company will drive everything across the country. By the time the truck arrives at our new apartment, I'll have explained all our plans to my parents.

Finally, we are ready to head to the airport. The apartment is now barren, leaving behind no echoes of the lives we lived in it. Our kitchen is now just a kitchen, our drawers just drawers, everything a meaningless object with no more sentimental value.

We stand beside each other, taking in the finality of our situation. Both of us understanding that now there is no going back, that our new lives begin today. He takes my hand, squeezes it gently.

"You ready?" he says, and in his voice I feel the brimming excitement and romanticism surrounding only the grandest of adventures.

I sigh, once, and take a last heartfelt glance around before internally beginning the process of turning something once loved into something faded dully into the past.

"Yes," I say with confidence, the trace of a smile playing on the corners of my lips. "I'm ready. Let's go home."

18
EVELYN

There are exactly two hours until the first guests will begin to filter in. I know this because I have these events down to a science. They are my livelihood, sometimes more so than motherhood or my career.

This party in particular must be perfect because it's Jenavieve's Harvard graduation party. It's not every day that your daughter graduates from college, let alone Harvard, and I am proud of her. And the way I show her this pride, the way I show her I love her, is by throwing her the party of the year.

You really have always lacked sentimentality, I tell myself as I deftly curl my bleach-blonde hair. My reflection stares back at me as I think about the ways in which I have lacked showing my daughters I love them. But then, my own mother wasn't the sentimental type, and I turned out successful.

James appears from the dressing room, and I watch him watching me in the mirror. He walks up to me, squeezes my shoulder. "You look lovely," he says, and he is smiling and I am remembering how very fortunate I am to have him.

"Thank you," I smile, finishing up my last curl. He kisses the side of my neck once, then turns and walks out of the room. I wait a moment before following, figuring it's about time to call Madeline down.

It's how it goes for every event. Jenavieve has always known when to be ready, has always meticulously planned so that she's downstairs, angelically waiting to greet the first guests right as they arrive.

Madeline is always ready in time, as long as I call her downstairs to remind her. She may not be as *aware*, per se, as Jenavieve, but she is respectful and cares about the parties.

Ashley couldn't care less, but she seems to listen to Madeline. I hear Madeline go into her room every time I call Ashley, and I hear her say it's time to come downstairs. I hear Ashley sigh and reluctantly make her way down, but then she disappears to God knows where.

It wasn't always that way, I solemnly remind myself. When she was tiny, Ashley would come bounding down the stairs earlier than Madeline or even Jenavieve. She would cling to me, ask me questions like three-year-olds do, get my dress sticky with her juice-stained fingers.

And I hate to admit now that it annoyed me back then. It was a nuisance, having a toddler clinging to me and following my every step while I was trying to prepare for guests. Jenavieve and Madeline hadn't been so eager to please when they were young. They didn't idolize me like Ashley did.

But I suppose I eventually scared her off, because she stopped coming downstairs early. Then she stopped coming down at all, until James and I took her phone away every time she neglected a gathering.

And now, she doesn't cling to me. She doesn't ask me questions or stare at me with those big, blue eyes. She barely even talks to me at all. I sigh, surprised at how it has hit me so out of the blue.

Her absence hit me hard, just as mine probably was a rough blow to her when she was young. *It's an unfortunate succession of abandonment, neglect and the inability to try to understand each other,* I think to myself as I stare out at the ocean.

That view. There's nothing but glass between this living room and outside, so all I can see is the infinity pool, the pink flower bushes lining it, the powdery beach and the glistening waves beyond.

The memory comes to me suddenly, making me stop for a moment. I stop what I'm doing, because I can't help but focus on the last true conversation Ashley had with me.

***

It was about two years ago, I suppose, making Ashley thirteen. I remember Elizabeth was sick, because her job making the appetizers had fallen to me.

It had been awhile since Ashley had stuck to my side as I prepared for a party, so I was surprised when I saw her bounding down the stairs toward me.

"Do you want some help, Mom?" she asked, and all I could do was stare at her blankly. I had expected a complaint or a request to go to a friend's house, or virtually anything other than an offer of help.

"I mean," she added, and I could feel the defense in her voice heightening, "you just don't have Elizabeth to help, so I figured you could maybe use an extra hand."

"Yes," I said quickly, because I knew that if I didn't respond fast I would scare her off, just like I always did. "Thank you, Ashley. I appreciate it."

She smiled a little, then, and I proceeded to show her how to toss the salad, how to roll out the dough for the mini pies, how to arrange the cheese and crackers the way Elizabeth did.

As we worked, it became more clear to me that we could not escape the formality. The time for truly connecting with Ashley had passed, and we both knew it. Neither of us knew what to say to the other, and neither of us knew how to chip the rock that had somehow formed an unbreakably solid wall between us.

I thought about this as I sliced onions and was thankful that onions make you cry.

Nonetheless, I didn't want Ashley to see me crying. I didn't like anyone seeing me cry. So I faced the kitchen wall, opposite from Ashley, and cut my vegetables, tears cutting rivulets through the makeup on my face—tears that weren't caused by the onions.

"Mom?" I heard a small voice from behind me and immediately wiped my face clean.

"Yes?" I said, and I saw as I turned around that Ashley was gazing outside, out at the view that had taken James' and my breath away twenty years earlier.

"Do you ever get tired of the view?" she asked quietly, and on her face was one of the most darkly troubled expressions I have ever seen.

I had to pause for a moment, because the nature of her question was so confusing that I had to stop and think.

"No. I don't. It takes my breath away every time."

She nodded, studying me for a few seconds, and then went back to arranging her cheese and crackers.

And all I could think about, as I gazed out at that magnificent view, was how I wished that what I'd said to her was true. *There must be something wrong with me,* I thought, because there was something strangely unsettling about the fact that I had lied.

After all, beautiful things should take your breath away every time you see them.

19
ELIZABETH

‿‿◦∞◦‿‿

It is a good day. Generally, I'm always in a good mood, but today is even better because it is finally Jenavieve's Harvard graduation party. I know how important this is to Evelyn, because it is her ultimate gift to Jenavieve, the ultimate way to show her she is proud.

I just hope Jen enjoys it. That everyone enjoys it, in fact. The numbers and grandeur of these parties can be overwhelming, and I can see it on all of the Blairs' faces from time to time. But this one should be fun and loose, a way for the family to genuinely celebrate.

Maybe Ashley will even participate. I don't know what she does, but I always see her quietly slip out the front door when she thinks no one is watching, usually with some type of alcoholic beverage in her hand. I wish she would be more in the center of it all. Talk to everyone, including her family. Including me.

Lost in my thoughts, I instinctively pull my hair into its usual loose ponytail, an ingrained repetition that has been part of my routine for years. I like predictability. It makes me feel secure, comfortable.

I go do what I do best: prepare for the guests. While I set up the tables and chairs and appetizers, Evelyn clacks frantically about, checking my work and adding on to it as she goes. I don't mind what she does, so long as she's content. It's my job and privilege to help her, and I'll do whatever I can to show her that.

Madeline appears just ten minutes before the party starts. She's wearing a dark-blue dress that shimmers a bit, and she has straightened her hair.

"You look beautiful, Madeline," I tell her, smiling encouragingly. For some reason, she looks a little on edge.

"Oh, thank you," she smiles quickly. Definitely distracted by something. I wonder what it could be.

She glances nervously about, her eyes flitting from place to place. Looking for someone.

"If you're looking for Jenavieve, I'm pretty sure she and Max are out back by the bar," I say, trying to fill in the gaps. Honestly, I can't really think of anyone else she would be looking for.

And then Noah walks in. He and his mom are some of the first people to arrive, which doesn't surprise me. Madeline's reaction, however, does. Her cheeks redden and I can practically feel the nervousness radiating off her.

"Wait," I smile, the realization suddenly hitting me. "Did you and Noah, like, *do* something?"

Her blush deepens. "No, no, we didn't," she mutters. I cock my head to the side and grin knowingly.

"I'm serious!" she whispers frantically. "I mean, there was just like, this *moment*, last time. We didn't kiss or anything. It was just different for us, and I don't know what to do. Shit, Liz, what do I do?"

"Calm down, for one thing," I smile at her, trying to ease her nerves. "And just act normal, I think. I mean, that can't hurt."

She nods, takes a deep breath, and turns to go talk to him and his mom. My advice could be horrible, for all I know. I haven't even had a boyfriend, so I suppose I'm not the most reliable source for dating tips. But being yourself must be good, right? Noah adores her as she is, and I know she feels the same way. I just wonder if they'll show it or not.

It could go well or bad, I think to myself as I watch them across the room. But this time, instead of feeling doubtful, I silently urge them to take the risk. Because two people who are so genuinely and wholesomely good for each other should know, really know, what that feels like. I have yet to find that. But Madeline has, and I want her to experience it as much, if not more, than I want it for myself.

So I go back to work, all the while silently willing them both to stop holding back.

20
MADELINE

I keep glancing over at him to try and catch his eye, but it doesn't do any good. Noah won't even glance in my general direction.

When I went over to say hi to him and Sherri, I could feel the nerves radiating off of my skin and my heart pounding. Something had happened last time, something different, and I thought for sure that it would create a different vibe between us.

But Noah seemed fine. Calm, put together, normal. He wasn't quite as outgoing as usual, though. He was more shy, probably feeling a bit vulnerable, like I am.

The aggravating thing is, though, is that nothing is happening. I don't know what I expected, exactly, but I expected things to be different between us. And they're not. My home is filling up with people, everyone is fake-laughing shrilly, and Noah is talking to various people around the room, seemingly not even caring where I am.

Doesn't matter, I repeat to myself like a mantra as I make my rounds. *Nothing has changed. It probably meant nothing to him. We're just friends. Always have been, always will be.*

I find myself back in the butler's pantry off the kitchen with Elizabeth an hour or so later, leaning against the counter as she prepares drinks. It's almost that lovely time of night.

"So, how's it going?" she asks, and I feel the amusement and curiosity in her voice.

"Honestly, everything is normal," I shrug. "I mean, we haven't talked at all tonight, but we usually go down to the beach around this time. I think I might just hide out with you tonight, though. He doesn't want to see me, Liz. I know he thinks it's awkward. And it kind of is, honestly —"

"Madeline," she cuts me off. "You're rambling. And I think you're reading too much into it. I'm sure he wants to see you, he just might be a little nervous, like you are. You shouldn't hide from him, though. You should go talk to him. It doesn't have to be any different than how you usually talk to him, but you should still go out there."

"So should you," I sigh, thinking about how Elizabeth never really has freedom at these parties like the rest of us.

"Ah, but I've got my routine," she says with a smile, pouring more champagne. "And as I recall, *you* have a certain beach routine with a certain Noah, who's probably wondering where the hell you are right now."

"Okay," I take a deep breath. "Alright, I'll go. Thanks Liz."

I make my way through the living room, trying to act confident, carefree. It's about eleven, which means that Noah is probably looking around for me.

Or not, I think to myself with disappointment when I see him with his back to me, laughing with a Detail worker.

I plop down on the couch in the corner in defeat, feeling lonely without Elizabeth or Noah or anyone else. My feet are aching; my heels have been rubbing uncomfortably against them all night, creating painful blisters.

I am seriously considering going upstairs and lying down in my bed, wondering if my parents would even notice my absence, when he appears. Noah, standing in front of me, the pounding bass and rising laughter of increasingly drunk individuals rising around us.

He peers down at me, and I finally make eye contact with him. Before I can think to say anything, he says curtly, "Let's dance."

"Dance?" I say aloud, incredulous, because dancing isn't our thing. We literally go down to the beach to avoid it.

"Yeah," he responds confidently, and I see the spontaneity in his eyes. "It's the biggest party of the year, and I'm feeling festive. Let's go."

"Noah, I don't really … my feet are killing me," I say, which is true. I don't know how much longer I can last in these things.

He laughs and kneels down, and I'm wondering what the hell he's doing when I see he's slipping off my shoes.

"Noah!" I laugh. "I can't go out there in front of everyone barefoot! You know my mom would kill me."

"Well luckily for you, we won't be in front of everyone." He grins mischievously and stands, holding out his hand expectantly.

After a second's pause, I take it. He pulls me through the throng of people to the side door and I know where we're going, wondering why we're running as he leads me across the beach, my bare feet sinking further into the sand with every step.

We reach the shore and he is twirling me, which is ridiculous because the music is nothing like what you'd hear in a ballroom—it's all bass and modernity.

As I finally stop twirling and try to regain my balance and my breath, I see a sizeable wave approaching out of the corner of my eye.

I shriek and Noah grabs my waist, pulling me away from the coming wave.

But it still hits us a bit, sending freezing cold droplets pelting against our skin. It's a shock in the warm night air.

His hands are still on my waist and we can't stop laughing. His hair is messy, so I reach up to push it off of his forehead and I can't help it, I can't stop myself from wrapping an arm around his neck, standing on tiptoe, and kissing him.

His lips taste like salt, which I know is from the wave that hit us. I pull away after a moment, trying to gauge his reaction. And I instantly realize it was a mistake.

He stands frozen, staring at me, a little stunned. I'm hoping he will say something, *do* something, but he doesn't. He doesn't.

My face burns with heat. *Now I've done it,* I chastise myself silently. *Gone and ruined the friendship forever, for real this time.*

Tears blur my vision and I fight to push them away. "I'm sorry," I mutter. "That was … I don't know what I was thinking. Just forget I did that, please."

I turn sharply in the sand and get no farther away from him than one step when I feel his hand gripping my wrist.

"Wait, Maddy," he says quietly. I'm trying to interpret his tone of voice as I turn around, but then I see the look in his eyes and think I know what's about to happen.

Sure enough, he pulls me in close to him, rests a hand gently on my neck, and kisses me, tentatively at first and then, as I lean in, more confidently, more passionately.

So we stand there, wrapped in each other's arms, and he is kissing me over and over and I don't see it stopping any time soon, and I don't want it to.

There must be no better feeling than this, I find myself thinking. This has to be as good as it gets. Anything beyond this, any better feeling is unimaginable.

All I know is the waves gently lapping against our feet, our arms holding each other steadily, the heat of his lips on mine, curious and explorative, and all I know is that this is all I ever want to know.

21

The afternoon hours are reserved for arts and crafts. As if drawing a picture can cure the depression experienced only by those who are acutely aware of how effortless it all is.

I can't create any art, as there's nothing lovely to create. This becomes clear as I continue to stare blankly at the paper in front of me, until a nurse makes her way over to ask me to draw something.

"I can't think of anything," I mutter despondently.

"Think of something that you consider beautiful," she encourages, "and do your best to recreate that beauty."

"There's nothing beautiful," I say curtly. And there's nothing to add to that.

"Well, then, think about what makes you happy," the nurse says, with a solemnity surpassing her usual cheer. "And don't say there's nothing," she continues, "because I know there is. It's part of being human."

I stare at my blank paper and think about, really consider, what brings me joy. Then I want to laugh, because I see that the only things that can bring me happiness surpass materialism of any form.

And then I want to cry, because I've realized this too late.

"What makes me happy," I say quietly, "is belonging. Feeling comfortable."

I sit back and watch her face, amused to see her struggle with the no-tion that my happiness can't be visually displayed.

"So that's the issue," I say aloud. "I can't paint 'belonging.' I can only **feel** *it. And I don't. I'm an outsider in my own goddamn family, and I will be for the rest of my life."*

Numb. That is how I feel, because to feel any emotion would be too painful to bear.

"So forgive me," I drip with sarcasm, "for not retaining a vast interest in maintaining my existence."

With that, I stand and confidently exit the room. No one tries to stop me, and no one interferes as I make it all the way to my room.

It's been a bad week, I suppose you could say, in the sense that I have refused to participate in much of anything. I figure that the fact that I'm speaking at all seems like progress enough to them.

It doesn't mean shit to me. None of it does. No matter what happens around me or what I do, the predicament won't change.

I feel my body starting to panic, so I initiate the breathing technique my therapist recommended.

It's simple. Deep breath in, deep breath out. In, out. In, out.

On the inside of the social strata. On the outside of the social strata. In love. Out of love. In a family. Out of a family.

It is one of the tragic ironies of being human, I think to myself. We bring all the beautiful things in, only to inevitably release them all.

There's no choice in the matter; it simply happens—a mind and entity separate from our desires. And it remains one of the reasons I lack partici-pation points in the loony bin.

22

ASHLEY

It's been a while since we've had an actual sit-down family meal, and it's a little awkward. Sometimes, when we're all together, it's easy to figure out what to talk about. Conversation runs smoothly if people are in high spirits, after all.

But other times, when you haven't been with people for so long, you don't even know how to begin. There's just a heavy, obvious silence stifling conversation.

Forks clink against plates as we all eat the stir fry that, of course, my mom made. I can't remember the last time my dad cooked us anything. He can barely even get back from work in time to join us for a pre-made meal.

Madeline clears her throat, signaling the start of some sort of conversation, I guess. A bit surprising, considering she's usually reserved. She's been in a weirdly good mood lately, though.

"Hey, Elizabeth?" she says, and I feel the way those two words echo around our unnecessarily cavernous home.

"Do you think you could give me a ride over to Noah's tomorrow?"

Everyone stops eating and stares at her. She and Noah may be best friends, but as far as I know, they never really hang out outside of the parties.

"I promised Sherri I would help her do some baking," she adds quickly, a blush deepening her pale complexion.

"Yeah, of course!" Elizabeth smiles brightly. For some reason, the exchange pisses me off.

I grunt and stare sullenly into my bowl, trying to keep quiet. I want this dinner to go smoothly so I can go upstairs and text Dash as soon as possible. We're hanging out tomorrow, *finally*. Except no one knows that I'm hanging out with him, because I always get dropped off at the Starbucks by his house to "meet up with Kelly," where Dash promptly picks me up. Dropped off tomorrow. Shit.

"Wait," I say a bit more loudly than intended. "I need a ride tomorrow too."

There are three cars in this family: my mom's SUV, my dad's convertible, and the sedan. I think the sedan is technically mine and Madeline's, but Elizabeth does all the driving.

Madeline never learned how to drive; my parents thought it was more important for her to focus on school than driving, especially since Elizabeth is capable of taking her where she needs to go.

"Well," Elizabeth says brightly, "I can take both of you, just at different times."

"No, that's ridiculous," my dad intervenes. "You drive enough as it is. It's unnecessary for you to take both the girls to different places tomorrow."

"Well, Dad," I say through gritted teeth, "it's not my fault that Madeline never learned how to drive. I have a commitment tomorrow, and you and Mom are both at work, so I kinda need to—"

"That's enough," he interrupts again. "Madeline asked first, so she gets the ride tomorrow. If that's a problem for you, ask Kelly to pick you up. I'm sure she wouldn't mind."

Except Kelly can't pick me up, because I won't be hanging out with her, I think to myself, because of course my family can't know. The sneaking around is usually exciting, but at times like these, I want to scream with frustration.

And I don't understand why my father always, without failure, sides with and protects Elizabeth in situations where he could just as easily back up one of his other kids. *Elizabeth isn't even part of this family, not really*, I find myself thinking. I momentarily hate myself for thinking it, but a small part of my brain argues that it's true.

"Can I be excused?" I ask in a monotone voice. I'm done with this conversation. Family dinners rarely go well, but this one is particularly bad.

No one is answering me, so I give myself permission to be excused and roughly push back my chair, the steel legs making a sharp, echoing screech that reverberates loudly around the room. I guess the hugeness of this house can sometimes help me make a statement.

Just after I've cleared my plate and am about to head upstairs and tell Dashton that I can no longer hang out with him tomorrow, my dad clears his throat. Goddammit.

"Ashley," he calls coolly. I turn around and try to refrain from rolling my eyes. I don't know if I'm successful, but I also don't really care.

"I think I have the perfect solution to your problem," he says. I can tell by his tone of voice that he's very pleased with whatever his idea is, which probably means I'm not going to like it.

"If you want to have the freedom of driving yourself to your friends' houses and such whenever you want, that's a freedom you need to earn."

Shit, I curse silently. I know he's implying a bunch of work around the house to prove that I'm worthy of rides, which is ridiculous.

Right when I'm about to say so, he continues. "Which is why I think Elizabeth should teach you how to drive."

My eyes widen. What the hell sort of plan is this? Everyone in this house knows that Elizabeth and I don't get along. Technically, it's one-sided. Perfect Elizabeth is nice to everyone, and is especially nice to me. But I don't know, there's just something about her that bothers me. It's admittedly unfair, but I can't control my feelings.

I glance over at Elizabeth, and she looks almost as uncomfortable as I do.

"If, of course, Elizabeth is willing to help you," my father quickly adds. So basically, Elizabeth gets a say in this but I don't.

I glance at her warily, awaiting her response. It's up to her now.

"Of course, yes," she says in a rush. "I would be happy to teach Ashley how to drive."

"Then it's settled," my dad says cheerily. It is just then that I notice my mom has said nothing to contribute to this conversation all night. "You can start tomorrow," he says with a smile.

"Lovely," I say in the most neutral tone of voice I can manage. But inside, I am seething, and I'm also profoundly uncomfortable. Elizabeth and I never bonded, and I never planned to. I thought I was in the clear with her leaving in a few months, but I guess not. At least not anymore.

Soon I will be forced to get to know my adopted sister for the first time. In less than twenty-four hours, to be exact.

As I close the door to my room, I am struck by the surprising revelation that I am scared of her hating me. Kind, welcoming Elizabeth, who likes everyone. Which means she will like me when she gets to know the real me. Right?

Snap out of it, Ashley, I chastise myself. *You don't give a damn about what Elizabeth thinks of you. Or anyone, for that matter.*

Yet I find myself continuously troubled for the rest of the night by the irony of my tough persona. I have always convinced myself that I am an unbreakable shield, the girl that no one can shake and no one can break.

But in reality, I know deep inside that Elizabeth is capable of breaking my shield. Maybe it's why I've never liked her, have always been unsettled by her. Because I know she may be capable of breaking down my walls and making me truly, fearfully vulnerable.

23
JAMES

I did love her, and she was everything I ever wanted. At one time.

When we were newly married, she lit up everything. I would find myself gazing at her in admiration in the most random moments when her beauty would shine through.

Her laugh was so genuine and full of joy, even over the smallest things. And she was quietly intelligent; although I knew she was smarter than me, she didn't realize it. I found this charming.

There were so many things to love about her: her vocabulary and the way she would use obscure academic words; the cool softness of her hand in mine as we walked into a cafe to do some work on Saturday mornings. The way her dark eyes lightened when there was sunlight shining directly on them.

I sincerely loved the little things about my wife, and that is how I knew without a doubt that I loved *her*. Everything about her was admirable, beautiful and engrossing.

In the beginning.

I think that after a few years with her as my wife, the stunning and unreal feeling that she was *mine* began to fade. Living under the same roof as her, I grew accustomed to everything about her.

And while it captivated me in the early years, I know that that was only because it was new. She was new. Being married was new.

But then it wasn't so new, and I found myself craving something that would surprise me, a flit of something new from Evelyn to reaffirm that her beauty was infinite.

And then I held Jenavieve for the first time, and I realized that I could hold more happiness in my heart than I had previously thought capable.

So I found myself searching for more. It was out there, within grasp, and I was tired of putting a limit on my happiness.

And that's when I met Sarah.

***

October 20, 1999. Almost five years I'd been married.

It was that day in the bar, when I had felt too defeated to go home and face my family just yet. I didn't feel like facing them much at all in those days. In all transparency, my life was a shit show.

Work was tough, time-consuming, mentally draining. I was good at my job, because I felt I had to be. My parents instilled the belief in me that I was only as good as the amount of money I made, and in order to make money, I had to do very well at a very high-paying job.

So I wasn't a natural. Most people assumed I was because of my increasing success. But in reality, I pushed my mind to what felt like its full capacity every day in order to be the man and provide for our little girl.

Evelyn didn't need provisions. Her intense focus, determination and ruthlessness got her far, and fast, with Detail. In the back of my mind, it bugged me that my wife was so financially independent. She wasn't dependent on me, and it seemed glaringly obvious in every way.

My wife did not need me. I knew with complete certainty that she would be fully okay if I weren't around. And I hated that fact from the bottom of my heart. I needed someone to need *me*, and it felt as though no one did.

Even my three-year-old didn't need me. She had her nanny and was attached to Evelyn rather than me. I felt alone, overwhelmed, unappreciated and ultimately unneeded by the people who were supposed to be closest to me.

So I don't blame myself for getting a drink that night in October. I don't blame myself for trying to take the edge off of the unrelenting despair that was my life. I don't even blame myself for trying to find something that would make me feel alive and loved again.

What I do blame myself for is the lengths I went to in order to get there.

When I saw her across the room, I was incapable of taking my eyes off her. She had this electric pull, and she gave off the sort of warmth and energy that made people want to be around her.

I had noted that she had come into the bar alone, but she had quickly acquired somewhat of a crowd. The people on either side of her at the bar seemed intent on listening to her talk, watching her gesticulate animatedly as she spoke. The bartender was slipping her drinks for free. She was that sort of girl.

Bright blonde hair, sharp blue eyes. You know, the sort of eyes that you see all of, every little speck and fleck of coloration.

The connection I felt with her when we first made eye contact was unlike anything I have ever felt in my life. Evelyn's confidently beautiful persona also pulled me in. But what this woman and I had was different.

When we looked into each other's eyes for the first time, we were both acutely aware that we pulled each other. We were magnetized by each other's everything.

So I had to talk to her. Not to would violate everything I knew about the despair of regret and yearning for the past.

She wasn't looking to pick someone up. I knew that, as did everyone else. She was put together, maybe had just come from work like I had. She was friendly to those around her, but not flirtatious.

But that didn't deter me because I hadn't been looking to pick anyone up in that bar either. Sometimes things just happen, and that night was the first and perhaps only time I have ever truly believed in fate.

I waited. I waited until those around her left, and I texted Evelyn that I had to do some late-night work at the office. I felt bad for the lie, but I was much more consumed with the prospect of talking to this striking woman, even for only a few moments, than I was about lying to my wife.

Finally, it was just us. We weren't the only ones in the whole place, but we were clearly the only ones in each other's vicinity. I watched her toss her long hair over her shoulder, delicately take the last sip of her vodka soda. Willing myself to shake the nerves, I tried to smoothly appear next to her by seeming to move so the bartender could hear me better.

"Hey, bartender," I called nonchalantly as I leaned against the bar right next to her. I could feel her closeness, the nearness of her body.

"Yup," he called from the back, on the side closest to us.

"Can I please get another round? And whip one up for her, too, while you're at it. Please."

I smiled at her then, not really sure where the hell I was going with this, but too intrigued to stop myself from finding out.

I sat down in the seat next to her and held out my hand, trying to appear professional.

"Hi, I'm James," I said warmly, and was surprised to feel most of my nerves dissipate with the inviting nature of her response.

"I'm Sarah," she smiled brightly, taking my hand and shaking it firmly. Even as the handshake itself ended, we stayed that way, hand in hand, for obviously longer than necessary.

I pulled away first, only because I was distracted by a text from Evelyn, signaling that she knew I was "at work" and would see me when I got home.

"Sorry, that was my coworker," I explained, trying to hide my blush at yet another lie. Somehow, I couldn't tell Sarah that I was married, let alone that I had a daughter. It was an awful thing, to not feel joy at the prospect of sharing my family with others. But Sarah didn't fall under the category of "others."

I only liked her more and more as time went on, as we continued talking with the ease of people who hadn't met only moments earlier.

She told me about her public relations job, about the company she worked for and how much she adored Malibu, to which she had moved about a year ago. She slipped in that she was twenty-eight, which was just two years younger than me.

I heard about her apartment, her little dog, how she liked to walk the beach at sunset every night, which was convenient because her office was practically on the beach. In the thirty minutes we talked over that one round of drinks, I came to know Sarah, and she came to know me

Keeping Evelyn and Jenavieve out of the conversation, I told Sarah about being a lawyer, how it was mentally exhausting much of the time. I told her about growing up in Malibu, how I couldn't imagine living anywhere else. I even slipped in bits about my money-obsessed parents, how they didn't care much about anything else.

And through it all, we understood each other, and were more and more attracted to each other. I knew we could both feel it, although neither of us made a move. That was probably due to the vibe I was giving off, as visions of my wife tucking my child into bed alone clouded my thoughts and made my chest ache with guilt.

It wasn't fair, and it wasn't right, and I knew I needed to stop right then and go home. But I didn't want to. Instead, I excused myself to the restroom.

Splashing water on my face, I leaned against the single-sink bathroom counter and looked wearily into the mirror. *What the hell are you doing, Blair?* I reprimanded myself defeatedly. Because it wasn't right. It couldn't be. Despite what I felt inside, there were people to go home to. People who may not have needed me, but whom I was still obligated to.

An obligation. It was fucked up, the whole thing, and I knew it. I knew it so well that I decided to go out there and politely tell Sarah that I had to go home because my wife and little girl were waiting for me. That would end whatever this was, without a doubt.

Unhappily determined, I took a deep breath and swung open the bathroom door, only to practically run right into her. She was there, right there, mere inches from my face.

We looked at each other, and I quite literally felt my heart skip a beat. She took the smallest and most cautious step forward, looking up at me timidly but also with a hunger I didn't believe I had ever seen in Evelyn's eyes.

And despite everything, I kissed her. I pulled her to me and kissed her, closed the bathroom door behind us and continued kissing her, even as I knew it was wrong. Despite Evelyn, Jenavieve and moral obligations, despite everything under the sun, I kissed Sarah passionately and could not hide that I liked—no, loved—it.

It was the most selfish thing I had ever done. Worse than sabotaging Ben to win class president all those years ago. I'd never thought I could ever do anything that would make me feel more terrible than that.

Ironically, I didn't feel terrible after kissing Sarah that night. And kiss was all we did. I didn't feel terrible leaving that bathroom with her, giggling like children while exchanging numbers. And I didn't feel terrible as I drove home.

There was no ache in my gut or pit in my stomach. Instead, I felt rejuvenated. I felt alive. I laughed out loud, then, because I realized that I was happy, unreservedly happy, for the first time in a long while. Despite the circumstances, I had found my *more*, and its name was Sarah Jenkins.

***

So yes, I did love Evelyn, and yes, she was everything I ever wanted. At a time. But love fades, burns slowly and painfully, and ultimately shrivels under the weight of life and incompatibility.

Yet here we are, continuing to live as we always have. I kiss my wife's forehead and stoically prepare for the party. I glance out at the same view, from the same house, paid for by the same job, and shared by the same wife and the same family.

It is one of the tragic ironies of being. Despite having joy handed to us on a silver platter, we too often revert to the safety of what we know. Which is often not joy.

24
ELIZABETH

G rowing up, I never felt a consuming urge to know my biological parents. Every single one of my memories consisted of the Blairs as my family. While it was clear to me that I wasn't quite aligned in the biological sense, it was even more clear that I was theirs as they were mine.

So I didn't need to know the details about my birth. I knew that my parents had left me on the doorstep like I was Harry Potter, and that was really all the information I needed. They were likely young, irresponsible and unable to provide for a baby, so they left me at a nice house where it looked like a child could flourish.

I came to the conclusion when I was young that DNA doesn't make a family, and I still stick to this. Yet now I find myself yearning to know who created me.

It all started when I was volunteering for the blood drive at school. Despite never having shared it with my family, I'd wanted to volunteer for years. But my fear of blood and needles always kept me from doing it. Since it's my senior year, I decided to be brave and finally go for it.

That proved to be difficult when I began filling out the paperwork.

It had never, up until that point, been difficult for me to deal with medical issues. I've always been extraordinarily healthy, have never had to go to the hospital and rarely need to go to the doctor. When I do, I'm always accompanied by Evelyn or James, who fills out paperwork.

So I never realized how much I don't know. Question upon question about my background: *Is there a history of heart disease in your family? Please explain. Is there a history of blood pressure abnormalities in your family? Please explain.* **Please explain.**

I couldn't explain anything. I so badly wanted to go home and just be a part of the natural order of things, ask James and Evelyn to fill out the paperwork for me so that I could go and do this thing that could help people. But I couldn't.

More aggravating was the sudden, lurching realization that I had no clue what sort of health concerns I could have inherited. Maybe heart disease does run in my family, and maybe blood pressure could be a concern for me one day.

So for purely this reason, purely because I must know my medical history, I have decided that I must talk to Evelyn or James about my biological parents. They must know something, or they must know how to help me find them. I figure they will be understanding. They're sensible people, and I think they would want me to know what I want to know.

James is at work, as he usually is, but Evelyn is working from home, as she usually does. I peek through the doorway of her office to find her sitting rigidly at her desk, bent over a stack of papers. I watch her rub her eyes tiredly, shake her body as though ridding herself of stress.

She's been on edge lately, working into all hours of the night. From the upstairs hallway, I can see the faint glow of her office light in the middle of the night as I use the bathroom or grab a drink of water.

Her frequent work sessions can't be good for her well-being. Yet she still throws herself into this work, into continuously perfecting Detail so that it can thrive forever.

I tap on the side of the wall, and she jumps only a little before turning to see me in the doorway. Smiling wearily, she invites me into her office and puts her papers off to the side.

"How's it going in here?" I ask her gently, hoping she'll see as I do that she deserves a break.

"It's ..." she pauses, sighs as she glances at the paperwork over-flowing her desk. "It's good. Busy, but it is what it is." She shrugs. Downplaying. I notice she does that a lot, especially when it comes to her own accomplishments. She doesn't give herself enough credit. Sometimes I wonder if Jenavieve inherited that part of her.

"But what's up?" she continues, swaying the subject away from her work.

"Oh," I am flustered, almost having forgotten the reason I came in here in the first place. "Well, I actually wanted to ask you about my birth parents." I'm surprised at how easily I say it.

Evelyn's face turns a bit pale, and she regards me quizzically. The few times we've talked about my biological parents, she was awkward and didn't say much. I'm hoping that things will be different this time.

"What do you want to know?" she asks after a moment.

"Anything, really," I say invitingly. "I want to know about them for health purposes," I clarify. "I just think it's important that I, you know, know my medical history. I tried to volunteer at the blood drive at school today, and when I was filling out that medical form they give you, I realized how much I don't even know about myself."

Evelyn glances down at the table, rubs her forehead. I instantly feel guilty for adding more stress to her life.

"It's okay," I voice quickly, before she can respond. "I know you and James don't know much. Obviously. I just ... any information I can find out about them, I'd like to know. For health purposes."

"I'm sorry, Liz," she says sadly, not quite looking at me. "I wish I could help you, but I don't know enough. And it's just … it wouldn't be good to try and find them, you know?"

Ouch. Even though she said it nicely, it still hurts. A reminder that there are people out there who didn't want me. People who were fine with leaving me with another family.

"You're right," I say quietly. "Yeah. I get it. It's okay, I'll be fine."

I get up to leave her office, knowing that this conversation is over and feeling bad that I even began it at all. After all Evelyn has done for me, what all the Blairs have done for me, it's not right to disregard them in any way. They are my family.

"I really am sorry, Elizabeth," Evelyn says quietly, almost so that I can't hear it. But I do, and there is so much regret and remorse in her voice.

"It's okay," I say, trying to sound as positive as I can. "Don't worry about it. And good luck with work."

But even as I'm up in my room, trying to focus on my homework, the feeling persists, nagging at me. As much as I try not to, I still want to know about my birth parents.

And I have a history of finding out things that I really want to know.

25
JENAVIEVE

When I was young, I was purely and innocently happy. There was beauty in every moment, a childlike sparkle decorating life.

And even now, even though I try not to, I struggle with the fact that my joy got punctured somewhere along the way.

When I met Max, I told him I wasn't perfect. I didn't want him to perceive me as something I'm not. Not that anyone is perfect—he just thought my world was devoid of struggle. Most people believe this about me. Maybe it's because I'm constantly smiling, or because my family comes from money, or because I have an Ivy League education.

All beautiful things, but at the end of the day, things can't bring joy. So I felt it was only fair that Max at least know that my life isn't always beautiful, despite the fact that I have beautiful things.

Something happened when I was younger, and I went to a dark place. At one point I really didn't think I would get out. And then Elizabeth found out, and she told me I needed help, and I couldn't do that. I didn't want to bring the strain of gossip to my family or myself.

I couldn't be someone I didn't want to be, and that simple realization drove me to skip the professional help and get better on my own. In retrospect, I probably should've gotten the help. There was a lot I, and others, could've done differently.

But I moved forward because the clock doesn't pause for anyone. Slowly but surely, the light came back again.

For a time, Elizabeth was the only one who knew that my beautiful life was falsified, that it wasn't even there at all. And then I started dating Max, and I find myself feeling that he should know what went wrong.

Max Grayson loves me. He has seen the beauty in my imperfections since that moment on Harper's balcony when I told him they existed. He laughs with me and never at me, makes me smile despite any sort of mood I am in, listens attentively to everything I say.

He is, always has been and always will be my person.

And yet, he still doesn't know about some of the darkest parts of me. For the longest time I didn't want our relationship to be anything but light. When I'm with him, I feel completely at ease. We laugh, do spontaneous things, have interesting conversations.

We don't talk about darkness, because when we are with each other, there is no darkness. It's a good thing, to have a relationship of pure happiness. But it's not real. There is no perfect relationship, and I believe that the more serious your relationship gets, the more you have to realize this.

I want him. I want to be with Max Grayson for the rest of my life. He is the person I love most in the world. But he can't be with me forever if he doesn't know everything about me.

He knows that I don't like wearing socks and that my favorite day of the year is Christmas Eve, that I hate red apples and love green ones. He knows my hopes and dreams, he knows how to read my emotions faster than anyone else. He knows how to make me smile better than anyone else.

But he doesn't know that there was a whole chunk of my life when I wasn't even me. He doesn't know how unhappy I was. He doesn't know that I lost my light, and that, as much as I wish it could, it won't fully return to its pure self again.

He doesn't know about my problems because I have denied their existence. What happened is in the past, and I worked hard to ensure that it stayed there. I did what I needed to do to bring back my light, but I can't deny the unsettling notion that it's not the same light.

Must the people we love know that there are parts of us that are unlovable? Or will they appreciate what we fail to love about ourselves?

I think I must believe that I am capable of being loved *because* of the things I don't love about myself, not in spite of them.

I know, deep inside, that Max will still love me. There is no doubt about that. I just hope that I can love myself enough to let someone else in—this time, voluntarily.

26
EVELYN

Sometimes I wonder if my mother thinks about my family. The last time we saw her was five years ago, when she unexpectedly dropped by two days after Christmas. She had come from Prague and brought the girls little gifts from the market. She visited with us, telling us of her travels, for about two hours. Then she abruptly got up and announced she had to get going if she was going to make her flight back to her home in Taiwan.

I walked her out, and it was only then, when it was just the two of us, that she stopped, took my face in her hands and asked sharply, "Are you happy?"

There was no lying to my mother. I reflected on everything that had happened in the past years. The problems in my marriage, the success of my company. The lack of connection with my children, the parties thrown in my beautiful home to celebrate anything and everything. The living in Malibu, escaping my broken childhood. Leaving my mother, even though she made it clear it was what she wanted.

So I looked her in the eye and said, "Yes, Mom. I am happy." I meant it, too. I didn't have to lie and say my life was perfect. It was certainly far from that. But there were so many things that made it so incredibly lovely, and I knew that my mother wouldn't leave without believing I was more than okay.

She nodded, looked into my soul with those piercing eyes and told me she was glad I was glad. Glad. Not happy. Never happy. Not even when I told her I was pregnant with my first baby, or when I had bought her a house in the middle of Beverly Hills—which, of course, she refused to accept.

∗∗∗

On November 5, 1995, I booked a flight to Los Angeles to go see my mother. The last time I had visited home was my second year of college, when I went there for Christmas break for my last time.

When the cab dropped me off at the doorstep, I was immediately thrown back to the vulnerability of my youth—when I lived with the notion that this was all that life was. Before I knew there was a way to climb to a top that I didn't even know existed.

And here I was, all these years later. The front door was still chipped in the same places. Nothing had changed. Yet everything had changed.

When my mother opened the door, she simply stared. I had shown up unannounced to surprise her. She looked surprised, that's for sure. But there wasn't exactly pleasure on her face. More like a strange sort of sadness interlaced with the faintest trace of fear.

"Evvy," she said. Then she smiled a little sadly when she softly said, "I almost wouldn't have recognized you." She gave me a once-over, and I found myself doing the same. I was wearing a long coat and cashmere scarf. I'd had my hair blown out, and I looked the part of the successful businesswoman. My mother, meanwhile, was dressed in faded blue jeans and an olive-colored shirt.

And my God, was I proud of myself to be where I was. My company was thriving. I was thriving. And James and I were thriving. I unbuttoned my coat, then, to show my mother the taut roundness of my stomach.

"You're going to be a grandma," I smiled, and a spark of light entered her eyes.

"Oh, that's wonderful," she said, and her eyes were a bit glassy as she stared at the stomach holding little Jenavieve. "I'm glad you came to tell me. And I'm glad you're glad."

Glad. There it was with that word. Even when it was clear to anyone that I was *happy*, having-a-*baby* happy, that was never what my mother seemed to think about my life. But it didn't faze me then because my joy was infinite. And hers was about to be, too.

"There's something else, Mom," I said, a small smile spreading over my face. And I had to just say it. I'm incessantly impatient and was too excited to hold back any longer.

"I bought you a house," I said. "The big, beautiful house that you've always deserved. It's really wonderful, lots of windows and light, and there's a sauna, too. I thought you would like that. And you know what the best part is? It's in Beverly Hills. Right in the heart of it. So you can be next door to those Beverly bitches and show them that you're not beneath them once and for all."

I don't know what I expected. Tears, a hug maybe? But certainly not laughter. It wasn't condescending or mean laughter. It was surprised laughter, the sort that happens when something is thrown completely out of left field.

"That's kind, Evelyn," she said finally. "Truly, it is. Completely and exceedingly generous. But I can't accept," she smiled sadly. But there was this trace of pride that I didn't understand.

"Yes, Mom, of course you can," I said emphatically. "Please accept this. You did so much for me, raising me on your own. I want to give back, that's what I've always wanted. You can accept this. Please do."

"The money is very kind," she said calmly. "And it's no secret I could use some," she added, chuckling a bit. "But it's the house ..." she trailed off. I looked at her expectantly.

"Darling, I never wanted to join them," she said softly, as if not to hurt my feelings.

"What?" I stared at her, dumbfounded. "But ... you always ... we talked about this!" I sputtered. "All those times you lost those acting jobs to those women who weren't any better at acting than you. The ones who got the part because they were rich and could do their hair and shit. We talked about this, Mom! I've wanted to buy you a house in Beverly Hills since the moment you first lost to one of them."

She sighed, looking at me with those blue eyes. "I let us talk about it because it was infuriating at the time, and I was glad you recognized that money was what differentiated us. Not skills or talent.

"It's like you said," she continued. "They weren't better than me. Never were. Hell, still aren't. So why would I feel any need to join them?" she asked simply. "I don't need to have a life like theirs to feel worthy of what I deserve. I know I *am* worthy, was always worthy. It's just that money places a dent in everything."

I was at a loss for words. I didn't understand, couldn't grasp what she was trying to say. Still can't, not really. To get what you want in life, you have to join those who have succeeded. That was what my childhood taught me, and look how it paid off for me! I had a beautiful house, a successful company, a loving husband, and a little baby growing inside me.

"Will you at least take the money?" I said softly, wearily. "You don't have to live in that house, just please take the money. Do what you want to do with it."

She stepped forward and hugged me, enfolding me in the strong warmth of her embrace. She thanked me and accepted the money I was keen on giving her.

And what she did with it was travel. There is an entire drawer in my room dedicated to the postcards she sends me from the most obscure places. Scandinavia. Iceland. Taiwan is her favorite, and she currently lives in a small apartment there when she's not backpacking around the world.

She rarely comes to visit us, but I know she still cares. She always sends the girls a little something on each holiday, calls them on their birthdays, and sends me postcards so that I have a little glimpse of her life.

But my mother stopped being my mother the moment I left for college. From that point forward, my life was devoted to rising up. Moving on.

And it always worked for me. There was never any flaw in it, until now. Now that Sherri Smith has told me we are losing profit. Now that my company is suddenly and unexpectedly sinking, the content losing its glamor in the sparkling sea of gossip.

It is exhausting to climb to the top. It is even more exhausting to stay there. But what is the worst, I see now, is the complete fear and hopelessness that comes with falling down, down, down to the bottom once more.

27

The tightness in my chest seems to expand with every passing day. There are these waves in which I am freshly aware of everything. The despair that shaped where I am racks my body with the urge to feel nothing at all.

I tried it once. It's what got me here the second time. I first came in because I hated my life so much that I barely refused to participate in it. Didn't speak, barely ate, barely moved. Felt myself slipping into a world of hallucinations, probably because I was deprived of food and fresh air and everything else necessary to live. So I checked myself into the hospital, because as much as I hated myself, I was too selfish to want to die.

After many months—could've been longer or shorter than that, I don't know, it was all a blur—I was deemed well enough to go back home. Except I didn't go home. Couldn't face them all. Instead, I bought an apartment near the mental hospital, away from everything and everyone I knew in Malibu.

After a few months of living in the place, I couldn't handle it anymore. I decided that if I had learned anything in the hospital, it was that there was no getting better for me. So I swallowed pills. Too many pills, all at once. It didn't have the effect I had intended, needless to say. When my whole body felt like it was on fire and I could barely breathe, the selfishness kicked in once again and I called 911.

Then I came back to the hospital, and haven't left since. Living in a mental hospital for several straight years isn't really standard protocol, but when you have enough money, exceptions can always be made. And when you're not only rich but consistently suicidal, the mental hospital doesn't want to risk any legal troubles upon your untimely release.

There are times when I feel like my life isn't so horrible. My pain seems tangible, identifiable and bearable. We talk it over, my therapist and me. My therapist has treated me since I first came here, and I think it really proves her dedication to being a therapist that she still accepts me as a patient.

I live this hopelessly cyclical life of trying to get through the "program" so that I can leave and get back to the real world. But the issue with that is, there is no real world. Not for me. Nothing is how it was, and nothing will ever be how it was.

The others will survive without me. I am not necessary for the maintenance of other humans. I contribute nothing to society.

No, that's not true. I pay this mental institution, and my therapist too. That's about all the good I am capable of.

There are different trigger points for the pain. There is the sharp remembrance of the breaking point, the breaking point that is specifically associated with someone's death.

Then there is the guilt, the guilt that it is my fault they are dead.

And there are the random flashbacks to different scenes of my life, different decisions I could have made but didn't to prevent this mess from occurring.

The problem is, nothing can change. They tell me here that change is possible, that I am capable of changing, but I laugh in the face of that idea. I can change? I can change the fact that someone died because of me?

There is nothing I can do to change that. They aren't coming back. They didn't deserve to die. No one deserved to feel any pain because of me.

I tried to live it well. I did what I knew how to do to live a good life that meant something. But my ideals were all wrong. The mistakes I made were irreversible.

So I live on, aware that there isn't a point to it all, aware that moving forward isn't possible when you are constantly living in the past. At least not moving forward in a positive direction.

28
MADELINE

For once, there's no special occasion for a party. My mother has been ultra-stressed with work lately, so my dad told her she should have a nice dinner party with some friends. He told her he would have her favorite restaurant cater and she could just enjoy a relaxing night.

Luckily, those friends include the Smiths. My heart beats a little faster as I wait for them to arrive. The last time I saw Noah was two weeks ago. I did go to his house to help his mom bake a pie—one that Elizabeth and I made for a party earlier in the year and Noah's mom had liked.

I didn't really get to talk to him though because he was coming home from the gym as I was just about to leave. He walked into the kitchen and gave me a side hug, and my God, were those arms of his nice. Everything about him is nice, and I'm more acutely aware of this than ever these days.

Finally, Noah and his mom arrive, and I realize with a flash of panic that I don't really know how to proceed. I don't know how to act with him in front of everyone. In all honesty, I don't even really know what we are. I haven't told anyone about the kiss, not even Elizabeth, for this very reason. I know I need to clarify things with Noah before I go running around thinking this means more than it may.

Noah watches me now and smiles a little shyly when he sees me. But he doesn't make any sort of move when I go over to talk to him and his mom. I carefully address the formalities, as usual—*yes, I'm good, the weather is beautiful*—and that seems to be about it until he discreetly squeezes my hand as he walks past me. He turns around just long enough to wink at me before disappearing to talk to the rest of the guests.

I smile to myself as I walk into the kitchen and frown a little when I can't find Elizabeth there. I spot her outside on a lounge chair, looking relaxed, sitting next to ... Ashley?

"Hey, you guys ..." I say tentatively as I walk outside. Never have I ever seen Ashley voluntarily sitting with, let alone talking to, Elizabeth. Ashley is not pleasant to any of us, but she has some weird issue with Liz that I've never understood. I don't think anyone understands it other than Ashley.

"Hey!" Liz smiles warmly. "Come sit with us! We were just talking about that time you made us all swim with you on Christmas."

I smile at that memory and see that even Ashley is grinning at the memory of that day.

Two years ago, on an especially balmy Christmas Day, I spontaneously exclaimed that we had to go swimming right then and there, all of us.

Everyone looked at me like I was crazy, and I knew there was no way I could get my parents to join me. But my sisters ... I thought there was some potential there.

"Come on," I whined. "Please! It'll be so fun, and we'll create memories."

"I'll go," Ashley shrugged indifferently, but I could see the trace of a smile on her lips. We dashed upstairs to get our swimsuits on and then ran together down to the beach, into the water.

"You guys are insane," Jenavieve laughed, but she looked a little regretful that she wasn't in the water with us. I noticed that Elizabeth had vanished, only to reappear a moment later in her swimsuit, running toward Ashley and me.

A few minutes later, Jen finally joined us, and we all cheered loudly. We dove and did handstand competitions, made sandcastles and had splashing wars like we were little kids again.

The sun was setting, and we were all laughing, having what was undoubtedly the best Christmas of our lives. Nothing was wrong with life. We were all happy—happy to be together, loving the waves and the beach and the pink-tinged sky.

I remember looking up to the house and seeing my parents watching us. They were both smiling. My dad's arm was around my mom's waist, and her head was resting contentedly on his shoulder.

I remember thinking to myself, *This is the best of our family.* We were all purely happy, awash in the loveliness that was living as a Blair.

"I remember that," I say, finally bringing myself back to the present.

"It was fun," Ashley says cheerfully. "We should do it next Christmas."

"Let's make it a tradition!" Liz exclaims, and she calls to Jenavieve, who's standing with Max a few feet away.

We fill Jen in on our plan, and she laughs fondly at the memory, reluctantly agreeing to go swimming with us come next Christmas.

For a while longer, I sit next to Ashley and Elizabeth, amazed at the peace and ease with which Ashley is talking.

Maybe the two of them will finally be friends, I think as I walk away to go find Noah. It's already that time of night again. I don't even have time to feel nervous before he waves to me from the side of the house.

I join him and tell him about the Christmas swim, and he watches me attentively as I speak, laughing in all the right places. We head down to the beach, and as we reach the shore, I kick my shoes off. Noah takes my hand and tells me a story about his friend's car breaking down when they were driving to school a few days ago. All the while I am amazed at how right it feels for things to be this way with us. Hand in hand, strolling along the beach.

We settle into our alcove, and it is only then that he asks, so innocently, "Can I kiss you again?"

I laugh, answering him by kissing him and not stopping as he pulls me to him. His lips brush mine, move to my cheeks and neck, and gently, slowly trace the path back up before he finally stops to gaze at me with those sharp, gray eyes. His arms still around me, he says, "So, if my mom asks about us, what should I tell her?"

He watches me carefully, trying to gauge my reaction.

"Why would your mom ask about us?" I ask innocently, watching his face redden. I probably shouldn't be messing with him, but I need to hear him say it. I need to know that we're more than friends, or whatever.

"Well, if I have you over or something, she just might ask, because it's not like you come over very often, but I want you to."

"Hey," I smile and put a finger on his lips, quieting him. "You can tell her …" Shit. What can he tell her?

"What are we, Noah?" I ask, and I really mean it. I really need to know.

He watches me for a second, then wraps his arms a little more snugly around me and takes a breath.

"I don't know about you," he says, "but I want to be more than friends. I think we kind of always have been, but I feel like it's about time we make it official."

There he goes with that half-smile again. Gets me every time.

"I agree," I say. "You and I just work, don't we?"

He absently reaches out and pushes a stray strand of hair behind my ear. "Yeah," he whispers. "We do."

And in that moment, I'm not thinking about Stanford. I don't think about him leaving, the futility of our relationship. In this moment, everything feels as it should. There is nothing that makes more sense than this, Noah and me, really together at last.

"Are you cold?" he asks, and I realize I am shivering. Sometimes I forget how chilly it can get near the water.

Without waiting for a response, he takes off his coat and wraps it around my shoulders. God, he is perfect.

We spend the next few minutes, hours—I don't know how long—just being. Talking, laughing, kissing, watching the stars. It is when we are watching the stars, one of his arms acting as my pillow and the other wrapped around my waist, that I ask him why he likes them.

He shrugs. "I don't really know," he says thoughtfully. "I mean, it's not like I want to go into space or anything. I just think they're cool to keep in perspective. It's like a way to see that there's so much more to life than us. We think we live in this little bubble that just concerns us and our own lives, which is ironic because the real bubble is Earth itself. It's just this tiny little speck in the grand scheme of things."

Wow. And that's why he is going to Stanford. He sees things differently. Everything is thought-provoking to him. And I adore him for it.

"You're pretty smart, you know," I say.

He laughs. "Nah, not any smarter than you. We're thinkers, Maddy. Do you remember when you would *not* give up trying to prove that that shell you'd found was some ancient fossil?"

"Oh, no," I groan, but I can't stop myself from laughing. I was about ten at the time, Noah eleven. We were playing on the beach, collecting little treasures from the shore when I found a shell I was convinced came straight from the Stone Age. Noah didn't buy it, but of course he still helped me research the shell and acted optimistic that it was a priceless prize.

"It *was* a pretty cool shell, you have to admit," I defend myself.

"It may not have been a fossil, but yeah, it was a cool shell," he admits, yawning. "I should probably get going," he sighs, propping himself up so that his elbows rest on either side of me.

"Noo," I protest, pulling him back to me. He kisses me once, slowly, then pulls away and stands.

"You know what? Let's just go together," he says, holding out his hand.

I barely hesitate, standing up and sliding my hand easily into his. He holds it tightly as we make our way back toward the house. And he doesn't falter in his grip as we walk up the path to the back door.

My heart beats a little faster as we walk into the main living room. I realize it's kind of a bold statement, but I also figure we might as well get it out in the open for everyone.

Elizabeth is the first to notice. She takes a look at our interlocked hands and smiles smugly, giving us a thumbs-up. Ashley, who looked bored over on the couch, now wears an expression of bemusement.

"Makes sense," she shrugs as we pass her. I turn around and roll my eyes at her, but I'm laughing a little.

I don't really know who else sees us, but I'm sure most of the room sees when he hugs me for a lot longer than a friend would.

"I'll see you later," he says with a smile. He's just about to turn away when I reach up and kiss him. He's surprised, I can tell, but he still kisses me steadily back until I pull away.

We're both blushing, seeing as the entire room just saw us kiss. But it feels good to not have to hide from anyone anymore.

"Goodnight, Maddy," he says. Then he kisses my forehead and

winks at me as he walks away toward his mom, who is waiting for him by the front door.

"Goodnight," I call after him, glancing timidly at Sherri. I hope she's okay with me dating her son.

She gives me a knowing smile and nods approvingly. Thank God.

I turn around and head upstairs to do my nightly routine. Just as I'm settling into my bed, I hear a small knock.

"Come in," I call, assuming it's Elizabeth. But I'm surprised to see it's my mother. She doesn't come in here very often.

She perches on the edge of my bed, looking glamorous as ever in her sparkling silver dress. There is light in her eyes, but there is also sadness there. I'm about to ask her if everything is okay before she interrupts my train of thought.

"So," she smiles knowingly. "You and Noah, huh?"

"Yeah." I grin at her. "I figured you and Dad would probably approve."

She nods, and looks genuinely happy. "He's a sweet kid, Madeline."

"Yeah," I sigh, thinking about all the things that make him so utterly good. Thinking about how lucky I am to have him in my life. "He really is."

"I'm confident he'll treat you right, and that's what matters most," she says. "But listen to me, Madeline," she adds. I look up to see her watching me carefully, ensuring she has my full attention.

"Sometimes you have to remember that there's more to it than that," she says. "It's clear that boy absolutely adores you, and I want you to know that that's what you should always look for in a relationship. It's the only way it's worth it."

I nod slowly, wondering how much my parents adore each other. They have a happy marriage, I know, but when I think about it, my dad doesn't really look at my mom the way Noah looks at me.

"Well, that's it," she sighs and stands up. "I'm happy for you, honey," she adds as she crosses the room. "He's always welcome here, as long as you welcome him."

"Thanks," I say. I can't help adding, "Are you okay, Mom?"

"Oh, yes, fine," she says quickly, evenly. "Don't you worry about me. You just have fun, enjoy being a kid while you still can."

She goes out the door, leaving me feeling a little perturbed. She can have that effect on people. Somewhat haunting, a constant trace of secrecy and darkness. A lot like Ashley, actually. Those two are more similar than they are willing to admit.

29
ASHLEY

I was surprised when my first driving lesson with Elizabeth didn't go as horribly wrong as I thought it would. We've been doing our lessons for about three weeks now, and it's becoming more difficult for me to find reasons to dislike her.

Of course, she's annoyingly cheerful and optimistic, but I think the thing that has really shifted my opinion of her is my realization that she's not fake-nice. She's just nice.

She didn't have to be nice to me when she was teaching me. I kind of figured that once away from the rest of the family, when it was just the two of us in the sedan, Elizabeth would act at least a little bitchy. I mean, I definitely would. Who wants to spend their free time teaching a fifteen-year-old how to drive?

But she's nice. Kind, patient, doesn't rush our lessons. At first, we spent a lot of time in the high school parking lot when no one was around, doing continuous laps. She's calm about things, even when I'm sure I scare the shit out of her by pressing the gas too hard or braking too suddenly. When that happens, she just tells me what to do different and we move on. I think she knows I don't do well with authority.

Elizabeth told me that the sooner I could master the parking lot, the sooner we could start going out on roads, which means the sooner

I can get myself to Dashton. So I started going out driving with her just about every day. After a little while, we became more comfortable with each other, and the lessons became more fun than obligatory.

Now I find myself asking her about the little things in her life that I have never bothered to ask about before. About her friends, the funny memories she has, her excitement about graduating soon and then going to Pepperdine. Her comfort at being close to home, because she doesn't want to be away from us.

Us. The whole family. Despite the complete and utter bitch I have been to her for basically forever, she still loves me because I'm family. How did I miss out on that? When I'm around Elizabeth, I find myself mourning the traits I lack. Why am I not kind like her? Why am I not as devoted to my family?

So the irony of it all, I've realized, is that I dislike her because she has what I would like to have.

But maybe I can overcome it. Maybe it doesn't have to be this way for the rest of our lives. She's sticking around. She'll be my future kids' aunt, for God's sake. I can't just ice her out forever. And maybe I don't want to anymore.

30
JAMES

In my clients' eyes, I'm a reliable man. I have to be, because I'm a lawyer. If people don't trust me, I'm out of business.

It is truly ironic: I get paid a considerable sum of money for an attribute I don't actually have.

I always did want to be a good, honorable person, as most people intend to be. I saw the ruthlessness of my father and the passiveness of my mother, and I decided I would not be like them. Instead, I would be good. I would be kind. I would be moral. And I would be trustworthy.

And then I kissed Sarah Jenkins and launched an era of dishonest living.

"James is good. With him, you'll win." My buddies at the office retain this belief that I'm the best in the business, that I will help just about anyone win their case. And I usually do. The problem is, being the best in the business means you get paid for constant immorality.

Just last week I got Annie Anderson as one of my clients. She's a popular singer who's trying to get custody of her child. Jason, my assistant, was so excited. He has always been eager to please me. To that end, he lands me new clients left and right. He's personable and well-liked, and he has helped me get a lot of the cases I've had over the years.

So when he barged into my office last week, a huge grin on his face, I instantly knew he had landed me something good, something he was proud of.

"Got you Anderson, Blair," he beamed.

"What, Annie Anderson!?" I exclaimed. Of course Jason was able to land me the most popular artist in Hollywood. Ashley is an especially big fan of her music, and I made a mental note to tell her when I got home. Anything to connect with her.

"That'd be the Anderson I'm referring to, yeah," Jason said proudly. "Custody case. Little two-year-old boy. Anyone else as her lawyer and she probably would've been screwed. But I told her, I said, 'Honey, James Blair is the best in the biz. He'll get you your kid, full custody. Don't you even worry.' And that got her."

"What do you mean, she would've been screwed with another lawyer?" I asked, confused. I didn't know a whole lot about Annie other than my daughter loved her music and she was big in Hollywood.

"Oh, she's a druggie, man. Was practically gone when she came and talked to me. But I mean, who in Hollywood hasn't done a little something? It'd be unbearable to be sober in that place," he snorted. "Anyway, it'll be fine. Easy for you. Nothing. But should bring in some good money, so that'll be nice, right?"

"Oh, yeah." I grinned wanly, trying to muster up the gratitude he deserved. "Thank you, Jason."

"No problem, buddy. I'll leave ya to it." He turned and left the office, leaving me to put my head in my hands and sigh.

So my newest project was to grant a drug addict full custody of a baby. *Someone has to do it*, I reminded myself, rubbing my forehead. *It's not a big deal. It's a job, it makes money, it's interesting. There's nothing wrong with it.*

Except there was something inexcusably wrong with how I made my living. I was about to ruin a child's life, set him up for failure. I had always thought my situation had been bad, growing up with my own parents. But this, this was significantly worse. And it would be my doing because I knew I would win. I always do.

***

What do we win at? I think to myself now, as I drive home from a meeting with Annie. We put her case together today, and the whole time we did, she was high.

We win for ourselves. Our actions are inexorably committed for us, and there is no escaping it.

I tried to be good. I tried to be honorable. I tried to be a good husband, a good father, a good contributor to society.

And yet. I cheated on my wife. I work so much that I can't be close to my kids. And my contribution to society? I give little kids over to people I know damn well won't be able to provide a good life for them.

Maybe I was just never really good. Maybe none of us is. Something inside us knows there's a better way to do things, but we never actually do a thing about it. We're programmed to do things that only wholly benefit ourselves, and it's a major flaw in the system.

I really did try. I still do. But it's no good. It's too late.

And I keep at it, succumbing to a lifetime of selfish decisions, severing the stitching that so meticulously holds together my life until, one day, something severs it completely and I bleed out.

God forbid that be any time soon.

31
ELIZABETH

I have always believed that people are good, that there is a way to connect with everyone, and that everyone's intentions are pure. That belief has never failed me, even when I thought it might.

Because, as much as I always hoped I would connect with Ashley, as much as I hoped she would finally come around to me, there was a part of me that thought it would never happen.

I'm not sure what it is about me. Since as far back as I can remember, Ashley couldn't get over me not being her biological sister. I think she resented the attention I got, the attention I took away, unintentionally, from her.

I never wanted to take anything from her, or from anybody. I know I'm a part of the Blair family, and I know they love me. But I also grew up with the notion that I didn't fully belong. I couldn't, because Ashley never felt comfortable with me. And if there was one thing I wouldn't do, one thing I will never do, it's take from them.

The Blairs have given me a home, a family and love. So I vowed to never take from them, or at least try not to.

For the longest time, it was not enough for Ashley. For fifteen years, actually, it wasn't enough.

And then I started teaching her how to drive, and she finally, slowly but surely, came around.

***

I don't think I ever felt more nervous about anything, even checking to see if I was accepted to Pepperdine, than when I first got into the sedan with Ashley.

It wasn't even about the driving. It was being in an enclosed space with her, alone. But the only thing I could do in the moment was be kind to her. Otherwise, I could aggravate her and she could very well crash the car. She's angsty that way.

So I was calm and tried to give her as much control as you can give a girl who's never driven a car. She hates authority, so I figured it was the best way to go about things. Let her take the reins as much as possible and then pray, I guess.

I was a little surprised, that first lap around the high school parking lot, to see that she was tentative. She wanted to do it right, actually wanted to be a good driver. Even more surprising, there were no snide comments, no eye rolling—nothing except a quiet, unfamiliar politeness.

She was trying, I realized that day, and it gave me hope. Maybe we could finally have a better relationship than just the generic, pass-each-other-by-quietly cadence we'd always maintained.

As the lessons went on, she got more friendly, more eager, more interested in what I had to say.

And now we drive just about every day. She has her permit. In fact, she has had it for a while because James told her as soon as she turned fifteen that he would teach her how to drive.

Needless to say, he never did. I don't think any of us really thought he would follow through with it. He tries, but he's very busy, and we all understand.

So she's close to being ready for the tests. She can technically take them any time, and I think she's on the right track there.

Which is why I'm taking her on the freeway now. Am I a bit terrified to drive at 60 miles per hour with an inexperienced fifteen-year-old? Absolutely. But I trust her, and she trusts me, too.

We are approaching the on-ramp now, and I look over to see her hands clenched tightly around the wheel.

"Hey," I say. "Loosen your grip a little. It's going to be okay. Remember what we talked about? You're going to speed up on the ramp, and then you just look for your gap. Check all three mirrors, because it's impossible to see someone in your blind spot if you don't. And make sure you don't veer when you look, just keep your wheel aimed straight ahead."

"Okay," she mutters, nodding to herself and looking attentively ahead.

"Oh, and remember, whenever you see brake lights, what do you do?" I prompt.

"I brake too," she says automatically, not blinking as she enters the on-ramp and speeds up. I track her eyes, making sure she's checking all her mirrors. I check to make sure there's no one in her blind spot.

She has an opening, but I want to let her find it. It'll give her more confidence.

Sure enough, she smoothly makes the transition and we're on the freeway, driving among everyone else, and we're still alive. I let out a breath I didn't even realize I was holding, and I relax my body.

Beside me, Ashley laughs, her scraggly blond curls shaking with the rest of her body. "Yes!" she exclaims, her eyes still wide and on the road ahead. "I could go pass this test, like, right now, couldn't I!?"

"You're getting there," I say with a grin. "We'll have to practice more, but your progress is great. I definitely didn't do my first freeway drive this well." I shudder, remembering how James had to grab the wheel before I veered us straight into the side of a Mercedes.

"That was with Dad, wasn't it ?" she asks, but there's no trace of bitterness in her voice. Dad. I don't think she's ever said it like that, like he's *our* dad and not *hers*.

"Yeah," I say tentatively. "It was pretty bad. I was so nervous, and he's not exactly the calmest person, so that just made me even more freaked out. When I merged, I literally almost hit a Mercedes. He had to grab the wheel and then made me get off at the next exit and switch seats with him. It was awful."

She laughs. "Thank God I'm not learning to drive with him. He would have driven me absolutely crazy. You're so calm. Like, way more calm than I would be, but hey, I haven't crashed yet!"

"And you won't crash at all because you're a good driver and won't get distracted," I affirm.

"Exactly," she says, and I look ahead to see we've almost circled around to our exit. She's getting ready to switch lanes when I think of something.

"Hey, let's actually take the next exit down," I tell her.

"Why?" she asks, but listens to me and continues past our usual exit.

"Because there's a much prettier route this way. Whenever I get off the freeway, I always go this way."

"You might like it, I don't know," I add, filling the void of her silence. "Just thought I'd show you."

"No, yeah, that sounds good," she says, and I look over to see her smiling a little.

I realize this is probably the first time, ever in our lives, that we've done something totally voluntarily together. Even though we enjoy the

126

driving lessons now, it's not like we came up with it ourselves. But this is something we didn't have to do together. It's something we want to do.

"Take a right here," I tell her as she gets off the freeway. She does, and I tell her to keep following the road.

We go on straight for a while, making small talk, until we're just about there.

"Okay, now take a left, and enjoy the magic," I tell her. Then I smile.

She turns obediently and then we are on my stretch, my favorite place to drive.

On either side, trees arch around us, the sunlight filtering through the car in stripes, the sand and ocean just visible through the branches on our right.

"Wow," Ashley mutters beside me, eyes wide as she steals glimpses around us.

I roll down the windows, letting in the balmy air, the sound of the trees rustling, the waves lapping the shore, and the smell of salt water.

I feel my body relax, as it always does here, and I let my hand rest lazily out the window. With my free hand, I connect my phone to the Bluetooth and play the song "Beyond," by Leon Bridges, as I always do when I drive this route. No one has ever driven it with me before.

We continue on this way, the warm wind blowing gently into our faces, the music filling the car.

And just as we're reaching the end, just as the sunlight is brighter than ever, Ashley says, so quietly, "It's such a beautiful road."

I look over at her, at the contentment on her face, her hair billowing crazily, and then I look out the other side at the beauty beyond.

"Yeah, it is," I whisper. "It really is."

32

I want to get the hell out of here. I don't know what my plan is, but I am aware that, whatever it is, it doesn't involve this institution.

So I'm following the rules. I participate in activities, I show up to meals on time and eat what they tell me to. I even make myself look a little presentable when I get up in the morning.

I can't stand it, my false engagement with the program, but I do it anyway. I remind myself that the better I do, the sooner they'll have a reason to let me out.

I know damn well they don't want me here anymore. I've been nothing but a continuous pain in the ass and a nuisance to the people here who are trying to get better. The people who still have hope.

I so badly want to tell them to stop. They're only fooling themselves. It works for a little while, especially when you're young, before you know how bad it gets. Before you know how bad you get.

It'll lessen their pain if they realize, like I do, how it all works. They may think I'm unstable and they may be right, but I'm no fool. I know exactly how everything works, and that is why I'm so unstable in their eyes.

You can't be okay when you come to the understanding that there isn't true goodness, that there isn't anything fair or right in the world.

I'm too negative for the system. No one wants anyone who knows the truth, after all. So I continue to do my best to fit in.

It mostly involves me not speaking. When I do speak, it's the bare minimum, and it's encouraging. They love positivity here. They like people who can hide reality and convince everyone that it's all okay and life is beautiful and we're so lucky to be alive.

When Sandra tells the group about her visits home and how she doesn't cut herself with any conceivably sharp object even though it's truly tempting, I smile at her and say, "That's great, Sandra."

It's not great. She wants that pain. She'll get it eventually. But the people in charge like positivity, they like the hope that energizes the others enough to get them out and bring the new shipment of screwed-up people in.

So I tell Sandra congratulations for not killing herself yet, tell the others that they're strong and capable even though they're not. None of us is.

I don't tell my therapist about my act, of course. She, more than just about anyone here, likes to get her constant assurances that the world is good. She's probably just as fucked up as the lot of us.

I'm almost there, I can feel it. I'm close to convincing them that there's a valid reason to let me out.

My time here is coming to a close. When they let me out, I will go elsewhere. Where that elsewhere is, I'm not sure, but I hope it shows me something I don't yet know. That's my last hope. I hope there's something more to it all.

33
JENAVIEVE

It is time. Max and I have been here for a good month now under the pretense that we're staying in a hotel for the summer. My parents still don't know that Max and I have actually been staying in our condo, which we now live in. Permanently. They also don't know that I've ditched law school to study psychology.

I'm afraid of what their reactions will be because I don't want to disappoint them. Max continuously reminds me that I'm following my dreams and considered everything thoroughly before making these decisions, and that I should be perfectly content.

Of course, he's right, but it doesn't stop me from dreading the moment my parents realize that I, their first-born child, am already neglecting their plans for me.

Their plans weren't bad. My dad makes very good money as a lawyer, and it would've been a secure lifestyle. It's just that it's not for me. I can't picture myself doing it, day in and day out. It would've lessened the blow a bit, I think, had I made the switch over to business, like my mom. Maybe then they would've understood a bit better.

But no. Instead, I am studying psychology, completely outside their spectrum. And I don't know what they will think about it. But I don't have much more time to consider, because Max and I are eating dinner at the house with them now. I am about to tell them, finally.

Ashley and Elizabeth are over at friends' houses, and Madeline is at Noah's. The two of them are finally dating, and I'm happy for them. I think everyone saw it coming, in a way, but I'm glad it finally came together for them. He's always been a sweet kid, and I can tell just by the way my sister looks at him what a good person he must be.

I'm shaken from my reverie by Max's sidelong glance, pointedly prompting me to start talking. There's an awkward lull in the conversation, and I know it's my time.

"Mom, Dad," I say, trying to make my voice sound less nervous than I feel.

They look up from their plates and smile at me, and I am struck by how much older they both look. It's not so much that their physical features have wizened as much as it is that the look in their eyes has. Their expressions are filled with a new weariness that I suppose accompanies whatever aging begets.

"I haven't been completely honest with you," I say, looking back and forth between my parents' faces. There. I tore off a corner of the bandage to let them see a little glimpse of what's coming.

"What haven't you been honest about, darling?" my mother asks. Both she and my father wear an expression of concern, like they think I've been hiding a health problem or something.

I look over at Max, trying to gather a last note of encouragement from him. His deep-brown eyes look into my own warmly, and he nods at me, smiling slightly. It's all I need.

"Max and I aren't staying in a hotel for the summer," I continue. "We are actually living in a condo, which we bought, and we're staying here. Permanently."

I watch their expressions turn from concern to surprise, and then to a little bit of happiness that I'm staying, and then the confusion.

"That's … well, I'm certainly glad to have you home," my dad says slowly, "but what about Harvard? Are you taking a gap year or something before starting law school?"

Here it is. Moment of truth.

"Actually," I sigh, looking down at the table for a moment before forcing myself to look back up at my parents. "I'm not studying law anymore."

My dad literally drops his fork and my mom's face goes a bit pale, but neither of them says anything. Shell-shocked. It's about what I expected, as an initial reaction at least.

"It's not that I don't like law," I add quickly. "I do. It's just not my passion. And I know chasing passions isn't always the most sensible thing to do, but I really believe it'll make me the most successful I can be, you know? I mean, if I'm truly happy doing what I love, I think I'll not only have a better quality of life, but my work will be better. And I'll be more successful."

I look at Max eagerly, and he smiles, nodding again with confirmation this time. We practiced this a little bit earlier today, and I'm pleasantly surprised that I stuck to the script. I said what I needed to say.

"And what exactly is that passion?" my dad asks, a tinge of exasperation in his voice.

Oh. Right.

"Psychology," I say, confidently this time. "I'm so fascinated with how the brain works it keeps me up at night. And I know it's not what our family does, but I know it's what I want."

Silence. Max doesn't add anything because there's nothing to add. I've said it all.

After what feels like an eternity, my mom says calmly, evenly, "Well. Thank you for telling us, Jen. I wish you'd come to us sooner, but I'm glad you told us. And I'm glad you're here. Glad you're both here," she adds, smiling at Max.

Wow. Never did I expect *that* response from my mother. As strong of a personality as she has, she mostly remains passive when it comes to things both she and my father have a stake in. I think that it's because of the notion that she, like me, doesn't want to disappoint.

But something about what I said must've resonated with her. When I think about it a little, I realize that she herself went against the grain when she left her lower-class Los Angeles neighborhood for Pepperdine. A part of her must understand why I'm doing this, then. After all, it sure worked out for her. Maybe it will for me, too.

My father simply nods, looking a little stunned.

"Can I take your plates, Mr. and Mrs. Blair?" Max interjects into the void.

"James and Evelyn, please, Max," my father says. "And that's alright, thank you. I'll take the plates and go clean. Goodnight," he adds a little stiffly, but he smiles at us politely as he takes our plates to the kitchen.

"He'll come around," my mother mutters, watching his back retreat as he goes to clean our plates.

"Thank you, Mom, for understanding. Or trying to, at least. I appreciate it," I tell her.

She nods elegantly, her slim hands crossed delicately with her chin resting on them, wearing that wise expression you can wear only if you truly understand something.

"You do what you want to do while you still can," she says quietly. "You're young. It's not too late for you. And your father isn't wrong about his thinking, isn't wrong at all to suggest some practicality, for it sees you through. It ensures your comfort, and that's something we all want, isn't it?"

Is there a touch of sarcasm there? I don't know, but I do know that it's practicality that got her this life, combined with the leap of faith she took when she launched Detail.

"Right," I agree quietly. I find myself wondering silently for the rest of the night about how much fulfillment she has and how much joy her success has brought her.

34
EVELYN

How do you tell your husband you're failing at what you yourself started?

For most people, I suppose the answer would be not telling him at all. I don't disagree. It would certainly be easier that way.

But I can't withhold it from him. I can't even withhold it from my children, if simply for the reason that they could help me.

People are losing interest in Detail's content, which means we need fresh content. And fast.

If we don't tell the stories people want to hear, we will be out of business. Just like if I don't have the juiciest gossip in Malibu, I'll be out of friends.

I don't expect James to be of much help in supplying gossip because he is a lawyer and would most certainly be fired if he disclosed any information about anyone he works with.

The kids, on the other hand … there are four young women in my family who could very well find something that could create at least a temporary explosion while Sherri Smith and I get things settled down.

We won't mess with the numbers. I believe that if I made it known to Sherri it was a viable option, she would go through with it because she's loyal. But she has a son, who is not only my daughter's boyfriend but is also her only family. And the influence of a materially manipulative parent is something no one needs.

I won't tell them all at once. James and James alone deserves to know first. And then I will tell the girls, with enough conviction that they will all feel compelled to find something, anything, that will temporarily halt the madness of this misfortune.

Is it selfish to ask my daughters for help with this? Maybe. But one of the great rules of morality is that family helps family, and it is this rule that may very well save my company.

***

The night I tell James about the impending doom of Detail, most of the girls are out of the house. Only Elizabeth and Madeline are home, working on homework upstairs. The only one who would eavesdrop anyway is Ashley, so I don't much mind Elizabeth and Madeline still being here.

I have to tell James tonight so that I can tell the girls tomorrow. And anyhow, I can't keep this secret from him any longer. Some people can bear to hold the burden of their wrongdoings, and others feel the weight of it as unbearable pressure. I am one of the latter. My husband, on the other hand … there is likely a lot he doesn't tell me.

I am pacing while I wait for him to return from work, late. It is the combination of the news I have to share and the fact that our worst conversations have taken place when he has arrived home late from work that makes me feel more anxious than ever.

There is an expression of apprehension on his face when he enters the room, and he pales just slightly at the sight of me sitting stoically, tensely, on the couch, a glass of wine anchoring me to the spot.

I don't often sit here, waiting for him to come home, especially on these later nights of his. Usually when he gets home from work, he's tired and worn out and just wants to eat something alone. And I am usually working in my office on something related to Detail. But now he must learn that there may soon not be a Detail at all.

"Hey, Ev," James smiles a little cautiously at me, slipping off his shoes and joining me on the couch.

I am struck, for the umpteenth time, at what gifts aging has given him. He looks almost more handsome than when I married him twenty-three years ago, his features chiseled and wizened, but not worn. His ocean eyes are still as striking as ever, his dark hair sprinkled with a gray that, of course, looks as if it was always meant to be there.

In these moments when I notice how attracted I still am to him, all these years later, I find myself hopefully, yet also hopelessly, wondering if he ever feels the same way about me.

I am about to ask, *How was work?,* and then I laugh silently at myself for the irony.

"There's something I need to talk to you about, and it's not good," I say calmly, staring steadily into the crystalline curvature of my wine glass.

Concern etches lines of worry instantly into his face. Is it bad that I feel relieved that my husband is immediately and attentively concerned?

"Detail is going to go under, and fast, if I can't save it very soon," I say slowly, emotionlessly. It is far easier not to feel than to let my emotions get the best of me.

"What?" he murmurs, now purely confused. "I don't understand. Detail is a multimillion-dollar business, and always has been …"

"Not lately," I say quietly. He needs to know the whole truth. "James, the truth is, we've been struggling for a long time. The glamour of our gossip is fading, and has been for some time.

"But until now, we've been able to keep it under control, Sherri and I and the others," I continue. "We've held on, done just well enough for people not to notice the struggle.

"And suddenly, now, we're falling fast. It's like we skydived, and the parachute had us going down at a steady pace in the beginning until it just ripped open. And now we are free-falling."

The look on his face now is sadness. He, more than just about anyone, knows how much my work means to me. It's what made me who I am, made my childhood dreams come true and provided the life of fantasies.

And now all of that is almost over. It's nearly comical, this turn of events.

"How do you fix it?" he asks softly, but with steadfast determination. "I mean, there's got to be a way you can fix this."

"I need something really, really good," I tell him. "A piece of gossip that's not only true, but incendiary. Something that I can get my hands on first, and that everyone would want to know. If that could happen, and in the next month or so, we could make it. There could be hope. Something big would boost us up a little, give us some headway to regain our grip. Which is why I need to tell the girls. I've been trying to conceal everything from everyone for so long, and I knew I needed to tell you. But it's also time I tell the girls."

My husband looks at me with apprehension almost akin to disgust.

"James, they're four young women living in the heart of Malibu," I say exasperatedly. "They have connections, debatably better connections than us. At least for gossip."

"So you want them all to go on some wild goose chase for a good piece of gossip?" he asks pointedly.

Well, when he puts it that way, it sounds a lot worse than it actually is.

"No, love," I say evenly. "I just want them to be aware that I need help so that they can be on the *lookout*. They don't need to chase after any geese; I just want their eyes open. What's wrong with that?"

"Nothing," he says quietly, conceding to the desperate nature of my predicament. "I don't want them involved, that's all. But keeping their eyes open for some gossip is hardly getting involved; they probably already do so anyway."

"Exactly."

James looks at me with that wholesome expression of sadness and tenderness, then reaches out, rubbing my back gently. He leans forward to look into my eyes.

"It'll be okay, Ev," he says assuredly. "You'll be okay, Detail will be okay. And if something goes wrong, at least we have financial security."

Financial security. At the end of the day, that's all this is, to everyone other than me. Of course, I understand what James is trying to say: That, ultimately, we're set for life, and set to provide for our family.

But it's way, way more than that to me. Detail may have been founded with the ultimate goal of making some money, but for me it has breached the steel of avariciousness and become something sentimental.

I nod, smiling with as much hope as I can muster.

James wraps his arm around me then, and pulls me close to him, holding me there steadily as I rest my head on his chest.

We aren't very affectionate, my husband and I. A long time ago I suppose that was different, but even this simple show of affection is almost foreign to me now.

It's ironic. Sometimes the people who should care about you the most only really care for you when you're in your worst place.

139

35
MADELINE

Throughout my life I have seen my mother's business as something completely and fully ingrained in the fabric of our lives. It has been a fixture of this family. After all, it is Detail that started all of the parties, Detail that brought me Noah.

Noah. It is not only my family that's impacted by the news of Detail's decline; Sherri, too, has devoted her livelihood to the business. At least we have my dad, whose job isn't going anywhere. Noah just has Sherri, who just has Detail, which may soon be nothing.

Since we heard the news about a week ago, I have felt determination, mixed with hopelessness, surrounding the situation. As much as I want to find something good to help pull Detail through, my sneaking off to the beach with Noah during every single party has meant that I don't get the scoop on anyone's life except his.

We haven't talked about it much, Noah and I. Elizabeth has been sick for the past few days, and the three of us talked about it a little while we were having a movie marathon. Other than that, though, it hasn't been discussed. I think he wants to deny it. And anyway, he's an optimistic person, even in the most dire of situations. I try to be too, but I'm not nearly as hopeful as he is.

I sigh to myself, staring up at my dark ceiling as I wrack my brain for the millionth time for anything that can help Detail. I come up short, as I have every time I've put thought into it.

It is nearing the end of May, which means the clock is ticking. We essentially have until the end of June to save Detail, and unfortunately, I doubt I will be of any help. Hopefully, I think to myself as I drift off, my sisters have paid more attention to the spectacles of socialites than I have.

***

Hours later, my phone wakes me up. Rubbing my eyes wearily, I glance at the time. 5:27 a.m. Wondering who in the world would be calling me at this time on a Sunday, I feel a small jolt of alarm when I see it's Noah.

"Hello?" I say a little groggily, yet I'm feeling more alert now.

"Good morning, Maddy," he says, and I can hear the smile in his voice.

Before I can say anything else, he adds, "I'm currently outside your house. I would come to the door, of course, but I didn't want to wake up the rest of your family."

"That's understandable, seeing as it's 5:30 in the morning! Noah, what are you doing here?" I laugh.

"You'll see," he responds mysteriously. "Just come out here. Trust me."

"Okay." I shake my head in amusement, even though he can't see. "I'll be out there in five minutes."

I hurriedly put on a pair of leggings and a sweatshirt, pull my hair back, brush my teeth, and text my parents that I'm about to leave.

It is only when I'm outside, walking toward Noah's car, that I realize with a lurch in my stomach that he's never really seen me without makeup, at least since we were little. Of course, I've always been done up for parties. And when I go to his house or he comes to mine, I at least make myself look somewhat nice.

But this morning he's getting the unconcealed, unhighlighted me, I think to myself a little grudgingly as I pull open the passenger door.

"Hey!" I say brightly as I busy myself buckling my seatbelt, telling myself to just act confident, act confident.

"Hey," he says, grinning. He, too, looks different than usual. Instead of his normal button-down shirt and slacks, he's wearing a faded lacrosse shirt and basketball shorts. His hair is also a little messier than usual, reminding me of when I first kissed him. I decide I like him better this way.

There's a pause then as he takes me in, likely noting the obvious plainness of my features.

"What?" I find myself saying, laughing a little to try to disguise my mounting insecurity.

"Oh, nothing," he says as he puts the car in drive, blushing a bit and smiling so that I can see his dimples. "You just look really beautiful right now."

Beautiful. Me, just woken up, nothing veiling my physical imperfections.

I lean across the seat and kiss his cheek as he pulls into the road. And it's then, as he smiles, ruffling my hair playfully with one hand and driving with the other, that I realize I love him.

I don't tell him though. Not yet. Besides, I think we both know we've always loved each other in some way.

Some things, I think to myself as we drive on, and in some particular moments, are simply better left unsaid.

***

"So you're probably wondering why I kidnapped you at 5:30 in the morning." Noah turns down our music to finally address where we're going.

"I mean, I'll hang out with you any time of day, but yeah, five in the morning is a little out there," I say with a smile.

"Well, I had to come get you so early because we're watching the sun rise," he responds.

"Here, actually," he adds as he parks the car in a little parking lot that I recognize being just off the tip of Point Dume.

"Stupid idea or good idea?" he asks me carefully, trying to gauge my reaction.

"Stupid?" I exclaim, wondering how he can possibly think I could find this, compared to most other ideas of "dates" in this generation, stupid.

"No, definitely not stupid. This is really sweet, Noah."

"Okay good, I thought you'd like it," he says with relief in his voice. "Also, I made us breakfast, so you might as well just call me boyfriend of the year," he adds with his signature half-smile.

"You're officially the best," I shake my head in amazement as he pops the trunk, grabbing a blanket and a big covered basket that must hold our breakfast.

"I know," he says, wrapping an arm around me and kissing the top of my head as we walk down the beach to find a good spot.

We settle down on our blanket in the sand, with a full view of the ocean and the reflection of the rising sun. I can't remember the last time I watched the sun rise, if I even have at all.

So I settle back, leaning against Noah as I watch the day slowly turn from darkness into something more absolute, something more definable by the softness of color and the loveliness of the rising light.

At some time when the sun is casting its freshly golden glow over everything, I take the perfect photo of him. I tell him the sun looks cool and to smile, and he obliges, but really, I just want to capture the moment. Noah, close-lipped smiling at me with his dimples, hair messy, leaning lazily on the blanket and looking at me with such simply and perfectly conveyed adoration. The waves behind him, the golden sun creating its beautiful, glorious hold over everything good.

I need these things, these little snapshots to hold on to. We all do.

***

"So, this meal comes in courses," he tells me as he opens the elaborate picnic basket, which has several little tiers holding different layers of our meal. At the top are two little covered glasses of orange juice.

"Cheers," I smile and clink my glass with Noah's. Drinking orange juice on a Sunday with my best friend, watching the sun rise. I didn't think it could be better than that first time he kissed me, but this morning gives that a run for its money.

The next thing Noah takes out of the basket is fresh-cut watermelon and pineapple, which I know by the jagged cuts he did himself. Of course he would spend the time to make me a multi-course breakfast.

"Okay, I swear I'm not trying to starve us," he assures me as we finish up the fruit. "In fact, I hope you're hungry, because this next one is pretty substantial."

"Oh, I'm ready," I say, rubbing my hands together in anticipation and smiling.

He carefully lifts a large, round wooden container from the bottom of the basket and hands it to me.

"For you," he smiles at me, but there's a sort of embarrassed, vulnerable look in his eyes that I don't understand until I lift the lid of the container.

Inside is about the biggest crêpe I've ever seen, and it looks delicious, perfectly cooked and dusted with powdered sugar.

But what really makes me gasp is the way the tiny little slivers of strawberries are arranged so that they perfectly spell out "PROM?"

In the midst of all that's happened lately, both with Noah and Detail, I almost completely forgot that it's prom season. I feel a surge of happiness that expands throughout my whole being. Never have I seen a more perfect promposal.

"This is amazing, I don't know how you … Yes! Of course I'll go to prom with you!" I sputter, wrapping my arms around him and kissing him as he pulls back to look at me.

"Thank God you were actually able to read it," he laughs. "That was some meticulous work, right there. It looked like a five-year-old did it for my first several attempts."

"Well congratulations, Noah Smith, this officially goes down as one of my favorite days," I tell him, still beaming.

He hugs me again, and when he pulls back there is so much pure, genuine love in his eyes that it's like he must express it with words.

Because it is at that moment that he says it.

"I love you, Madeline," he says quietly, but with self-assuredness. "Honestly, I can't remember the day I didn't, and I can't imagine the day I won't."

I'm not the emotional type, but this. I force back the tears that are threatening to well so that I can fully see him, fully memorize the way he looks, the way it all looks right now.

"I love you, too," I whisper. "So much. Always have, always will."

I know we are young, but there is nothing that can tarnish the truth of my words. Or his.

I believe there are people in our lives who we can say with complete conviction that we love. Past, present and future.

Really, I'm not one for cheesy romance, not one who takes feelings and words lightly.

But there are some things that make you wonder. These little snippets of the human experience that are so profoundly, movingly beautiful. Things that remind you that you get to experience the magnificent glory of being alive.

And who am I to ever deny myself these most precious moments of being?

***

The rest of the day goes by in tones of lightness, nothing capable of popping the bubble of my buoyancy.

After staying on the beach a while longer, finishing our breakfast and wading through the shallows, Noah drives me home—and I spend the rest of the day, while as normal as ever, floating with the confirmed knowledge I am loved.

It's funny, I think absently later on. *Despite the fact that we know, deep down, certain things to be true, it is only when they are publicly affirmed to us that we allow ourselves to feel the full weight of their meaning.*

36
ELIZABETH

Deep breath, *Elizabeth,* I tell myself. *You've got this.*

I have just signed into the doctor's office, by myself. It feels strange but shouldn't, because I'm legally an adult.

I tap my foot nervously on the floor, trying unsuccessfully to calm myself. No matter what I do, it's hopeless. There's no escaping the guilt that's gnawing its way through me, reminding me that what I am doing is wrong.

What I'm here to do today is get a DNA test.

Over the past week, for most of which I've been sick, I've incessantly mulled all of the options over in my mind as to how to proceed with finding out information about my biological parents.

Asking Evelyn didn't help, which makes me rule out James because he surely wouldn't know anything if Evelyn doesn't. I wish I could just not care so much and could continue living my life the way I always have. I wish I could feel that I don't need this, that I don't need to know who made me, but I can't get rid of the desire to have answers.

I keep telling myself it's simply for health purposes, but I think it runs deeper than that. I love the Blairs with all my heart, but I've never been fully a part of that family. And that makes me think that I am fully part of a family that I don't even know.

147

My parents probably aren't even together anymore, I remind myself sullenly, because it's probably true. Any people who can leave a baby on someone's doorstep probably lack the maturity for a relationship of any kind.

My nervous trance is broken by the nurse ushering me back to see the doctor. I realize as I follow her into the exam room that I didn't fully think this through. I mean, I'm assuming it should be as simple as a blood test, and I'm authorized to make all my own medical decisions because I'm eighteen. *Stop.* I interrupt my own thoughts. *I'm doing nothing wrong.*

The nurse asks me, "What brings you here today, Elizabeth?" The little brass name tag pinned to her scrubs tells me her name is Brenda.

"I just have a few questions for Doctor Buchanan. Some DNA questions. I'm adopted," I add quickly, replying to Brenda's slightly confused expression. "And I don't know my biological parents, don't know anything about them, in fact. So I figured my doctor could maybe help me with that?"

"Okay then," Brenda says, making a quick note on her tablet, seeming slightly annoyed at the nature of my visit. I should probably just be here if I'm sick, but I didn't know where else to go for this sort of thing.

"Doctor Buchanan will be with you shortly," she tells me as she opens the door to leave the exam room.

Within a few minutes, I hear a quick rap on the door. I suppose it didn't take long for Nurse Brenda to fill my doctor in on why I'm here.

Doctor Buchanan enters the room, smiling warmly and reaching out to shake my hand. She's always been kind and easy to talk to, and I feel my nerves dissipating. This will be okay. This will go without a hitch.

"Elizabeth, good to see you! It's been a while," she remarks. "On second thought, I guess it's not so good to see you, here at least," she adds with a little laugh.

"Oh, no, I'm still in perfectly good health," I assure her quickly.

She raises her eyebrows in surprise. Did Brenda not tell her why I am here?

"Oh. Well, what brings you here?"

There's something off in her voice. Her steady gaze flits away from mine, and she fidgets slightly. After years of homing in on suspicious characteristics, I know one when I see one. She knows. My doctor knows why I'm here, but she doesn't want to address it. I immediately feel uncomfortable.

"Um," I start, my nerves returning. But I realize the importance of speaking with confidence, asserting the importance and rationality of what I have to say.

"I would like to know who my biological parents are," I say calmly. "It's very important to me that I know. For health purposes."

Again with a statement that hovers just on the periphery of a lie. I do want to know about my parents for health purposes, but there is a hint of something more, an undeniably pressing urge to know what it is to fully belong.

Doctor Buchanan nods slowly. "I see," she says quietly. "And how would you like me to help you with that?"

It's not sarcasm or rudeness I hear in her voice. It's a legitimate question, with aversion at its core. But I still have to keep at it. I don't know why she is seemingly unwilling to help me, but I have to persist. She's my doctor—she can't deny me a blood test.

"Well, a blood test, I was thinking," I respond. "I figure a simple DNA match should do it, to which I could take the results elsewhere, to proceed."

Maybe that's it. She doesn't want to deal with an extensive search, doesn't want to be involved in more of a patient's life than she needs to be.

"I'm sorry, Elizabeth," she says calmly, as she looks down at the floor. She takes a breath then, as if summoning the strength to look up. Then she looks me in the eye. "I can't do that for you."

"You can't give me a blood test?" I ask incredulously. This doesn't make any sense. Maybe I should feel angry or upset, but I'm merely confused.

"No," she says quietly, but she reveals a hint of sadness, too.

"I don't understand," I say calmly, watching her carefully. "Are you out of needles or something?"

"No," she says again. But this time, she can't bring herself to look me in the eye. "I'm sorry, but I have been specifically ordered to not administer any testing on you. And even if I could perform a blood test, that wouldn't be sufficient information to identify your biological parents ..."

Screw the science behind finding my parents! I scream in my head. *What the hell?*

"Specifically ordered? What do you mean, specifically ordered?" My voice is rising, but now I'm angry. I'm eighteen years old, and my doctor has been ordered to not administer tests on me?

"I'm sorry," she says, "but I can't say any more."

She's so full of apologies, and yet she doesn't do anything to make it better. I want to laugh, then, at the ceaseless contradictions of human nature.

"You *can* say more, you're my doctor," I tell her, and I'm a bit surprised at myself. I'm not the sort of person to question authority—that's more Ashley's arena. But this is too important to ignore.

"I'm sorry," she says quietly, adjusting her iPad and making as if to leave.

"If you're so sorry," I say calmly, trying to suppress the anger building in me as she takes a step toward the door, "at least tell me one thing. Just one. Who ordered you to refuse to perform a blood test on me?"

We are in a standoff. I watch her steadily, determined to keep my gaze unwavering. She looks back at me, thinking the situation over.

Maybe the determined look in my eyes intimidates her. Or maybe she can see the desperation that's burning a hole in me, driving me close to breaking.

I don't know what makes her decide to respond to me. And I don't know what I expect her to say. But when she does speak, I'm so shocked by her response that I can't think of anything else.

Doctor Buchanan sighs, looks up at the ceiling as if seeking divine strength, then looks back at me, a little tired and a little sad.

"Evelyn Blair," she says.

37
ASHLEY

I duck my head into my mom's office, hoping this will be fast and I can leave quickly.

"Bye, Mom, I'm going to Kelly's," I tell her. I wait for her to register what I said as she types furiously on her keyboard.

She rubs her face in her hands. Shoulders slumped, she turns to face me, looking like she didn't hear a single word I just said.

"Going with Elizabeth?" she guesses.

Normally this sort of indifference to my life would bother me, but it's different this time. This time, my mom's company is going under. The least I can do is cut her some slack.

"No, I'm going to Kelly's. She's out front," I tell her patiently.

"Oh, yes, okay," she says a bit despondently. I turn to leave, having gone no farther than a few steps before she calls me back.

"Hey, Ashley, before I forget, I need you and Elizabeth to go get the sedan serviced," my mother tells me, and there's a hint of the usual focus kicking back in. "There've been some recalls on the car, so you need to take it in soon. Can you two do it in the next week or so, please?"

"Yep," I say, telling myself to try to be patient, but I can't. I have places I desperately need to be.

"See ya," I call to her and whoever else is here—God knows who's ever here in this sea of glass—as I march out the front door, heels clicking all the way to the waiting car.

Kelly doesn't even drive. I tell my Uber the name of the hotel, and he raises his eyebrows.

"My boyfriend's famous," I smile, shrugging off his dubious glance.

Dating a famous person has its perks, but it has way more downfalls. Most notably that I can't be seen with him in public, which means I can see him only when he's holed up in one of his regular Malibu hotels.

It's been several weeks since the last time I saw Dashton, and I feel my heart rate rising as we near the hotel. There is no one who brings me more to life, and I sometimes find myself brimming full with the energy of it. It makes it all the more exhilarating to be with him when I'm actually *with* him. Other times, it's all I can do not to tell someone.

But I can't tell anyone because we both agree it wouldn't be wise. The media would be all over it, and everyone would freak out about the age gap.

People say they understand love, but they clearly don't when they're willing to abuse it for the sake of being accepted by meaningless people.

Before too long, we pull up to the glamorous Four Seasons. I hand my Uber driver a crisp wad of bills and thank him as I step out of the car, walking briskly up the steps and into the lobby. I flip my shades on and pull my long, blonde hair back as I walk past the front desk, flashing my key card authoritatively.

It's not like anyone knows who I am, but the less they know, the better. Everyone at the front desk here recognizes me by my Prada sunglasses, bright blonde extensions, and key card that signifies my importance to Dashton. He must've paid them considerably to not tip off the media. Or maybe they just don't care enough.

I step into the elevator, daintily pressing an acrylic fingernail for the floor that contains the deluxe suites.

Moments later, I'm striding down the hall to the end, until only a door separates me and the person I love most.

I smile as the door yields to my key. I rap lightly to let him know I'm here.

"Knock, knock," I sing as I step into the room, looking around for him. The bathroom door opens and he walks out without a shirt on, toweling his damp hair as he smiles that glistening smile at me. My stomach leaps.

"Hi, gorgeous," he says. Then he tosses the towel aside and takes me in his arms, kissing me slowly. I feel the heat of his bare, muscled torso, and I force my mind to resist the temptations of his body.

"Hi." I smile at him, reaching up and running a hand through his damp, golden curls. "I've missed you," I say with a sigh.

"Me too," he says, wrapping me in a hug. "I'm sorry I haven't been able to see you lately. But I should be freed up for at least a little while now."

I nod earnestly, hoping it's true. I know he'll always be busy, but it is a continuously gnawing fear of mine that he will someday be too busy for me.

We settle down on the couch, Dash rubbing my feet while he tells me about the movie scripts he's been given recently.

I don't like to listen to anyone but him. Most people don't have very interesting things to say, and when they do, they almost always adhere to a version of the story that others neither need nor want.

But with Dashton Little, it's different. Maybe it's the fact that he's an actor. Whatever it is, his words have the power to draw you in, inviting you to cling to their melodious flow. It's no wonder that so many people watch him speak on a screen. I could listen to him all day.

"And what's new with you?" He smiles expectantly at me, as if I have something to report that's comparable to acting in Hollywood.

"Oh, nothing really," I shrug. "Well, on second thought," I add, "I'm learning to drive. Elizabeth is teaching me."

"How's that been?" Dash asks me. He knows I don't, or at least didn't, much care for Elizabeth. That slipped out after about my fifth glass of chardonnay the night I met him.

"You know, it actually hasn't been bad at all," I respond thoughtfully. He lifts his eyebrows.

"The more time I spend with her, the more I realize she's not as bad as I made her out to be," I admit. "I think I kind of loathed her for being three times the person I'll ever be, even though she's not technically in our family. Which I know is a bad thing to think, but I couldn't suppress those feelings. Now, though … I don't know. I think it's time to just accept that she's a good person, and maybe learn a thing or two." I laugh, but I mean it.

"You are not a bad person, Ashley Blair," Dash says softly, taking my hand. "I'm glad you're getting along with Elizabeth, but her good traits don't take away from your own. You're beautiful, and funny, and smart, and witty, and a whole lot more. Don't you forget that, okay?"

There is a guilelessness in his eyes. His conviction that I am a beautiful person of substance practically radiates off him. And I love him for it.

"I love you," I tell him, for about the millionth time.

He leans forward and kisses me. I can feel the heat of his chest pressing against me and my heart pounding beneath him as we lean back on the couch.

We have gone about as far as you can get without going completely over the line. He has never, and would never, push me to do anything I'm uncomfortable with, which is how I know he truly loves me. Most guys in their twenties are after sex and little else, especially the ones in Hollywood.

And in the year we have been together, we haven't done that yet. But moments like these make me very much want to.

It's not that I'm scared of Dash—no one makes me feel more comfortable, more myself, than he does. It's that I'm afraid of the act itself, afraid of the vulnerability associated with it. *But*, I remind myself, *that fear won't change unless I face it.*

It's what I do with all of my other fears: look them in the eye and confront them head-on. Maybe this is no different.

"I want to be with you, Dash," I mutter so quietly that he almost doesn't hear me.

But sure enough, he pulls back, watching me carefully. "You do?" he asks skeptically.

I'm slightly annoyed that he doesn't believe it. "Yes," I voice confidently, kissing him. But he pulls back again.

"Are you sure?" When he asks me this time, there's a sort of light in his voice. A trace of hope. So he *does* want this, then. Well. Of course he does.

"I've never been more sure of anything," I say, and I mean it. At least I tell myself I do.

"But not here, not now," Dash says, as if it's the most obvious thing.

"Why not?" This seems fine to me—all I really need is him, not our surroundings.

"Because I want it to be special," he tells me, and I can tell by the look in his eyes that he means it. I decide it can't hurt to suspend my desires, at least for a short while longer.

"Okay." I smile at him and sit up on the couch. "So when?"

"How about next weekend?" He runs a hand through my hair. I wonder if he knows it's fake.

"That should work perfectly," I tell him, realizing that next weekend is prom. I'll just tell my parents that I'm going with my older friend, Jeremy, who I'll pay to keep quiet. I trust him not to tell anyone that I won't, in fact, be going to prom.

Moments later, Dash gets a phone call.

"I'm so sorry, Ash, it's my agent," he frowns at me apologetically.

"No, it's okay, you take it!" I exclaim. He is famous, after all, and if I didn't support his career, I don't know what sort of girlfriend I'd be.

I swing my coat over my arm and slip on my stilettos. I'm about to leave when I go to him and stand on tip-toe, kissing his cheek.

"I'll see you next weekend," I whisper into his ear so as not to interrupt him, but I use the most seductive voice I've got.

I stride out of the room, turning back only long enough to register his flushed skin, his eyes watching me longingly.

I text Jeremy immediately.

38
JAMES

I find myself thinking a lot lately about how, for the first time, I might be the only source of income for our family. Of all of the things to feel—sadness, fear, confusion, worry—all I can think about is how strange the situation is. And how, ironically, this is the situation I always wanted.

All this time, I wanted to be needed. It's why I felt alone, isolated in my quest to provide through a job I didn't thoroughly enjoy for people who did not thoroughly need what I provided.

But now, I see, for me to be needed by my family like I always secretly desired, it requires my wife to fall down.

It is a remarkably unstable scale we are all balancing on, a scale that tips and recedes under the shifting merits of its inhabitants.

I don't know why it all brings me such sadness and a new kind of awareness. I never want to see Evelyn upset, but nothing ever breaks her. Nothing means more to her than her business and the stability it has provided over the years.

And now it is all falling, and she is breaking. And my words can offer no condolences, because I created some of the fissures.

I did not break her. My actions didn't hurt her enough for her to fall apart, but they certainly didn't help her stability. What I did, all those years ago, was wrong and unfair and unbecoming of a man. Unbecoming of a person who is supposed to be committed to another.

Now I must be here for her to make up for the absence of years past, to help her during the one time she will likely ever need me.

I am not upset at her, or at Detail, or even at myself. I am upset at the life I created for myself, from the day I spread the rumor that Ben Hatching impregnated Angela Shelling so I could win class president.

It's simple to blame your faults on other things and other people, but it's deceiving. Because, at the end of the day, it is you. Your life, which is yours even when it doesn't feel like it. It's your actions that lead to your wrongdoings, that lead to the adverse impact you have on others.

Am I saying what is happening to Evelyn is her fault? No. Not necessarily. It's not fault that's the point. It is just reason. For the unspoken but exceedingly persistent law governing human nature declares that we are the products of our doings.

If I told any of my clients this after we lost a case, I would most certainly be fired.

39
JENAVIEVE

On the night of Elizabeth and Madeline's prom (and Ashley's, too, who's going with her older friend), Max gets a call. It is from the psychiatric inpatient clinic where his brother lives. Today, they tell Max that Jacob had a manic episode and almost hurt others. He is now restricted from group activities for the time being, forced to live in virtual confinement.

Max told me his brother is schizophrenic shortly after we started dating. It wasn't really the sort of topic that could be avoided. When family came up, I had my sisters, biological and adopted alike, to tell him about. He had his younger brother, who was too unstable to live without close medical supervision.

Max had been that supervision until he came to Harvard.

Now he sits with his head in his hand, rubbing his temple like he can find there the solution to the problem, pinpoint how he can help his brother in a way the medical professionals can't.

When he gets like this, there's nothing to do but be there for him and wait out the wave of emotions as he processes his brother's ceaselessly painful situation.

I rub his back and rest my head on his shoulder, murmuring the words of condolence that signify you care about, but can't relate to, another's condition.

"You don't understand," Max says stiffly, moving his shoulder out from under me.

"I know," I say quietly. "I don't understand what it's like to have a sick family member, and I'm lucky. But I'm here for you always, okay?"

"No," Max mutters wearily, looking up at me out of the corner of his eye. "You don't understand how it *feels*. You don't know what that pain feels like."

Ouch. A flush rises to my cheeks, and I try to brush off the slight anger I feel at him. I can't be angry, not now. But I also can't let him believe I'm naive any longer.

"I do know what pain feels like," I tell him quietly.

"I'm not referring to, like, sprained ankle pain, Jenavieve," Max says exasperatedly. Now he's not being fair.

"That's not the sort of pain I was referring to," I respond, a bit more sharply than was intended. Or maybe with just a bit more con- viction than was expected.

He raises his head then and looks at me, and I know that he's thinking about that night on Harper's balcony too. Since then he never really followed up on why I "wasn't perfect," and I didn't need him to. Not until now. Now he doesn't think I understand what pain feels like. He thinks I've lived all wrapped up in my privileged little shell. He needs to know how fragile that shell is.

"Then what are you referring to?" he asks softly. His eyes are on me now, and I realize that pain demands to run its whole course. And that can't happen until you've said it out loud to those you love.

"Please tell me," he adds. I realize now that he knows this runs deep, all the way back to the night I told him that I'm not perfect.

"Okay," I say quietly, and, finally: "I'll tell you."

***

"It's not that bad," I tell him, "compared to all of the other things that people go through, and I'm aware of that." I feel it's important to start with this.

"But then," I add, "I don't believe pain is measurable. Because even though what I went through years ago may sound like nothing, frivolous even, it meant something to me. It hurt me badly. So it's not stupid or dramatic, because it put me in a place that I wouldn't wish upon anyone."

I have his full attention now. He looks at me with concern, because it's not often that I talk like this. Things are light with us, and that's how I prefer them to be. But he has to understand the bad parts of me to understand all of me.

"I had an eating disorder, Max," I tell him, ripping the bandage off swiftly. It feels okay, surprisingly, to hear the words coming out of my own mouth.

"And it was a bad one. Not that any of them are good," I say, laughing hollowly.

He looks interested, and still concerned, but I know he's wondering just how badly it impacted me.

"I didn't understand how bad it could be until I dealt with it myself," I continue. "I would hear of people who starved themselves to be thin even though they already were, and I didn't get it. It was almost annoying to me, how people could make that, of all of the things, their problem.

"And then, sometime around the time I was fourteen, I looked in the mirror and it all changed. I no longer looked to brush my hair or take out my contacts. I looked in the mirror to scrutinize my appear-

162

ance, to tell myself how completely horrible I looked.

"I decided I needed to lose some weight, and the simple way to do so would be to cut down on my portion sizes. I had been eating a lot, but I was also a teenager who was growing. Of course, I didn't see it that way. I told myself I needed to eat minimally, just to cut off a few pounds. I hated how much I weighed, and I wanted to fix it. Just a little, of course.

"There were so many people around, too, all the time. Party after party being thrown in my house, where people made flash judgements the moment they walked through the door. So there was this constant reminder that I needed to look presentable, not merely for myself but for all the people who saw me in my day-to-day life.

"Sure enough, I reduced my portion sizes, and slowly lost a little weight. And then a little more. I became a little hungry, and all the time. But the strange thing was, the more I looked at myself in the mirror, the worse I thought I looked.

"It may sound shallow, and even made-up, but how I saw myself only got progressively worse as time went on. I bullied myself over the way I looked and truly believed I was repulsive. When I weighed myself every week, I thought there was something wrong with the scale, even as the number decreased.

"So I started eating less and running more. I started weighing myself every day, and I still hated the way I looked more and more.

"And I hated the inside of myself, too, for focusing so much on the outside. I hated myself for being moody and upset at everyone all the time. In retrospect, I had good reason to be upset. I was hungry, painfully hungry, until all hunger went away. I gave away my lunch at school and ate a few bites of salad, a granola bar halfway through the day to give me just enough energy to keep up my grades and focus in school.

"I ate less and less, and weighed myself more and more, until I was weighing myself about five times a day. I had to be good at being secretive with everything I did because I didn't want anyone to know.

"And I was good at it. In public I ate enough to not raise any concern, and then punished myself the next day by running a little longer or eating a little less. I had to always know what we were going to be having for dinner so I could plan accordingly. If it was something high in calories, I had to make sure I didn't eat all of my daily granola bar, or if it was something I considered healthy, I could maybe eat a few more bites of salad at lunch.

"I felt like I was losing my mind, and as time went on, I got worse and worse. At night, it took me hours to fall asleep, hours in which I cried silently and berated myself for being the person I was. There was never a moment I considered hurting myself in any way. But there were many times when I thought the world would be better off without me in it."

I have to stop here, for a moment, to take a breath. Saying it out loud makes me remember the realness of it, remember the complete hatred I felt toward my own pain all those years ago.

Max is still watching me and sitting completely still. I can see there are tears in his eyes. I take another breath and continue.

"I remember my lowest moment. One time, in the middle of the night, I felt so delusional and fed up with myself that I could no longer stand it. I was terrified at the idea of my family waking up to see me ravaging the kitchen, so I got out of bed and started searching my room, trying frantically to find something, anything, to eat.

"Finally, I found a granola bar deep in a desk drawer. God knows how old it was, but I didn't care. I sat in the middle of my floor in the pitch black and devoured that stale granola bar in a matter of seconds. I remember thinking to myself, numbly, *This is the lowest of the low, and I'm only fourteen. At least it can't get any worse.*

"I was a living paradox. A large part of me never wanted anyone to know about my eating disorder, but deep down inside, it's all I wanted. I wanted someone to force me to get help. I just didn't want to ask for it myself.

"It's no one's fault, any of it. I was exceptionally good at hiding it, and my friends and I were only in eighth grade. I wouldn't expect them to get it, wouldn't expect the thought to even cross their minds.

"As for my family, Elizabeth of course had her hunches. Madeline and Ashley were too young to notice anything out of the ordinary. And my parents, they did notice. They noticed my weight loss, the way I picked at my favorite meals. But they didn't see the full severity of it, and there was just no way they could have. How could they have any way of knowing what I kept so relentlessly guarded?

"A few times they mentioned the idea of me maybe talking to someone, but I shut it down so fast. I couldn't do that to myself, couldn't do that to my family. People couldn't know I was in therapy for an eating disorder, because that wasn't me. I was the straight-A golden girl in the perfect Blair family, not an emotionally unstable teenager.

"Except I was, and I just kept getting worse. By the end of eighth grade I had lost almost twenty pounds that I didn't need to lose in the first place. All of my clothes were loose, and I could see the bony curves of my hip bones, could count my ribs.

"There were constant dark hollows under my eyes from not sleeping, and my skin was pale. I looked skeletal. I lost my period for several months because my body wasn't nourished enough to support itself, and my hair fell out in increasingly large amounts in the shower. I was depressed. Almost nothing could make me feel any joy. I even passed out once.

"These were the side effects of starvation. Here I was, trying to make myself be beautiful, when I just was damaging my body almost beyond repair in the process.

"One of the saddest things was, my thinness was celebrated. Adults at the parties marveled at my tiny body, complimented me on my thinness. They asked how I was doing it, asked how a fourteen-year-old girl was rapidly losing weight.

"Even one of my teachers complimented me. And what a horrible, awful thing that is. For me to see my harmful actions validated by someone who is supposed to be a wise role model.

"So, yes, it was terrible, and it made me into a person so completely unlike who I ever was, or ever want to be again. Before, I was all light, pure joy. During, I literally felt dead inside, like I was next to nothing in value, both inside and out. And now I feel almost as I once did. Almost as buoyant, but not quite. I missed out on just being a kid, and the childlike innocence left. But I guess it does for everyone, at some point."

I feel I am about finished, now. Said everything I needed to say. There is a momentary silence as Max processes my story, regarding me solemnly.

"So how did you get better?" he asks me quietly, gently.

"Elizabeth had her suspicions, and one night, she told me how worried not just she was, but my parents, too. That's when I knew I had to get it together. They were beginning to grasp the severity of my condition. My secrecy was fading. And it became very clear to me, during that talk with Elizabeth, that if I didn't put my life back together, someone else would have to.

"I think I would've been institutionalized, eventually. The path I was going down clearly wasn't a good one, and it wasn't just me who was seeing it. It's like, that night, the fact that others knew what I was putting myself through solidified just how bad it was.

"There was no way I was going to be in a hospital. And, honestly, I was lucky. My will can be so powerful, and that night I figured to myself that eating again would be a clearly suitable alternative to living in a hospital and seeing my family put through that.

"So I ate. I was lucky, because I know it's not that simple for most. And, truth be told, it's not that simple for me, either. I ate, and I grew so much happier again, but I haven't looked in the mirror the way I did before I was sick. I still scrutinize my appearance—which I figure just about every girl does. But I don't remember the last time I looked in the mirror and truly thought I was beautiful. I find myself wondering if that'll ever happen, and I realize how sad that is.

"There are also still days when I feel this heavy kind of sadness weighing down on me, out of the blue, and it's like a flash of how I used to feel all the time.

"But it's not all the time anymore. It's infrequent, fleeting. One day I hope it will go away altogether. For now, though, I'm perfectly fine as is."

Max still is barely moving, watching me with love and attention but also with that underlying sadness.

"Do you think the world needs you now?" he asks me quietly, almost at a whisper.

"Oh, yes, Max," I tell him emphatically, because I can't have him concerned about this.

"If there's one thing I took away from it all, it was my worth," I tell him, laughing a little at the irony of it.

"It took me receding into a sad, hopeless shell of a creature for me to see that I was so much more than that. I wouldn't have been able to get my life back together if I'd believed otherwise. I worked hard throughout high school, and ever since, to fulfill the potential that I know I have.

"And now, Max, I'm happy. I always wanted to give back doing something I love, which is why I'm going to be a psychologist. I can do my part to ensure other people don't feel the way I did, and if they do, I can make it better for them. And I always wanted to end up with someone I fully and completely love, and we both know I checked that box."

I nudge Max's shoulder with my own, and he gives me what I think can almost count as a smile.

"So it all did work out, in the end. Life has a funny way of doing that, I think."

***

Later, when we are settled into bed and Max is drifting off, I know I must ask him before he falls asleep, or I won't be able to fall asleep myself.

"Max?" I whisper, and he turns groggily to face me, his long lashes making small shadows on his face.

"I just … you believe I know pain, right?" I ask him. "Not your pain, or your brother's," I clarify, "but pain. You understand that I know it now, right?"

He wraps his arms around me and says, quietly and surely, "Yes. I'm sorry I ever felt otherwise."

Then, with the ghost of nostalgia playing tricks of light on his face, he says: "And besides. You said it with just enough conviction that I couldn't help but believe you."

40
EVELYN

⤬⤬

Time, I believe, moves differently when you are viewing it through the lens of someone, or rather some*thing* in my case, that has so little time left.

This evening, I watched Elizabeth, Madeline and Ashley get ready for their prom. I saw Elizabeth in shimmery pink, Madeline in deep purple, Ashley in jet black. I saw them beautiful, buoyant, happy—Elizabeth knowing she's graduating in two weeks, Madeline happy as could be with Noah, and Ashley seemingly awash in the glamour of going to prom as a sophomore.

I watched them and had a pang of regret that I probably hadn't seen many of their other beautiful moments. It was like I was really seeing them this evening, seeing the innocent joy of their lives. I realized that I had sacrificed seeing more of that in exchange for a relentless lifestyle that is collapsing before my eyes.

There isn't much more that can be done. It is the first weekend of June, and we have three weeks left to pull something extraordinary together.

It should be simple. I've poured countless years into carefully dissecting the lives of the wealthiest and most privileged—maybe as payback for how many times people like them had defeated my mother.

169

Maybe because I wanted to become just like them. I don't know. It doesn't much matter now.

What does matter is that I have nothing. There is an apparent lull in the lives of America's Most Watched. My girls are unable to find anything either. They regard me tentatively now, sadly, even a little guiltily. Madeline, especially, seems remorseful that she can't find a good piece of gossip.

Even if she could, though, even if any of them could, it likely wouldn't be enough. The truth is, this company needs to dig up something astounding to expose if there's going to be any possibility of rising up again.

For one thing to flourish, another must fall.

And it must be me who flourishes. There is simply too much that counts on it.

My life wouldn't be my life without this company. The parties, the house, the husband, the family—they would never have been mine if Detail never existed.

It can't die yet. If a foundation crumbles, the entire system collapses in on itself.

I'm thinking about my family and the things I have done to keep them secure, to provide the best opportunities. If my company disappears, the value of what I sacrificed, of the choices I made, disappears as well.

And that cannot happen. I can withstand plenty, but not the notion that what I did wasn't right.

Maybe it's entirely selfish, and maybe it's entirely not—I don't know. In any case, I believe there must still be something out there, for there is always a way. I would know.

So I make the call to Sherri Smith in the spirit of good faith and determination, and I tell her we'll be pulling an all-nighter at the office tonight.

41

I sit poised on my therapist's couch a little more eagerly than usual. I've known her for quite a while now, and I have passed virtually all of our meetings with a blank stare and a bland distaste for the world.

Through all of that, she has continued to see me and has continued to let my disinterest run its course. She must be thrilled that I'm leaving soon.

For it's true. I have done everything so well, for so long, that surely we are meeting here now to discuss my discharge.

Sure enough: "I'm so glad to see you've been participating so much more."

She smiles at me a little—not an over-the-top, proud mom smile, but just a little show of pride.

"Yes, I'm feeling good lately." I force my face into a smile. Time to pretend, once more. It's ironic that the only time I wasn't pretending here was the blurry period I spent in a psychotic break.

My therapist tells me that she doesn't think we need to adjust my medications because my activity has been so much better lately. She says my improvement is notable, and I should be proud of myself.

She says nothing about discharge. I wait for that little ghost of pride again, wait for her to announce that it's time I move on, but there's nothing.

Okay. I prepared for this, because you must always anticipate and prepare for your worst-case scenario. It's simply time for me to convince her I'm ready to go.

171

"I appreciate all you've done to help me," I start, gushing with graciousness. People tend to do more for you when they think they are pleasing you. God only knows why we all give so much of a damn about what others think.

"It really means a lot," I continue. "And I feel that I've made a lot of growth these past few months. Of course, things have been hard, but I think I've displayed resilience. As you said, I'm actively participating in activities and group discussions; I make myself look presentable. I'm really trying. And I'm ready to be a productive member of society again."

Am I ready to be a productive member of society again? Likely not. Society is tainted for me now, as is just about everything.

I do know I am ready for something more than this. I am ready to go. Whatever it takes to convince her, I'll do it.

"I see," the therapist says thoughtfully. "You want to be discharged."

"Yes," I respond confidently. "I do."

"Well, there's definitely a profound improvement in you, one that I haven't seen before," she agrees. "Even when you were discharged before, you were not like this. I agree that you're doing well. Very well, in fact. But I can't discharge you."

Damn it. Remain calm, remain cool. If you blow up now, your efforts will be set back.

"And why is that?" I ask cordially, hopefully not through gritted teeth.

"You know why, I think." She's watching me now with her unyielding, fixed gaze. I wonder if she knows it unnerves me. Not much gets to me, but this look does. As if challenging me to bring forth something she knows I have.

"I don't, actually," I say, and now I'm a little annoyed. "What more do you want from me?"

"You can't move forward by carrying the past with you," my therapist says slowly. "If you try to take those steps with the burden of the past on your shoulders, you might get places at first. You might get pretty far, in fact. But eventually, your back will start to ache. And you'll keep walking, because you're still capable, but it will get more and more painful. And you'll still keep pushing, but you'll start to resent every step. And eventually, you will collapse."

"What am I supposed to do about that?" I ask her, flustered at the truth behind her little analogy. "I've told you about my family before, told you that one of them died. And I told you it was my fault. You know that's what led me here. What more is there to say?"

"I want you to walk me through it," she says, watching me carefully.

"Walk you through what?"

"The death, the events leading up to it. I want you to tell me all of it, in detail."

"That's ... that's just stupid," I sputter. There is no way I can do what she's asking.

"If you want to be discharged it's not stupid," my therapist tells me. And there is that look. That challenge. "In order to move forward, you need to leave your past behind. Not forgotten, but behind you. And you can't do that until you say it out loud. All of it."

It is my turn to stare at her, now. I see in her face that she means it. She won't let me out of here until I walk her through all of it.

If I didn't desperately want to get out, I wouldn't do it. It simply wouldn't be worth it.

But I do want out. I want it so badly, I can feel it every day, every minute, every second. I have to leave. And I can't leave unless I leave the past behind me.

Every time we leave, it's never just places we're leaving.

"Okay," I tell her. I take a deep breath, because we might be here a while. "I guess I'll start with prom night."

42
ELIZABETH

⸎

It occurs to me, as I stand beneath the shimmering lights and vaulted ceilings of our prom venue, that this is one of the last, and most significant, high school memories I will have.

I'll graduate in two weeks, leaving behind all the people who stand before me now. Some, like Noah, I've known since I was five years old. Many of them have been so ingrained into my life for so long that I now realize with a pang that I've taken it for granted. The long-lasting friendships that are a part of so many of my memories are soon to be severed.

But I try to focus on the beauty of the night, on the elegant venue that I myself helped set up. As the senior class secretary, I played a significant role in putting prom together—and I must say, it turned out beautifully. We had enough funding to afford an elaborately extravagant ballroom venue, complete with marble floors and sleek furnishings. Of course, it's the sort of venue the trust-fund babies from my school would likely expect, but that doesn't taint the splendor of this evening.

I watch everyone in the dimly lit expanse now, laughing and dancing. Each person here is exuberant, and how could they not be? They're lost in the thrill of gowns and elegance and the notion that this is the last of high school.

And I find myself wishing, with an unfamiliar resentment, that I felt the same way.

In essence, my night has been made just as beautiful as any girl's fantasy. Evelyn and James bought me a glittering gossamer gown, light pink crested with shimmering silver sparkles. My blonde hair has been curled and pinned expertly on top of my head with a heavy silver clip, leaving a few strands to dangle around my face. My makeup has been professionally done, making my eyes a significantly more electric blue than they actually are.

I have been made to look and feel like a princess tonight, and it would all be perfect, more than perfect, if I didn't know what I know.

After my doctor's appointment a few weeks ago, I was full to the brim with emotions that I wasn't sure how to handle. What I knew to be true was that Evelyn knows something no one else does about my birth parents. It was she who had ordered our family doctor not to administer testing, and I assume she must've paid the doctor a considerable sum to comply.

So then, the question was: *Why?* What does Evelyn know that no one else, including me, does?

The question dominated my every thought, but everything I came up with fell short of an adequate answer. No matter what sort of birth parents I could imagine, none of them merited eighteen years of scrupulously kept secrecy.

There was a plausible explanation, however—one I couldn't bring myself to face until last weekend. As I sat in my bed in the dark, mulling over more possibilities about my birth parents' identities, the thought struck me:

Evelyn is my mother.

When I thought it through, it wasn't any more ridiculous than my other ideas. If anything, it seemed like the most realistic thing I could come up with.

Evelyn must have not wanted anyone to know that she had an affair that led to my conception.

It wasn't all that surprising when I allowed myself to think about it. Evelyn was in the public eye, and had been since she was in her early twenties. She had created an instant name for herself through Detail. Then she had married James, a handsome and intelligent lawyer who even further accelerated her societal strides.

It must all have been going so well for her, until she had an affair. A mindless affair, I choose to believe, because I don't think that she would deliberately choose to sabotage her secure relationship with James.

She must have wanted me enough to keep me, enough to raise me—so she let me live a comfortable, secure, happy life with a hint of separation from the rest of the family. Just enough so that no one would suspect I was her illegitimate child.

The thing I still can't figure out is how she hid her pregnancy and gave birth to Madeline nine months later. Maybe James knew, but somehow I doubt it. There is a softness to him, and I believe he has always pitied the way I was raised. I believe if he knew the truth about Evelyn, he would've told me long ago.

In any case, I decided I would give it until the end of June to confront Evelyn about it. I'm full of questions for her that I desperately want answered, but I can't bring myself to put this on her while her company is on the line.

She's been working virtually around the clock to pull things together for Detail before it is too late. And although I badly want my answers, I can't help but want Evelyn to be okay first. Because no matter what, she did raise me. She did choose me.

Besides, I know there is always an explanation. When I finally unveiled the reason behind Jenavieve's mysterious darkness all those years ago, she had a good reason. She explained her eating disorder to me, and although I couldn't relate to it on a personal level, I could understand how it had led her to be so utterly unlike herself.

And after that conversation, things got better. For her as well as for the family, who were relieved to see her improving. We had our follow-up conversations and still occasionally do, just to make sure she's still okay. But getting her issues out in the open created a peaceful sense of clarity.

That is what I need. It's what I have needed for the past eighteen years but have been too afraid to ask for.

And Evelyn needs that peace just as badly as I do.

But for now I wait. I am giving her the time she needs to focus on her most pressing and immediate concerns. I've waited this long, after all. What's a couple more weeks?

Despite all of the thoughts swarming in my head, I am still at prom, and I remind myself that I must enjoy this moment while I'm still living in it.

So I dance, choosing to lose myself in the loveliness of childhood's fading grasp, before the inevitable changes of my near future take their hold.

43
ASHLEY

‹§›

It didn't take much to get Jeremy to pose as my prom date. All I had to do was promise him a couple hundred bucks, and we were on our merry way to a dance I had no intention of attending.

We took the obligatory photos, and I fancied myself up for the occasion, which I didn't mind at all. I want to look nice for Dash tonight anyway. I smiled and pretended to be excited about the dance, just to ensure my family wouldn't suspect anything. Not that any of them would care.

Besides, I'm sure Elizabeth and Madeline won't even notice my absence at the dance—Elizabeth will probably be too busy running it, and Madeline will probably be too busy hooking up with Noah. It is prom night, after all.

After the photos, we proceeded to Jeremy's family limo, where I am seated now.

"So where do you want me to drop you off again?" Jeremy asks me, eyes squinted suspiciously.

"In Point Dume Village will be fine," I chirp. "My Uber's expecting me there soon."

"And where is it you're going?"

"Jeremy, darling, I already told you that's confidential," I smile cloyingly. "Nothing for you to have any concern over."

Maybe if he were more like the Noahs of the world, he would care more and wouldn't let me dip out on him so readily. But, he is not a Noah, which is precisely why I chose him for my mission in the first place.

He merely shrugs, his interest fading almost before he had any at all.

Minutes later, the limo stops in the Village and I step delicately out. "Thanks again, Jeremy. Check your bank account in about a minute," I call to him as the limo pulls off. Then I deftly unlock my phone and transfer the money I promised him.

There. That's finished. My Uber arrives promptly and I hop in the backseat. "Four Seasons, please," I tell the driver, settling back for the ride. Dash has upgraded us to a suite even nicer than the one he already had. He wants it to be special, so he booked the nicest room in the hotel.

I find my nerves mounting again as we near my destination. Dash has texted me that he just checked in, which means he'll be waiting once I get there.

I don't know why I'm nervous. It was me who instigated all of this, me who wanted this. Me who wants this. And it's Dash. Dashton Little, who I would trust with my life. Dashton Little, who has listened to me and cared about what I have to say when no one else has. Dashton Little, the person I love most in this world.

And so it is that as we approach the hotel and I step out into the warm night, I find I am barely nervous at all anymore.

***

I swipe my key card at our room, knocking before entering to signify I'm here.

Not a second later, he appears, taking in my dress, carefully done-up hair and makeup.

"Wow," he mutters. "You look beautiful."

"Thank you," I smile at him and stand on tiptoe to kiss him, and it is a kiss that doesn't stop as we make our way to the bed, or as we lie together on top of it, acutely aware that our relationship is about to change.

I know what I'm about to do is meaningful. Sure, you could call me impulsive, and I probably wouldn't object, but this move isn't one I made rashly. It isn't the sort of thing you do just to do, and even I know that. It's what you do when you love someone with all your heart.

And if it's true, if you really do both love each other, then what's wrong with it? I may be fifteen to his twenty-one, may be the relatively unknown daughter of Detail's creator while he is a famous movie star, may be a seven at best to his perfect ten, but none of it matters. None of it matters because I love him and he loves me, and *that* is what means something. That is what means everything.

"We'll take it slow, okay?" he tells me.

"Okay," I say, a little breathlessly and pull him back to me.

***

Later, when it is all over, I lie awake in bed, Dash asleep next to me. One of his arms is slung around my waist, the other tucked under his head. He sleeps like a rock, not snoring or moving.

I, on the other hand, am wide awake. I don't want to lose consciousness yet, don't want to lose all that just happened.

I feel different yet the same, entirely changed while entirely the same girl I was in Jeremy's limo a few hours ago, the same girl I was on the night I twirled drunkenly in my golden dress, before I had ever even spoken to Dashton Little.

And here I am now, my life so entirely different than how it was before tonight. My loneliness is eased by the presence of someone who actually gives a damn. The void in my life is filled with a love I didn't know could exist, a love I didn't know I was capable of feeling.

And yet. No one in my family knows I have a boyfriend. And as secretive as I've been, I realize that I haven't really had to be. Because they have never asked. In fact, the only person who ever asks me anything about my life is Elizabeth.

Little do they all know that I am currently sleeping in a bed with Dashton Little.

I've always been the wild child. It's simple that way. My mother doesn't have to keep tabs on me at her parties because she can just roll her eyes, shake her head and laugh it off with her high society friends.

"She's a wild child, that one," she'd say, because she would much rather attribute my absence to an inherent personality flaw than actually try to find me.

And my father doesn't worry, probably because he's invented the excuse that I'm too crazy to be tamed. He can go to work every day with a clean conscience because none of his efforts would keep me from doing whatever crazy thing my wild-child self wants to do next. Right?

If only they knew. If only they had any clue or cared about what I have done tonight, and with whom.

But maybe it wouldn't even surprise them. Maybe it wouldn't surprise anyone.

No. It would probably matter to my sisters. I don't see Jenavieve that often because she doesn't live in the house with us, but Madeline and Elizabeth would care. They haven't abandoned me like my parents have. They have just had things of their own, Elizabeth being the hostess, Madeline being with Noah.

In any case, I tell myself as I feel my eyelids finally getting heavy,

I have someone who loves me. Right here, right now. And isn't one person more than enough?

It is. Tonight it is more than enough. So I take his hand, close my eyes, and let the thought that someone loves me, really loves me, soothe me into the most restful sleep I've had since I can remember.

44
MADELINE

∽∽

The night of prom proves to be dazzlingly beautiful. Malibu has granted us one of its most stunning sunsets to date. Noah and I take our photos right in my backyard, with the pink flower bushes and sandy serenity as our backdrop.

It feels like the epitome of something, like the countless hours we've spent growing up together have all built up to this. It's come to this moment, with Noah and me beaming with pure radiance for the snapshots I know I'll want to safeguard.

I wonder, as I watch them taking their countless photos of us, if my parents see how happy I am and how loved I feel. And I wonder, too, if they know what it feels like.

I remind myself how lucky I am that, at the age of seventeen, I know what love looks like. I'm beginning to realize that people with well over double my life experience don't always know what it is.

To me, this night is for the sort of sparkly, romantic glamour that Noah and I have usually seen conveyed falsely at all the parties we've sought to escape. For us, I think to myself as my group boards our party bus, this is a real celebration.

It never crosses my mind that it could be anything more than that, not as Noah tells me how beautiful I look, not as we dance, not as we laugh with our friends.

It's only when Noah leaves me for the other side of the party bus to talk with a lacrosse teammate that my friend Ally comes over and completely changes my perception of what this night should be.

"You look *stunning*," she gushes, gaping at the deep purple dress my parents bought for me. "And I bet Noah thinks so, too," she winks.

I laugh, blushing a little. "Thanks, Ally. And you look amazing!" I stare awestruck at her gorgeous, bright-red gown.

"So," she says coyly, leaning toward me conspiratorially, "is tonight the night?"

"What do you mean?" I laugh uncomfortably, a little confused.

"*You* know, you and Noah …" she trails off, letting me fill in the blanks. "It *is* prom night, after all. Totally the perfect time to hook up. Everyone will be doing it. Plus, he's hot. And you guys are the perfect couple."

Everyone will be doing it. I've never been one to bow to peer pressure, ever, but something about what Ally says brings a strange sort of tightness to my chest. I glance over at Noah, who's smiling his sweet smile as he listens to his friend.

It never even crossed my mind. It's not that I don't love him, or anything like that. It's just that there hasn't been anyone, ever, before Noah. He's the first boyfriend I've had, and although it's always kind of been him, I don't have experience. I'm young, or at least I feel like I am. But maybe he's not.

Plus, he's hot. For all I know, he has all sorts of experience. He's a year older than me, smart, charming, athletic, and yes, hot.

"Oh, I don't know," I try to shrug nonchalantly, but I can feel my nerves mounting instead of dissipating when Noah catches my eye from across the bus.

My boyfriend should not be making me feel nervous, I scold myself, and I suddenly feel inadequate in so many ways. This is his night, and I love him, and why wouldn't I want to be with him?

"Hey, Ally?" I have to raise my voice to be heard over the pounding bass. "Do you want to take shots?"

"Oh, honey, when do I *not*?" she exclaims, and I laugh, because I can. And I take a shot, and then another one, because I can. And I dance with Noah, because I'm really not so nervous any more. I say cheers with Ally for that.

***

By the time we reach our prom venue, it's safe to say I'm not sober. I'm not flat-out drunk, but just tipsy enough to make the venue look more sparkly than it actually is and to make me hold on to Noah more than I actually should need to.

I don't like to drink. In fact, practically the first and only time I drank was with Noah this past New Year's Eve. We snuck a bottle of champagne down to the beach and passed it clumsily back and forth, laughing, barely even making it through half the bottle.

So no, I don't drink, and neither does he. But after regularly attending high-society events for about as long as I've been alive, I know what being a little drunk does to people. It makes them a little less inhibited, a little more likely to let loose and have some fun.

I didn't drink enough to embarrass myself, but Noah can definitely tell I'm not quite there, for he holds me steadily as we dance. Well, I guess he would hold me steadily regardless, come to think of it.

All around us, there are people, many of whom I know, but many of whom I don't know, or at least not nearly as well as Noah does. These are his people, and this is his night, and I am constantly reminded of the probable importance of this to him.

Even if he wouldn't admit it, it's clear to see the magnitude of this event for any senior. It marks one of the last, and most significant, things they'll do in high school. It's also one of the last times they will be with these familiar people before they head off to meet new people at college.

College. That's something I try not to think about. That, and the doom of Detail, and the annoying twinge of fear about what might happen tonight.

But right now, those things fade. They lined my thoughts before, but the alcohol has made the lovely parts of tonight stand out most: Noah's hands on my waist, all the beautiful gowns, the music that sounds so much better than it actually is.

As people start to file out, I can see our group starting to gather together, getting ready to leave.

"So, are we still planning on going back to Ally's?" Noah asks me. Yes, this was originally the plan, because Ally is throwing an after-party that the group is invited to. But now, things have changed a bit.

"We could," I shrug furtively. "Or," I add, leaning toward him a little, "we can go back to your place. Our moms are pulling an all-nighter at the office."

His face immediately reddens, and I find myself pleased with how readily I suggested the idea. Sober Madeline probably wouldn't have done that.

"Okay," he says, watching me carefully. "Yeah, we can do that."

"Good!" I chirp, grabbing his hand and leading him over to the bus. "I'll just ask the driver to drop us off on the way."

There is a sort of tension between us on the bus, but not necessarily a bad one. I sit close to him. There's an expectant sort of electricity in the air, and I'm aware of how badly I want to kiss him, and I think he's thinking the same thing.

But, no matter what my state of consciousness, I am not one for PDA, and I know Noah feels the same. So even though it could, nothing happens on that bus ride.

At long last the bus stops in front of Noah's pretty, beach-side home, and people whistle at us as we get off.

"Have fun, lovebirds!" Ally calls after us as the bus pulls away. Noah holds my hand so I don't wobble as we walk through the door.

The house is dark and quiet, and I think we realize at the same time that we're completely alone. Sure, we may be alone when we're in our beach alcove, but even then there are people just above us. Here though, it's just the two of us. And in this moment, I know what I want.

Before Noah can say or do anything, I twist around and kiss him, and he kisses me back, and there's a sort of different feel to these kisses, a sort of passion that wasn't there even the first time he kissed me.

We don't stop kissing, and before I know it, we're kicking off our shoes and he's leading me up the stairs into his room, which I realize I've never been in before. I'm a little too preoccupied to take in many of the details, but I see blue walls, a clean floor. Bookshelf, flat-screen. Made bed.

He's kissing my neck now and that's it—my hands almost intuitively reach for the buttons of his shirt, undoing them with surprising ease. He doesn't stop me as I pull his shirt off him. His kisses move down to my collarbone as I feel the warmth of his skin and firmness of his muscles. My hands run along his abs and his arms, and my God, I have never been more aware of just how nice his body is.

Noah's hand moves to the zipper of my dress but stops there, questioningly. I nod and keep kissing him as my dress loosens and then is on the floor. This is okay. This is more than okay.

Just as we've reached his bed, he stops. We're both a little out of breath, a little flushed, but we still have done nothing other than kiss and get half-undressed.

His eyes search mine, and I'm wondering what he's looking for when he speaks. "Maddy, we don't have to do this," he says quietly, sincerely.

"What? No, I want to," I kiss him, but he pulls back.

"Look, you've had a little bit to drink tonight, which is totally fine," he says, "but I just don't think this is the best idea right now."

"Oh. Do you not want to?" I ask, a little defensively.

"No! I do," he stammers, blushing, "I do. Just not like this. I want it to be the right time, for both of us, and there's nothing wrong with tonight not being that night."

The way he's looking at me brings tears to my eyes, because I know how much he means it. And I know how much of a complete letdown I am, even if he doesn't think so.

"Hey, why are you crying?" He gently wipes away a tear with the pad of his thumb, concern etching lines in his face.

I shake my head, and he pulls me into a hug. "I'm sorry," I sputter into his bare shoulder.

He holds on to me and says soothing things, and I am filled with the notion that this is what matters to him most right now: my feelings. So many boys, I think to myself, can learn a thing or two from Noah Smith.

"You know it's not that I don't want to be with you, right?" I ask him earnestly, because he has to understand that. "It's just that I don't right now."

"I know," he says, and I know that he really does get what I'm trying to say. "And it's okay. It's completely okay. We've got time, Maddy. And besides," he adds, pulling back to look me dead in the eyes. "Why I love you has nothing to do with this," he gestures around. "I love you because you're *you*. You're my favorite person," he says with that half-smile. "You're the kindest, smartest, most beautiful girl I know, and that's why I love you. Not for this. I mean, not that I wouldn't love that too, but ..." he smirks, and I laugh, swatting at him playfully.

"You're a fantastic person, you know that?" I tell him, and he smiles at me with the love that underlies just about every way he looks at me. And I am so glad that he is mine then—my Noah, with his sweetness and ability to see things not as they are but as how they should be.

"I'm sorry I'm ending your night on this note," I sigh, thinking that I should probably just leave.

"What?" He feigns shock. "Who says this night is over?"

I look at him questioningly, wondering what he has in mind.

"You can still sleep over, if you want." He grins, and I feel a smile stretching across my face. We can still sleep together ... without sleeping together. Of course we can, because it's Noah Smith we're talking about.

He tosses me one of his worn, cozy t-shirts and I slip it over my head as he pulls off his slacks, exchanging them for a pair of sweatpants. We crawl into his bed and he snuggles up against me, wrapping an arm around me and cradling me perfectly against him.

"Goodnight, Maddy," he whispers, and I can feel his body relaxing into sleep.

"Goodnight, Noah," I whisper back. "I love you," I add, even though I think he's already out, and I almost instantly doze off. Ironically, I've never felt more completely comfortable in my life.

***

I awake a little drowsily the next morning, forgetting momentarily where I am. Then I hear Noah breathing soundly beside me, his arm still wrapped around me.

I turn to look at him, moving carefully to avoid waking him. He's a peaceful sleeper, I note. His face is smooth, his hair a little messy, his breathing quiet and slow.

He opens his eyes a few minutes later and smiles groggily when he registers me.

"Hey," he says, looking at me in a way that makes me feel like I look a lot better than someone who just woke up.

"Hi." I smile at him and push the hair off his forehead. I'm feeling warmer, safer and more content than I believe I've ever felt.

We kiss for a few minutes and then Noah turns on his TV. We lean back and I rest my head on his chest while he plays with my hair. We watch "House Hunters," deciding which houses we like best and why.

"Ugh, that one's too modern," I shudder at an all-steel-and-glass home in Florida.

"Really? I think it's kinda cool," Noah shrugs. "But yeah, some homeyness would probably be nice."

"Tell me about it," I grunt, thinking about my own modern, relatively colorless home. I want a colorful house someday," I tell him. "Somewhere nice, maybe here, I don't know. I just want it to be happy. And even though I don't like to cook, I'll make cookies and stuff so it'll always smell good."

"A bright, colorful house that smells good," I can hear the smile in Noah's voice. "That sounds pretty great."

"Yep," I smile contentedly, and even though I don't say it out loud, I don't think I need to. He knows that I would want him there, in my bright, colorful house that smells like cookies.

"Hey, speaking of good smells, how do pancakes sound?" he asks me, flipping over to look at me so that his arms rest on either side of me.

"Um, amazing," I gush.

"Chocolate chips, whipped cream, syrup, what do you want on them?"

"All of the above!" I exclaim.

He laughs and kisses me, letting it linger, then lifts himself up and hops out of bed. "Alright, let's go have ourselves some breakfast."

I smile giddily and follow him to the beautiful silver-and-white kitchen, which is filled with top-notch stainless-steel appliances.

Noah flips on the grill and whips up the batter as I sit on a bar stool, watching him, still shirtless, sprinkle in chocolate chips and shake up the whipped cream.

I open my mouth and he squirts way too much Reddi-Whip in. We're both laughing, and he leans down and eats the stray whipped cream from the corner of my mouth. Then we're making out, and he almost burns the pancakes.

He slides a plate of slightly crispy, golden-brown pancakes toward me, and I smile at the heart that he's drawn on top with the whipped cream.

We eat our pancakes and finally, when I'm so full and happy that I can feel myself getting tired again, Sherri texts Noah that she'll be home soon. It's time to go.

Noah calls me an Uber and grabs me one of his mom's old, long coats. It hides that the only thing I'm wearing is his big shirt underneath.

"I figure this is probably better than you wearing your prom dress home," he laughs.

"Definitely, thank you. I'll wash this and get it back to you soon," I gesture at his shirt as I button up Sherri's coat.

"Nah, that's okay, you keep it," he smiles, shrugging, and I wonder if he realizes just how much girls enjoy big, cozy shirts, especially ones that are from their boyfriends.

When my Uber is here, Noah walks me out. I wrap my arms around him at the end of the driveway, holding him there for a second and then pulling back to look at him.

"Thank you," I say quietly, meaningfully.

"For what?" he asks.

"Just for being you," I tell him, and that's really all that needs to be said.

I climb in the Uber, and Noah blows me a kiss as the car leaves the driveway. And my goodness, isn't it a remarkable thing? That there really are people like Noah out there in the world, people who love you for entirely the right reasons.

45

JAMES

Annie Anderson's case is nearly over. This weekend I will go to court with her and present her as the loving, rightful parental guardian of her two-year-old son, Liam. Her curly-haired, innocent child with rosy cheeks has no idea that I'm putting his life in the hands of a drug addict. All in the name of justice.

Law school was tedious. Preparing for the LSAT took years of arduous dedication to knowledge. Major mistakes and slip-ups were not tolerated. There were areas of the law that I was genuinely interested in. But more often than not, the years I spent preparing to practice law felt obligatory.

My father was a businessman, too. It wasn't as if law had been built into the family crest, a birthright for any son of William Blair. But the thing about law was that it was impressive. My parents raised me with the notion that I had to pursue what they considered the holy trifecta: business, medicine, or law.

I didn't like the risk of building myself up to great heights through business, and I knew automatically that medicine was not for me. I realized it takes precision, diligence and an ability to thrive under pressure. As you would guess, these were all things I didn't think I could do. And so, I chose law. It takes hard work but it is relatively safe and sturdy, and it generates a sizeable income if you do it right.

Maybe if I didn't care so much about what my father thought, I wouldn't have done it. Maybe I wouldn't have spent so much of my life trying to perfect something I didn't have the passion to be fully invested in.

But me being a lawyer proved to parallel just about every other aspect of my life. It dominated in the face of my reservations, consuming me with a life that was comfortable yet not all that I wanted.

I believe I will win this case, but I hope I don't. And I can't tell if that hope is ethical or unethical of me.

I'm tired. Tired of the life I have created for myself, the life that I am subpar at. Here I am, with a beautiful home, a beautiful wife and beautiful kids, and I have never been good enough for any of it.

The ironic thing is, I was good enough when I was a child. I didn't see it then, but I was a good kid. I was kind, hard-working, innocent, eager to do the right thing. But my father made me feel inadequate. I just didn't know that it was his fault—not mine.

Now I truly am not good enough, and it's no one's fault but my own. I made a commitment to someone I had the deepest reverence and awe for, but didn't love, and she unfairly paid for it. I raised four children who I've never been able to fully commit to, all because of a job I don't enjoy.

And yet everything will continue. I know it because it has never stopped continuing, and never will.

I will win Annie Anderson's case, and little Liam will grow up severely disadvantaged because of it. I will continue to be a lawyer, and I will go home to my wife and daughters at the end of each day.

Maybe Jenavieve is onto something. When she told me she wasn't going to be a lawyer, I was shocked. But I was also secretly envious.

I envied her tenacity, at such a young age, to abandon what the safe thing is in order to search for what's right.

It's an ability people many years older than her, myself included, don't have. I find myself wondering how she got there. Was she always this way, always willing to chase her dreams, or did she have some flash of insight? What are the secrets to living life well? It's funny that I want to ask my own daughter these things.

So perhaps I did do something right, by her at least. And maybe there is hope for Elizabeth, Madeline and Ashley. Maybe they will live and love unapologetically, chasing after all the fulfillment they desire. Maybe they will be okay.

It would be ironic for them to turn out good despite my bad.

Yet there is a strange sort of balance governing every aspect of the world: In order for anything to be good, there must be something bad to compare it to.

So maybe it is alright. If my subpar lifestyle and questionable morals mean my daughters turn out genuinely good, then it has all been worth it.

For while the circle never stops spinning, revolving in its steady abyss of nothing and everything, there must be ways to make it all mean something. If there weren't, after all, what would be the point?

46
JENAVIEVE

E ver since my conversation with Max, there has been a small, yet perceptible, shift in our relationship.

For the first time, I went with Max to visit his brother at the hospital. Taking me with him was important to Max, but I know he also felt vulnerable doing so. I got to meet Jacob Grayson in the sun-filled parlor of the nice hospital nearby that Max transferred him to so he could be closer to us.

I quickly discovered that Jacob, who recently turned twenty, is not only a spitting image of his brother, but a person with kind eyes and a deep admiration for Max.

When Max and I don't have class—marketing and business management courses at Pepperdine for him, psychology classes for me—we take leisurely strolls on the beach or sip martinis on our little patio.

Not that we didn't do those sorts of things before, but it's different now. Because now, sprinkled in with our witty banter and light stories, are conversations about the sorts of serious topics relationships need if they're going to grow and strengthen.

Max tells me more about Jacob, about how he worries for him and constantly struggles with the guilt that he's not a good enough brother.

Of course, I tell him he's a wonderful brother and that Jacob will be okay. But I also listen to acknowledge the pain, to nod quietly. I assure him that what he's feeling is okay to feel, because the darkness existing in his life is real.

As for me, I tell him more about my perfectionism, and how it's functioned as both the greatest blessing and biggest curse throughout my life. I explain how it fed both my eating disorder and my academic diligence, my self-debilitating thoughts and my drive to make a difference in the world.

I tell him that it's something I try to manage, a part of me that both boosts me up and weighs me down. He listens to me attentively the way he always has, completely immersed in what I have to say. But now he knows that I'm not a stranger to psychological pain.

We also talk about the future. We discuss my plan to become a psychologist specializing in eating disorders, and Max tells me that he'll try to help facilitate an opportunity for me to shadow Jacob's own psychologist. We talk about buying a house once we've both become more financially stable—a house close by my parents' so that we can be around my family.

We talk about raising children in the house, too, something we didn't speak much about until recently. We toss around the idea of a big wedding occurring sometime in the next few years, with a beachside theme and pink-frosted cupcakes.

We talk about the future in a way that makes me believe it is truly on its way, my life with Max solidified by our dreamy conversations about our shared existence five, ten, twenty years down the line.

Perhaps the best thing about my current life is that I am feeling something I had suppressed into near oblivion, something I haven't felt since I was thirteen.

I am beginning to get some of the old buoyancy back. I'll never go back completely to the innocently joyful, beaming young girl I used to be. But I'm starting to see that the best parts of her aren't lost to me completely. They went away for a while, but they are beginning to return, peeking out in little glimpses at a world they will eventually participate in once again.

Besides, when I feel surges of happiness as Max and I walk along the beach to the setting sun, I realize that I don't want to be that little girl anymore. She was a nice kid, but she wasn't me. Everyone leaves their youthful self behind, and it's not a bad thing. The person I am now is a good one, one who has learned how to love and find joy and, most importantly, make meaning out of the madness.

Maybe this stability won't last forever. Life likes to throw in its unsparing curveballs every once in a while, and who knows? I could be subject to one at any time.

But the thing is, it will be okay. I have Max and I have myself, and I have the knowledge that life goes on, and it is up to us to determine how it goes on. And whatever comes next, I know, is simply a facet of this truth.

47
MADELINE

One week after prom, I awake to a sun-filled day, the sort of bright Saturday morning that signifies a warm, summer weekend lies ahead.

Noah is coming over soon, and I'm thinking that maybe we'll stroll the beach today, bask in the sun, go swimming. Anything to enjoy the first bits of summer. School is out in a week and a half, and after that will be long, blissfully free days that I can spend hanging out with my friends, adventuring with Elizabeth, and spending time with Noah.

I pull on shorts and a summery blouse, brush my hair and apply my makeup in front of my vanity. I am just passing Ashley's room to head downstairs when someone calls out my name.

"Madeline?" I hear a small, slightly tentative voice that doesn't sound at all like my sister's usual sass but must belong to her.

I circle slowly back around and walk into her room, where she leans back on her bed.

"Hey, Ashley, what's up?" I try to sound casual, but inside, I'm trying to remember the last time Ashley invited me into her room to chat.

"How was prom?" she asks me with a slight smile. Huh. So she really does just want to chat.

"It was good. Really good, actually," I smile. "And how was it for you?"

"Good," she says dismissively, and then: "Did you and Noah sleep together?"

I feel my face redden, shocked at her bluntness and the uncomfortable nature of her question. I don't know why I even respond to her, but it probably has something to do with her pressing, unrelenting stare.

"Um, not that it's any of your business," I tell her, "but no. We didn't."

She nods, watching me carefully, as if trying to decide if I'm telling the truth. Her gaze keeps flitting between me and other spots in the room, as if she's still deciding something. I've had enough of this little talk.

"Okay, well, I'm going downstairs. Noah's coming over soon," I mutter, turning and walking briskly out of her room.

I've just reached the landing of the stairs when I hear her say, so quietly, "I did."

I stop in my tracks, and I need to know what she's talking about. I walk slowly back into her room, scrutinizing her for a few moments.

"You did what?" I ask her carefully, realizing I'm kind of afraid to hear her answer.

"Slept with someone. On prom night," she says, and I'm impressed that she doesn't break my gaze.

She's not lying. I can see it in her eyes. But there must be some part of her that regrets it, or at least some part of her that wants to connect with someone about it. I'm her older sister. I have to be that person for her.

"Ashley, you slept with Jeremy?" I try to mask any tones of judgement with concern because I am concerned. "He's two years older, and I didn't realize you two were more than friends."

"I didn't sleep with Jeremy," Ashley says firmly, and now I'm more confused than ever. If she didn't sleep with Jeremy, then who was it?

"I slept with Dashton Little," she says confidently. I can tell by her expression that she's also proud of this.

"You *what*?" I sputter. "Dashton Little, like, *actor* Dashton, who's at all the ... ?" Oh. At all the parties. And suddenly, it makes more sense. Why I've never really known where Ashley sneaks off to during the parties. I've always simply assumed she goes up to watch Netflix like a normal fifteen-year-old.

"At all the parties, yes," she says impatiently.

"Ashley, he's so much older," I say quietly. "Are you okay? I mean, did you consent to this? Because, if you didn't—"

"He's my boyfriend, Madeline," Ashley interrupts, a twinge of annoyance in her voice. "We've been dating for a year. So yes, it was entirely consensual. It was my idea, actually."

Never have I been more shaken by anything in my life, ever.

"Where? It wasn't *here*, was it?"

"No, of course it wasn't here," she rolls her eyes. "It was at the Four Seasons, and it was really nice."

I don't even know what to say. While I was watching "House Hunters" with Noah, Ashley was probably sleeping in a bed with Dashton Little. It's too much to absorb right now, but I know that what matters most is if she's okay.

"Are you sure you're okay, Ash?" I ask her tentatively, looking at her with what I hope she can see is care and concern. "That's a really big deal, and I would know because I haven't even done it myself, yet."

Ashley watches me for a second, formulating a response. But it isn't fear or violation that I see in her eyes. I know deep down that she really did orchestrate it all. But then, why is there so much sadness in her face?

"I'm okay, really," she tells me, and there's an unusual trace of kindness in her voice. "I don't regret it, and it wasn't a bad thing at all.

I just wish that people knew."

Knew that you had sex with Dashton Little? I think to myself scrupulously, but of course I don't say it out loud. Right now, I just need to listen.

"Not, like, *that*," she says quickly, as if reading my mind. "I just wish people knew I had a boyfriend, you know? I mean, this is all such a big shocker to you, and it would be to everyone because no one knows that I have a boyfriend.

"And it's the sort of thing you don't want to keep inside. You would know," she looks at me with the ghost of a smile on her face. "After you've hung out with Noah, you smile like you just heard the best news of your life. But I've never been able to do that. I've had to keep it all inside because I'm dating a celebrity, which is cool and glamorous, until you realize that no one can know anything about it.

"You would really like him. He's so caring and smart, and he listens to what I say like I'm not just a dumb teenager," she says earnestly.

I think to myself how sad it is that my sister feels she needs someone to validate that.

"I can't change anything, though, because no one can know about our relationship," she sighs. "He's famous, and I'm young, I guess, and it just has to stay hidden. That's a price I'm always willing to pay, because I love him.

"But I just wish people asked more, you know? Because no one has ever actually asked me about boys. No one really cares. And I know I haven't always been the nicest, and that's my fault. But I still want people to care."

"I care," I tell her, crossing the room to give her a hug. She immediately stiffens, and I pull back quickly. "I care, okay? And you can always talk to me. You shouldn't have to keep these important parts of your life hidden."

She nods, and I can see the gratitude in her eyes. Just as she's about to say something else, the doorbell rings and I can hear Noah's voice cheerily greeting Liz as she lets him in.

"Okay, well, that's my cue," I say apologetically. "But let's talk about this more later, alright?"

"Okay," she says quietly. "Hey, and Madeline?"

I turn around to face her once more.

"Thank you," she says steadily. "You're, like, the only person I trusted to tell this stuff to."

"You're welcome, Ashley," I smile at her softly. "Anytime."

And as I walk down the stairs to see Noah, there is one thing in my conversation with Ashley that fully registers in my brain.

This is all such a big shocker to you, and it would be to everyone.

***

Noah and I walk the beach, a warm wind gently blowing the smell of the sea into our faces, the sun beaming brightly overhead. He holds my hand and tells me a funny story about a graduation rehearsal that apparently happened last week, but I'm only half-listening to him.

Everything would be more than good if I didn't have this *thing* eating away at me, this thing that I have to figure out how to act on.

I know deep down that I shouldn't even be taking this into consideration, but I'm unable to let it go. Ashley trusts me to protect this huge secret of hers that she felt she couldn't share with anyone else. When I think about breaking that trust, I feel a deep, guilty ache inside.

But I could save everything my mom worked for. She's been so distraught lately, so desperate for help that no one has been able to give her, and now I have something. Something that would get Detail back on its feet again.

It's not just my mom I'm considering, either. It's Sherri Smith and her job that, all on its own, provides for her and Noah.

If I tell my mom about Ashley, I risk losing Ashley's trust forever. If I don't tell my mom about Ashley, my mom loses a company, her employees lose their jobs, and my boyfriend's mom loses her one source of income.

Telling my mom will help more people than it will hurt, I know that. But would helping people destroy my guilt? Would it compensate for it at all?

I mull over the options to no clear conclusion. It is impossible for me to differentiate between right and wrong, impossible to clearly separate the two. I know, then, that I have to run it by Noah, the person whose opinion I value the most.

I wait until after he's finished his story, and I take a deep breath.

"Noah, I have to talk to you about something," I say, looking up at him so that I can see his gray eyes, which look brighter and clearer today in the sunlight.

"What's up?" he asks me, watching me attentively and keeping my hand in his as we walk.

"Ashley slept with Dashton Little," I say quickly, watching his face turn from concern to shock, and then back to concern again.

"*What?*" he exclaims. "Ashley, your little sister Ashley, slept with *Dashton Little?*"

"Yes," I say quietly, waiting for him to process it a little better.

"Whoa. That's statutory rape, isn't it?" he mutters softly.

"Yeah, it is," I respond grimly. "She's fifteen, and he's twenty-one, so yeah, it's definitely not legal."

"Is she okay?" he asks, the familiar lines of concern etched into his face. "I mean, did he force himself on her?"

205

"No, it really doesn't sound like it," I tell him. "She's apparently been dating him for a year. She even told me she loves him."

"God, it can't be a good relationship," Noah remarks. "And it's sad that she thinks it is, you know?"

Yes, it is sad. But there's something else.

"Yeah, it's terrible, obviously," I say. "But there is one good thing that comes out of this, I think."

"Really? What's that?" Noah asks me skeptically.

"It's the story," I say, making sure that it's loud and clear enough that I don't have to repeat myself.

"The story?" He's not grasping it. "What are you talking about?"

"It's the story that saves Detail," I tell him patiently. "It's big, and it's shocking, and no one is ever going to get their hands on it before Detail does."

Noah drops my hand, stops walking, and looks at me like he doesn't even know who I am.

"Are you serious, Maddy?" he asks me softly. "You're telling me that you're going to tell the whole world something so personal about your little sister? And for what, a business?"

"It's not just a business, Noah," I shake my head. "It's my mom, everything she's worked for. And not only that, but it's *your* mom, too, and every other employee working for Detail. This is bigger than Ashley."

He watches me for a long moment, speechless.

"Don't do this," he mutters, shaking his head. "I know that Detail matters, I do. But this isn't the way to save it."

"There are no other ways to save it, Noah," I respond impatiently. "They're running out of time. There's going to be nothing else this good before their deadline at the end of June."

"I can't believe you think this is 'good.'" He looks up at the sky, exasperated.

"I obviously don't think it's good," I snap. "But I do think it's necessary."

"Maddy, our moms are loaded," Noah says quietly. "You know it's true. It's going to be really sad if Detail doesn't make it, but it won't be the end of the world. They all have more than enough money. But Dashton and Ashley? They won't be okay from this."

"Releasing this story will help more people than it will hurt," I say firmly. "And besides, our moms may have enough money, but that's not all it's about."

"Isn't it, though?" Noah says softly. "To them, it is about the money, and I've always known that," he continues slowly, with so much sadness in his voice. "I just never thought money would ever be what it's about for you."

I stare at him with disbelief, not even knowing what to say. After all the years I've known him, the years we've shared our deepest feelings about the parties and the lives we live, without any filter, this is what he thinks of me.

"Noah, you know that's not—"

He cuts me off. "I just need some space right now, okay? I'll see you later."

He turns to leave, retracing our steps as I stand there watching him, numb. There is no half-smile. There's nothing except him turning away from me and not taking the time to look back.

With that, I pivot in the sand, walk up to my house and through the doors to my mother's office, and don't even hesitate before saying it. Because this isn't about the damn money. It's about my family, and helping more people than I hurt.

"Mom," I say to her, and this is the right thing. I know it is. "I know how to save Detail."

48
EVELYN

Out of all of the emotions I should be feeling—sadness, surprise, guilt, a mix of all three—what I feel instead is a wave of calm. As if this is how it was meant to be, as if this whole time there was an answer to the question, How do we save Detail?

Because now, there is an answer. The only strange thing about it is that the answer is my daughter.

When Madeline told me a few hours ago, I did not speak. I simply listened as she told me that Ashley has supposedly been dating Dashton Little for a year, that she is in love with him, and also that there is proof.

As it turns out, Ashley made a little slip-up when she was talking to Madeline by telling her exactly where she and Dashton had stayed. Madeline figured it wouldn't take much for me to get the security footage from the Four Seasons, and she was right.

I watch the tapes now on loop, and marvel at how excellent the quality is. Anyone can easily depict Dashton Little, his wavy golden hair and leisurely stroll.

And you can see my daughter, too, her long, bright blonde curls swinging as she enters the hotel lobby just half an hour after Dashton.

The footage is so clear that you can zoom in on the key cards the concierge gave the two of them, seeing for yourself that the room numbers match.

The two even left the hotel together, holding hands.

Privacy will always be violated in the name of good gossip. And, of course, money.

When Madeline told me all of it, I knew what she was thinking. She was thinking that a twenty-one-year-old celebrity sleeping with a fifteen-year-old is plenty to be talked about.

She's right. It is a career-saving story. And everyone will be eager to soak up all the details.

But what will make headlines, more than anything, is that Ashley is my daughter. Me releasing something about my own child is what will make this story the most successful, and that's something that I know Madeline didn't even think of.

It is almost comical. To save the lifestyle of my family as we've always known it, I have to sacrifice one of them.

It's like what Madeline told me: *This will help more people than it will hurt.*

This is true, I know it is. So then why do I feel as though there's something so wrong with it?

I suppose it's all a question of morality. Is it moral to exploit my child for the sake of my other children? Am I even doing this for my children?

The thoughts are horrible and swarming, overwhelming my brain with more than it can handle.

I can't answer these things. I don't know the answers to life's most pressing questions. No one does.

What I do have is a solution to this question: How do I save Detail? I do know the answer to this one. It's sitting in front of me now, in the neatly compiled security footage and notes I have ready to go for Melissa, my head publicist.

Right and wrong is all construed on the basis of subjectivity, but this story is not. My company is not. People can take what they want out of the stories I release, but the stories themselves are always accurate.

I tell myself that this must be enough—accuracy must be what I can base my decisions on. To base them on anything else would be illogical and inevitably unsatisfying.

So I email Melissa, order her to release the blast. And with that, the silken ribbon of interwoven postulations and inner musings is completely cut.

49
ELIZABETH

I stare at my computer screen, tapping my fingers idly. For the umpteenth time, I scan the article, my eyes drawn to the video clips of Dashton Little and Ashley leaving the Four Seasons hand in hand.

Since I've worked with Ashley to teach her to drive, she's opened up to me more than I ever thought she would. But, throughout all our time in the car, she never told me a thing about Dashton. We didn't talk much about boys at all. I don't have much to speak of in that department, and neither did she. At least to my knowledge.

It was a brilliant business move on Evelyn's part. The article was released just half an hour ago, and already there are thousands of shocked commentators making the connection between Evelyn Blair and Ashley Blair.

There isn't much time before Ashley finds out. In fact, I'm surprised she hasn't already.

When she does, there's no telling what will happen. I know she'll be shocked, and then infuriated. Things will get bad between her and Evelyn very fast. God only knows when it will blow over.

I sigh, lowering my head into my hand. It's not kind or considerate of me to do this, but I have to. I have to talk to Evelyn before everything explodes with Ashley.

Even though I told myself I would wait until the end of June, there's no need to do that anymore. Detail is undoubtedly saved, so the only thing holding me back is the imminent family feud that's perhaps just minutes away.

Jenavieve is at her condo with Max, Madeline and Ashley are in their rooms, and James is at work. As for Evelyn, she's downstairs in her office, likely basking in her success.

If there's any time to talk to her, it's right now. Because I know there will always be an excuse to hold off. I realize I'm pretty good at coming up with excuses when it comes to anything involving the Blairs.

But now is not the time for that. It's time to do this thing for *me,* before I lose my mind in all of my confusion about how I came into the world.

So, for maybe the first time in my life, I abandon all other factors in reckless pursuit of what I want. It feels like some sort of strange, selfish violation, but still I go on.

I shut my laptop, walk down the stairs to Evelyn's office, knock on the door, and am invited, finally, into the conversation.

***

I think a part of her knows what's coming because she doesn't look all that surprised when I enter the room.

Then again, not much can probably surprise her right now, considering her own recent actions are a surprise in and of themselves.

"I guess you saw the article?" Evelyn looks up at me fleetingly, and although her voice is calm, I can see the fearful sort of guilt in her eyes. Her few pages of words hold the immense power to unhinge Ashley's life, and she knows it.

I feel a slight pang, a sort of empathy toward her. Because I'm likely about to unhinge Evelyn's life myself, at least a little. I close the office door and take a seat on the chair across from her desk.

"Yes. I saw it," I mutter quietly. "But that's not what I'm here to talk to you about, actually."

She looks up at me and holds eye contact this time, raising her eyebrows in confused interest. Here we go.

"I know you have a lot going on right now, and I'm sorry about that, but I can't not talk to you about this anymore."

"What's going on?" Evelyn prompts.

Deep breath. "I went to the doctor a couple of weeks ago."

"I'm perfectly healthy," I reassure her in response to her bewildered expression.

"Then why did you go to the doctor?" Evelyn's face scrunches in confusion.

"I went to get a DNA test," I say quickly, but surprisingly firmly. My anger is starting to mount. I keep my eyes on her face as I watch it go pale, watch as she tries to figure out what to say to me.

I feel some satisfaction in seeing her squirm, because it's only fair. She withheld information from me that no one should have the power to withhold from anyone. And because of what? Her own fear? Her own desire for me to not ruin her life completely?

"I wasn't able to get the test, unfortunately," I say stiffly. "Even though I'm eighteen, I'm not allowed to have a DNA test. A little strange, right? It's fine, though, because Doctor Buchanan actually told me that getting a DNA test isn't even the way to go about tracking my biological parents. Which is what I was there to do."

It's unlike me to be this way, and I feel the guilt already bubbling up. But on a much deeper level, I feel the need to know.

"Look, I know this isn't ideal to talk about right now," I say with a sigh, "but it's never going to be ideal, is it?"

She hasn't moved, not since I mentioned going to see Doctor

Buchanan. I can't read her face, and that's saying something, coming from me.

"I wasn't just left on the doorstep by some scared, unstable teenagers like I always believed, was I?"

Evelyn shakes her head slightly, and I see her cheeks reddening with shame.

My eyes water a bit, and there's so much that I'm feeling, right now. Anger and fear, mixed with a strange sort of relief, and even excitement. Excitement to finally understand that I'm not an outcast in this family, excitement for Evelyn to explain the answers.

"You're my mom, aren't you?" I whisper, my voice trembling.

Evelyn sighs, looking at me for a long moment. There is such sadness, marking deeper and deeper crevices in her until she becomes an endless chasm of it all.

I almost think she won't answer, but I won't even consider leaving this office until I have my explanation.

Evelyn must know this, because after a long moment she takes a deep sigh, rubbing her face defeatedly with the palm of her hand.

"I'm not your mother, Elizabeth," she tells me wearily, and she says it with such sincerity that I know it's true.

Well. I guess I was wrong. But even then, I'm not going to let it go that Evelyn won't let me have a DNA test. I don't know what it is. Maybe she's afraid of me leaving the family or something.

If that's the case, she doesn't have to be. I'm not going anywhere. But I still need to know the truth.

I'm trying to formulate what best to say, when I hear it. Clearly, candidly, and with such deep sorrow, she says:

"But James is your father."

50
JAMES

I told myself I would never see Sarah Jenkins again.

After that night in the bar, the giddiness and childlike joy that came with meeting her and kissing her eventually left. I lived the next day, week, month with my wife and child, fully aware that they were my wife and child and this was my life.

I realized I was being childish for still texting her, and so I ended it. I'm sorry, but I can't be doing this. I pressed send, and then couldn't help myself from adding: I really am sorry.

Because I was. Not just sorry for her, but sorry for me.

Life went on, however, as it always does—regardless of whatever the hell is going on with its participants. I watched Jenavieve grow, watched her play and laugh and learn her letters.

I watched Evelyn's joy in seeing these things, watched her watching Jen with proud mom eyes. I saw her beam at me when I walked through the door after work, and it was good. It felt good to live this life. I had made the right choice, and I knew it.

And then there came the night.

It wasn't a particularly different night from all the others. I had gone to the office that day, done my work. Its difficulty tired me out a little more than usual.

I didn't stop at any bars on my way home. I just wanted to see my wife. I thought maybe if I talked to her, saw her face glow when she saw me, I could go to sleep feeling happier.

When I walked through my door, the house was dark and quiet. On the countertop was a note, scrawled hastily by Evelyn: *Jen and I were extra tired, so I put us down early tonight. Left some dinner for you in the fridge. xx*

I sighed, rubbing my face in my hands. I heated up the dinner, ate it as quietly as possible so as not to wake my family. Then I crept upstairs and ducked my head into my daughter's room to check on her, then checked on Evelyn.

There she was, curled up on her side of the bed, not moving, barely even audible. On her bedside table, inches from her face, lay a haphazard stack of Detail reports she had clearly spent the evening poring over.

Her face was so peaceful and quiet, I didn't want to wake her. The selfish part of me wanted her to be here, present, asking me about work and telling me about the interesting or funny things Jenavieve had done that day.

But she had had a long day at work, which she loved, and was now sleeping peacefully, which she needed. My wife bounced around each day's events wide awake, and that fulfilled her. I didn't fulfill her, I reminded myself, because I wasn't a part of those days.

I watched her for a moment longer before quietly closing our door, walking downstairs and heading out to the driveway. I sat in my convertible and, without thinking, pulled out my phone and texted Sarah: Where are you right now?

Then, in a separate text: I don't expect you to answer that. But I hope you do.

A minute later, she sent me an address, one that I assumed was hers but couldn't know for sure. I drove to it.

I pulled up to a little beachfront apartment that looked a lot like the one I remembered her describing to me in the bar. And because I wasn't enough, and my wife's joy came from work and not me, and because my daughter didn't need me, and because my life wasn't enough for me, and because I didn't know what to do with all of these thoughts, I knocked on the door.

She answered, dressed in jeans and a black tank top, and as she looked up at me with those big, bright blue eyes, I literally felt my heart skip a beat.

"James, what are you doing here?"

"I needed to see you," I told her firmly and earnestly, because that was the truth.

I took a small step closer to her, shutting the front door behind me, and she moved closer to me so that if I moved even a fraction of an inch, we would be touching.

"But I thought you said you couldn't do this," she said, and I knew she didn't want to be involved in the dishonest, immoral thing. But I also noticed she had moved toward me, not away from me.

And so I did the dishonest, immoral thing. I kissed her, again, and didn't stop there.

I woke up beside her at the crack of dawn, fully aware that I had done something utterly rash and irresponsible. But, like that night at the bar, I didn't really feel bad. That was the worst part of it all: I had to remind myself to feel bad.

When Sarah woke up, she knew with just one look at my face.

"You have a wife, don't you," she whispered.

I nodded, not wanting to mess it all up, but then, of course, I already had.

"We can't do this again, then," she said, so softly that I could barely hear her.

I knew at that moment how genuinely good Sarah Jenkins was. I knew that I had dragged her into something that a woman like her shouldn't be a part of. Maybe I was a terrible person, but she wasn't. And she didn't have to become one.

I kissed her one more time and then I left, hoping that the look in my eyes explained everything to her, but knowing it couldn't say it all. How sorry I was. How I had to be a good man. How aggravated I was that I had to try so hard to be that man. How wonderfully beautiful, inside and out Sarah was, and how truly tragic it was that we could not be together.

At first, the guilt gnawed at me incessantly, consuming me completely. I was reminded of what I had done as I played with Jenavieve, kissed Evelyn, came home every night from work.

I lived with the knowledge that I had, once again, screwed up. But I tried to not let it screw things up for others. If it meant my wife and daughter lived on happily, content, I would bear the burden of my infidelity indefinitely.

Gradually, I found it got easier to live with. I had to accept the fact that the past was behind me, and that the only thing I could do was focus on the future.

Although I don't believe that the past is always behind us. If it were, then how come I continued to see Sarah in strangers' blonde hair, or the sound of a joyful laugh? How come my guilt never really left?

But it did get better, and my life became comfortable. I looked forward to working and coming home, where I ate my refrigerator dinners while Evelyn lazily twirled a glass of wine, telling me about Jenavieve and work and listening as I told her about my day.

And so when I saw the incoming call from Sarah, about eight months after our night together, I was shaken from the reverie. I had forgotten that I'd never erased her number—another sign of my unceasingly idiotic negligence—so I was taken aback.

I almost didn't even answer, but I was alone in the car, having just parked in the driveway at home. I knew deep down that I couldn't avoid her.

"Hello?" I tried to say in the most neutral, even tone I could conjure, not quite ready to hear the sound of her voice.

"James? Hi, it's Sarah," she said, and I noticed that her voice was a little frantic.

I didn't say anything, not trusting myself to try and conduct a conversation with her. After all, I hadn't been the one who'd called.

"I'm sorry to bother you," she continued, and there was so much apology in her voice that I cringed, "but I need to see you. Right now. It's urgent, James."

I felt my heart sink. Something in the tone of her voice made me ready to drop everything.

"Are you okay?" I asked, focusing on the sound of my breathing, counting in my head to keep the breaths even.

"I will be, I think. Just please come over now."

I nodded even though she couldn't see that. I put the car in reverse, texted Evelyn that I had to deal with an unexpected work emergency, and drove to Sarah's apartment, knowing the way there perfectly by memory.

I wasn't sure what to expect when I knocked on her door. I believe a part of me didn't want to think about it, didn't want to think about all of the reasons she could possibly be needing me now.

So when she opened the door and I saw her, I was completely speechless.

"Oh my God," I muttered, telling myself to calm down, calm down.

Sarah Jenkins was pregnant. Very pregnant.

51
EVELYN

I have never before seen this sort of look in Elizabeth's eyes. In fact, I've never seen this look in anyone's eyes.

For a moment, I am afraid about what Elizabeth might do. There is so much aggravation and anger in her face. She surely doesn't know what to do with it all. I feel a twinge of fear that she might take it out on me.

But of course, she doesn't. She is even-keeled, forever calm and composed. Much like her father.

"Tell me everything, right now," she says. But it's not anger I hear in her voice, because anger is never what she wants to convey to anyone. It's just hollowness.

So I do what she asks. I tell her everything, exactly as it happened.

***

"On the night I found out," I start, "I was so excited. Excited because I had just found out I was pregnant with Madeline, and I could barely wait to tell James.

"I sat on the couch, poised there eagerly as I heard him pull into the driveway. I noticed that it took him a couple minutes to come inside, but I didn't think much of it. I was just so excited that we were having another baby.

"He walked inside, and I looked at him and knew that my pregnancy news had to be held off. There was clearly something wrong with him, and it worried me enough to put aside the news and focus on whatever was bothering him.

"Before I could even say anything, he took a deep breath and said 'Ev, I need to talk to you.'"

I stop the story for a moment and take a breath. The memory of those next moments are acutely embedded in my mind. It's not just the memory of what he said next, but also of how inadequate I felt. What had I done to make him do this? Why was I not enough?

Questions I still ask myself.

"He sat down on the couch next to me, looked into my eyes, and told me that he had had an affair with a woman he met one night, about a year before, at a bar. He said her name was Sarah Jenkins, and that it had been one time. One time, eight months earlier.

"I thought he was finished, and I didn't know what to say. I was infuriated, sad, overwhelmed. And then he told me that he had just been at Sarah's house, where he had just found out she was eight months pregnant."

Elizabeth nods slowly, looking at the floor, not saying anything as she waits for me to continue.

"That was when he stopped talking. As if the rest of it explained itself. As if that was it, for us, for life as we knew it. And Elizabeth, as much as I feared what his cheating meant for us as a couple, I feared him leaving me even more.

"'I'm pregnant,' I told him, and I must've said it emotionlessly, because I don't think I could've spoken otherwise.

"His eyes got really wide and he looked at my stomach. Of course he didn't see anything. I was only six weeks along. But he still knew what this meant. It meant he was bound to me, more so now than ever.

"He told me we would figure it out, and that he was so sorry. But he never once mentioned staying out of your life, which is how I knew he needed to know you. I knew I could not keep him in my life without you in it. He cared about you very much, Elizabeth.

"I cared, too, mostly because I knew none of it was your fault. I made myself consider your tiny, innocent little self, almost ready to make your grand entrance into this world, and I didn't want you to suffer for it.

"But I also needed my life to be what I wanted it to be. I had done nothing wrong. I had been a good, faithful wife, and we both knew it. Clearly though, that wasn't enough. He would hurt me, it seemed, but he would never hurt his children.

"And so I looked him in the eye and told him very calmly, 'No one can ever know about this. Your affair.' He was confused, clearly. Of course people would know, his look told me, because there would be this new baby girl in the world soon who was unmistakably not mine.

"'As I see it,' I continued, 'you have two choices. You can never see Sarah again, and she and the baby can move far away. Or you can never see Sarah again, and she can move far away. The baby could live here. But not as our child. Not as your child.'

"He was angry at this, I could tell. He thought it was unfair, but I didn't care at the time about what was fair to him. Still, he told me that he was sorry, but he had to be in his daughter's life as her dad. He just had to.

"It was cold, what I said next, but it was also necessary. 'Okay,' I told him calmly, 'then you will never see Jenavieve again. I mean it. Oh, and you'll never see this baby, either,' I added, pointing at my stomach.

"His face paled, and I knew he was stuck. 'Trust me,' I told him,

'I will make absolutely sure you don't get visitation rights. I don't give a damn that you're a lawyer and have your connections, because I have mine too, and I will use them.'

"I had him cornered. He knew how serious I was. But I had made the choice simple for him. He could either move away with Sarah and you, never to see Jenavieve and Madeline again, or he could stay, where he could see all his children, all the time.

"He looked at me like I was the coldest person ever, and maybe I was. But I knew what option he would choose. He cared about his children. And yes, he cared about me. Not as much as he should have, but he did care.

"So he chose you, and Jenavieve, and Madeline, and me. I know that he loved your mother, in a different way than he could or would ever love me. I know how much it must have hurt him to go and tell her that she had to leave as soon as you were born.

"I'm sure she didn't want to leave you—of course she wouldn't want that. I don't know what her ideal plan was, but I know it took her eight months to gather up the courage to tell James about you. She didn't want to hurt anyone, I think. Much like you.

"She knew, though, from what I had James tell her a few days later, that she had to leave. Some digging showed me that her adorable little beachside condo and Ivy League education was overwhelming her in debt. The offer I gave her wouldn't just cover that debt, but would allow her to live without fear of debt ever again. I was willing to do just about anything for her to leave and for my life to be in my control again, and money is the classic motivator.

"It worked on her, clearly, because she left. I know she left the state, but I don't know where exactly she went. I never met her, but I wouldn't be surprised if you look a lot like her. I see a bit of James in you, but there's definitely something else. Someone else."

Elizabeth is frozen in place, staring at some distant point on the wall behind me. I pause, waiting for her to say something, ask me a question, but she just stays still. So I continue.

"It was difficult for me, I admit, to take care of you. I couldn't really get over the fact that you weren't mine, but I also could never get over the fact that you were completely innocent. As you grew older, and then there were three of you, I saw just how well you fit into the family. Just how wonderful of a girl you were.

"I like to think that James and I rekindled something. It took time, and I know I hurt him, but he also hurt me. We hurt each other, but at least there was some part of both of us that wanted to save our relationship.

"Ashley was a bit of a surprise, and we were a little overwhelmed at the prospect of raising four children. Quite honestly, two had always been the plan for me. For James, also, I think.

"Which is why I'm so glad that you turned out the way you did," I tell her, looking into her eyes and hoping she can see how truly, wholly grateful I am that she is okay.

"I know I did wrong by you," I continue, "and I don't expect you to ever forgive me for that.

"But I look at you and the way you act toward your sisters, toward all of us, and I am filled with relief that, despite all the turmoil surrounding you, you emerged so beautiful.

"I wish I could say the same for Ashley. I wish I had been prepared for the both of you. For you, it turned out better than I had hoped. For Ashley, well. It turned out worse than I had imagined."

I think I am finished, and I think Elizabeth knows it, but she doesn't say anything. My eyes move between her and my desk, wanting to give her whatever sort of space she needs to process it all.

I have almost forgotten, in the midst of mentally going back in time, what conditions are surrounding my present. Until I hear Ashley's feet pounding down the stairs.

"Mom?" she shrieks.

Elizabeth and I look at each other and, without saying a word, we get up and leave my office. We walk together toward the living room, me in the lead. I have to deal with this. Me alone.

"What the hell is wrong with you," Ashley says, much more quietly than I had expected. Right now, she simply looks confused. She must have just read the blast, then. Must still be processing, like Elizabeth.

"Ashley," I try to say calmly, because I can't show her any emotions that may trigger her further. "What happened was illegal, and ..."

"I don't give a fuck if it was illegal!" she yells, and now she is losing it. "I love him!" She's still yelling, and now she's crying, too. "And I know I'm the family outcast, and always have been, but *this*? This is the most selfish, fucked-up thing you could ever do."

She shakes her head at me, and I'm at a loss for words. My face is burning, and suddenly I feel so terrible for all of it. For the pain I inflicted on her and on Elizabeth. And for what? For what.

"I'm done. I'm fucking done," she says, spinning around and marching toward the front door.

"And you?" she turns to face Madeline, who's standing a little shocked on the landing. "I hope you go straight to hell," her eyes burn daggers into Madeline's, but her voice shakes with those last words. I can tell how broken she is.

I don't know where she's going, but I know that a walk is probably the best thing for her right now.

And then I hear the car engine start up.

"What the ..." I run to the door and throw it open in time to see Ashley peel out of the driveway in my SUV, taking a sharp left.

"Oh my God," I wail, and now I'm hysterical. After everything that's happened in the last ten minutes alone, this sends me over the edge.

"She can't drive," I cry, and Elizabeth and Madeline look at me with terror in their eyes. "She doesn't even have her license, damn it."

I put my head in my hands for just one second and then look up at the girls.

"I'm going," I tell them. "I need to go after her, find out where she's going, I don't know. I just need to go."

"Mom," Madeline interjects frantically, "I don't think that's the best idea. You're really shaken, and the last thing we need is two emotionally charged people on the roads."

"I'll go," a small voice says behind me.

I turn around to look at Elizabeth, and I am amazed, for the millionth time, at her grace. She has no obligation, no fathomable reason, to help me right now.

The look in her eyes, nevertheless, tells me that this is what she wants. To help, always, even when we're undeserving.

"Thank you. Thank you so much," I tell her through watery eyes, and I register her soft, stoic nod in return.

She grabs the keys to the sedan and runs to the car. I can feel Madeline beside me as we watch Elizabeth reverse and screech out of our driveway toward whatever is coming next.

52

ASHLEY

It was bad when my mother left me in Dior when I was five. It was bad when she forgot about my fifth-grade project, which I had spent the entire year planning, failing to show up because she had a work meeting.

There were the bad moments throughout my life, bad moments that reminded me constantly about how unprepared and unwilling my mother was to accommodate my existence.

But this. This is by far the worst. It's a new, fucked-up level of thoughtless and cruel, selfish negligence.

My hands clench the steering wheel of my mother's SUV. I like the feel of it, the feel of being completely in control of one of her prized material possessions.

I am seething, burning with rage, my heart beating on overtime. I have to get to Dash, and fast, because he will surely flip his shit.

If he hasn't already.

It's a good thing that Elizabeth taught me how to drive because I don't know what I would have said or done to my mother had I not had this to fall back on. I just had to get the hell out, and now I am out.

Do I have my license? Still no. I do have a permit, but it's not on me. I have no credentials for driving this car. But fuck it. I give my own damn credentials.

I cruise down side streets and main roads, making my way to where I think Dash is staying. I don't really know for sure—he's a little bit nomadic that way, preferring to move around as much as possible.

For a second, I humor myself with the thought of driving to the Four Seasons. Flip off the security cameras, cause another scene for my mother to document on Detail for the entire fucking world to see.

But I laugh, a little manically probably, and keep going. I have more important things to accomplish, more important places to go, and more important people to see. I think I'm done with my family, after all. I can't stand to look at my mom or Madeline. And the others could never really stand me anyway, so why bother anymore?

As my time on the road passes, I'm starting to get a little calmer, a little more composed. It's just me and the open road, blue skies, Malibu sun. My family may have stabbed me in the back enough times that I can barely walk anymore, but at least I live in a pretty place. At least I have pretty things. Because that's what matters, of course.

I almost don't notice it. I'm calmly and steadily focused on the road in front of me, enough so that I haven't paid attention in several minutes to what's behind me.

Sure enough, when I do look in my rearview mirror, I see that I'm not alone. There's one other car that's right behind me. A familiar, glistening white vehicle that I recognize.

The sedan. And the only one who would have the nerve to drive it right now is my mother.

I can hardly believe her audacity. To follow me like this, the one time she's ever given any sort of care to my whereabouts.

"What about all the times you had no idea where the hell I was at all of your parties?" I yell, even though I know she can't hear me. "Then again, you probably weren't even thinking about me at all!"

I shake my head, and the rage has returned. Now I'm crying, the road becoming blurry through my tears.

I try to catch sight of her, see if my mom is pissed or crying or what, but the sun is too bright and I can't see her. All I know is that it's her, in the sedan, tailing my ass.

What does she even think she's going to do? Corner me at my destination and tell me to not drive? What the hell is she trying to accomplish here? I'm the one in control.

I'm the one in control.

My grip on the wheel tightens, and I flex my fingers, watching them curl and uncurl on the steering wheel. My breathing is shallow and rapid, and there's no one around. There's no one around other than the sedan.

I'm so mad, so unbelievably angry. She can't get away with it. She simply can't. My mother has had the control for fifteen years. She has neglected me and played with my life only when she felt the personal need to. She has cared about me only when it directly benefited her. And that's the problem with it all.

If I'm ever a mother, my child will never be my personal chess piece. They will never be Mommy's little toy.

And I won't be anymore, either. I'm done. So done.

And I'm the one in control.

I slam on the brakes suddenly. The fast and automatic motion of my foot surprises me a little.

I don't know what the point was, what I'm trying to do—it all happens so fast in a manic, impulsive flame of anger.

What I do know is that I slam on the brakes so powerfully that the sedan crashes hard into the back of the SUV, sending me flying into the airbag.

***

When I come to, my thoughts are a little fuzzy, but I know I am okay. Okay enough to register something, something that makes my stomach sink and churn. Suddenly I don't want to get out of the car and see the damage I have done.

Because, in the middle of all the turmoil of my thoughts and headache and airbag and pain, I remember that I never did something. Something important.

I forgot to service the sedan.

53
ELIZABETH

〜∞〜

I try to distract myself as I follow Ashley, and distracting myself turns out to be an easy thing to do. There's a lot to think about right now, after all.

James is my father. And Sarah Jenkins, whoever she is, is my mother.

I find myself wondering about her, wondering what sort of person she was. Maybe I can talk to James about her sometime. Maybe I could even talk to Sarah myself someday.

Evelyn did a vile thing to preserve the perfect Blair family name. But I can't say I'm too surprised. I've grown up under her roof for eighteen years, years in which I've watched her be perfectly prim and proper in the face of the outside world.

She was afraid, I remind myself, *and hurt, and angry, and she didn't know what to do with it all.*

And it didn't turn out so badly for me. I know this, deep down inside, and of course so does Evelyn. She had to feel justified in what she did, so she gave me a great life. A room overlooking the beach, private school and now Pepperdine. Maybe she has treated me better than my own mother would've. After all, Evelyn isn't the one who traded me for money.

I'm right behind the SUV, trying to keep a safe distance, but Ashley keeps speeding up. I furrow my brow as I watch her shoot ahead spastically, then lag back a little, only to slam on the gas once more.

She's in a rage. A rage that should not be channeled on the roads.

I sigh, speeding up a little myself to get closer behind her. It may not be the best choice, I know, but if I can just get her attention …

She must be so concentrated on the road ahead that she doesn't notice me, or she simply doesn't care. Well. I'll just see this through to wherever she's going and try to reason with her there.

I'll tell her that I understand why she's mad. She has every right to be. Her mother—and Madeline, and I guess all of us—took something from her that they had no right to.

I'll tell her I understand how that feels, more than she knows. I'll say it's okay to be angry and upset and hurt, and everything else, because those feelings are completely normal.

But at the end of the day, what good do those feelings do? What good does it do to wallow in all the most unpleasant emotions? It surely doesn't make life good again. And isn't that what we all want? For life to be good?

So, I will tell her it's better to choose forgiveness. It doesn't have to be for Evelyn if she's not ready. It can just be for herself, so that she can move forward with the goodness of things.

But I hope she forgives the family. I hope she chooses to forgive them for who they are, because there is so much goodness in them.

There's so much goodness in all of us.

I will try to explain these things to my sister—my sister!—because she needs to hear them. I believe I can explain them to her in a way that might actually make her listen.

I'm still thinking about all of this when I register the sharp, sudden stop of the SUV.

In the seconds before the collision, I am able to register just a few things:

First, that in my rush to get to Ashley, I forgot to fasten my seatbelt.

Then, a memory of Madeline's laugh, Jenavieve's kind eyes.

Ashley driving along the shore to "Beyond," blonde hair billowing. Peaceful.

James and Evelyn smiling, watching the girls and me swimming in the sunset.

And then, poof!

Like magic.

Gone.

The Scene

A sedan and an SUV. The SUV has been hit in the back, and it shows. But it's the sedan that is truly wrecked.

The front of the car is crumpled and the windshield is shattered. Little rainbows glisten on the shards of all that glass.

A girl lies limp across the front of the vehicle.

She is facedown, her blonde hair visible. Blood.

The girl has crashed through the windshield. There were no working airbags by the looks of it. Probably no seatbelt, either.

Died on impact.

Blue and red flashing lights, sirens. Police officers. Ambulances. Yellow tape.

A hysterical girl. Bright, scraggly blonde hair, mascara marking dark trails down her face.

The girl is sobbing, shaking, unable to take her eyes off the dead girl.

The police are trying to calm her down, but she's inconsolable.

Honey, why don't you go over to the ambulance and get yourself checked out. You hit that airbag pretty hard, a female police officer with warm, brown eyes tells her.

No, she sobs, shakes her head. I can't. Damn it, damn it, damn it.

It wasn't supposed to be her, she cries, and now she has all of the officers' attention.

What do you mean, it wasn't supposed to be her? The warm, brown eyes have now gone cool.

It was supposed to be my mom in the car, the girl wails. Not Elizabeth, damn it!

She cries and continues muttering this to herself, in shock, and now the police officer with the eyes is pulling out handcuffs.

Because it wasn't supposed to be her. It wasn't supposed to be her.

54
JAMES

I am driving home from court. Annie Anderson was granted full custody of Liam. I won the case.

But it doesn't matter, none of it matters, because Evelyn just called me.

Elizabeth knows.

I smile to myself a little bit, glowing in spite of it all. After eighteen years, I can finally be her dad.

I guess I always was, but Evelyn certainly didn't make any of us feel that way.

I think about how I will tell Elizabeth about Sarah. I will tell her about Sarah's blonde hair and blue eyes that so closely resemble her own. I'll tell her about how happy she was, how selfless and generous her heart was.

I'll tell her about how great Sarah was at listening to me, how she was attentive and warm and lovely in every possible way.

My daughter inherited all her good traits from her mother. And she deserves to know it.

I doubt I'll ever speak to Sarah again—I basically forced her to give up her child, after all. I hurt, beyond repair, a person I loved, but it was never destined to end well. I was never destined to end well, and some part of Sarah must have seen that from the start.

But maybe Elizabeth can know her. I'm not sure, but I think Sarah went to London. I imagine Elizabeth meeting her for the first time, and the thought makes me feel a warmth inside that I always used to associate solely with Sarah.

She would invite Elizabeth in, and the two would talk and laugh about the eighteen years of each others' lives that they missed. Maybe Elizabeth even has more siblings, younger ones who she can grow to love as much as she loves all of my other daughters.

I know Elizabeth is probably angry at me, and rightfully so. It may take some time for her to want to speak to me.

But when she does want to talk, I will be waiting with open arms. I have been waiting for this for eighteen years, waiting to be the father I'm supposed to be, waiting to speak to someone about all of Sarah's goodness.

It'll be okay, I tell myself as I drive on, getting closer to home. *There's time to make things right again.*

And so it is that when I get the next call from Evelyn and hear my wife in hysterics on the other end, it all goes dreadfully, shockingly, horrifyingly to waste.

Of course there's no time left. Things will never be right again.

Then again, things were never right to begin with.

55

EVELYN

The vibrancy of the pain is sudden and blinding and consuming in a way I didn't know was possible. I see now how people can sink into the sort of despair that becomes illness, because I am now falling into this myself.

Each time I wake up from sleep or from purely subconscious darkness, the force of it hits me again. I replay the phone call from the police, the clear image of what must have transpired embedded into my mind.

The sedan, almost completely useless in providing protection because its defective airbags were never replaced.

Elizabeth, propelled through the glass windshield and so suddenly gone.

And Ashley shaking uncontrollably. In shock.

Because it was supposed to be me.

Maybe they wouldn't have told me this if it didn't involve my daughter being in police custody. But they had to explain why Ashley was handcuffed and sitting in jail.

She meant to hurt me. She admitted it openly to the officers at the scene. It was supposed to be me in the car.

It wasn't supposed to be Elizabeth. The feeling of it, of knowing I let her go, is entirely separate from the pain. It's guilt, which is gut-wrenching and torturous and always present.

I never did right by her. I never treated Elizabeth the way she should have been treated. And now, right after she'd learned the truth about the circumstances of her birth, it's too late for me to make it up to her. Of course, the likelihood that I would have changed, that things would have changed for Elizabeth and me, is slim. I am a treacherous human being, after all. Treacherous enough to compel my fifteen-year-old to kill somebody.

So the pain and guilt don't leave. They seep through every crevice of my thoughts incessantly. This is who I am now—a woman who lies in bed, overcome with all of the worst there is to know.

Because it was supposed to be me.

I am supposed to be dead.

56

Her death has been explained.

It is out there, spoken and outside of my own head now. Even though my therapist obviously knew what had happened from my file—knew, that is, that I voluntarily checked myself into this mental institution because I could no longer stand my life—she didn't know about all the events surrounding it.

All people give a damn about is the thing itself, after all. Not the circumstances of the thing.

I suppose my therapist cares, though, to some extent at least. It is her occupation.

She watches me now, carefully, but also with satisfaction. At least I think that's what it is.

Sure enough: "So you didn't do it."

"What?" I mutter, a bit dazed.

"You didn't kill Elizabeth," my therapist says, as if it's the most obvious thing.

"I may as well have," I grunt, and force myself to stop picking at my cuticle and look her in the eyes.

"Evelyn," she says slowly, watching me attentively. "You were not driving the car. You were nowhere near the scene. You're experiencing survivor's *guilt, and you have to release yourself from it. This was not your fault."*

Survivor's guilt. Fucking survivor's guilt. Don't laugh, Evelyn. Don't do it, or else she'll think you're manic or something, and you won't be released.

"Sure, it could be survivor's guilt," I concede for the therapist's benefit. "But the guilt is justified. It isn't justified for, like, plane crash survivors, or something. Because in that case, they're completely unrelated to the incident.

"They got on a plane one day with a pilot and people surrounding them who they hadn't had any previous contact with, and the plane crashed. And no. It wasn't their fault.

"But this was my family. Elizabeth may not have biologically been my daughter, but I raised her. I was responsible for her, and I was supposed to do a much better job of it. I was supposed to care about the right things. Instead, she died protecting all of us, I guess. Maybe the others deserved protecting—I don't know. All I know is that I certainly didn't deserve protecting."

The therapist nods, considering what I said. "She sounds kind," she says softly, eyes warm. "She sounds like a truly lovely person, and I'm so sorry she's gone."

No tears. Just numbness.

"You made mistakes," she continues, "mistakes that you regret. You're justified in that regret."

My head whips up. My therapist says I'm justified in my self-hatred? She's finally catching on.

"But, you know," she says thoughtfully, taking a big sigh. "I don't know how we live with it if we don't think of it all differently."

I'm fully intrigued now. My peppy, positive, perfect therapist speaking this way? Maybe I've rubbed off on her. Another reason to want to escape my own self.

"Maybe it's not about the acts of right and wrong," she continues, "but about the interaction of all of these acts.

"Equal opposite. I've always liked that. Yin and yang. Thermodynamics. For every bad thing, there's a good thing. For every entity, there's something equivalent in quantity and opposite in quality.

"You deprived Elizabeth of her mother, but you provided her with a beautiful home. You weren't attentive enough to Ashley, but you worked hard enough to be able to provide high-quality education for all your girls. Elizabeth followed Ashley that day in the car but Madeline didn't. You didn't.

"It in no way devalues Elizabeth's life or death," she says quickly to my appalled expression, "but it means something. It means that there's some sort of balance in this universe. A universe that I know can be cruel and unsparing, but that also has so much beauty. No matter what, beauty abounds. And I have to tell myself that it makes it all worth it. We have to tell ourselves that, Evelyn."

I feel something. I don't know what—it's been so long since I've been anything but numb. But this. This is something.

I reach out and initiate my first contact in years, resting my hand on top of hers.

"Okay," I whisper, and it's not for me. It's for her. I've done a lot of horrible, unforgivable things, but if I can be of any reassurance to her, maybe there is truth to the equal opposite.

So, again: "Okay."

57
ASHLEY

There's a lot of time to reflect in prison.

In the month after the crash, everything happened fast, with varying degrees of my conscious participation.

I was tried as an adult and pled guilty to avoid an extended trial, which I knew wasn't worth it because I am guilty. I was charged with involuntary vehicular manslaughter. I will be in prison for four years.

I still don't know what I was trying to do in the car. What I do know is that I am guilty of ending Elizabeth's life.

I have refused to see my mother. Madeline hasn't come to see me. My father has seen me briefly, but he was despondent and detached.

Jenavieve is the only one who wanted to visit. She held my hand in hers and simply sat there while I cried. Minutes? Hours? I don't know. All the while, it struck me that it was exactly the sort of thing Elizabeth would have done.

Dashton has a year in prison for statutory rape. Not an unbearably long time, but long enough to end his acting career. He'll forever be labeled a rapist, and I'll forever be labeled the insane rich kid who tried to kill her mom and got her sister instead.

Jenavieve told me about Elizabeth, about how my father had an affair and Elizabeth is—was—our half-sister. She and Madeline must've found out sometime in the wake of everything.

It made sense to me then, after Jen explained. Of course Madeline couldn't see me. I killed not only her best friend, but her sister. And of course my dad couldn't see me either, couldn't *really* see me. I killed his daughter.

The Blair family, it appears, has irreversibly fallen.

Under different circumstances, I would probably give up. I would sink into the deepest of depressions and never even try to claw my way out. I would sit in this cell and not try. I would make my life worse than death itself. At least that would get me closer to what I deserve for what I did to Elizabeth.

But I can't give up.

Because somehow, in the midst of it all, some little form of goodness prevailed. And it's growing tiny human features inside me.

I'm pregnant.

There is a strange, shocking sort of marvel to it, to the fact that something pure and wholesome came out of all this. That some part of Dashton and me lives on.

This child will be okay. More than okay—I will see to it. I may deserve whatever shit life can throw at me, but this baby does not.

I pass the days thinking about if it's a boy or a girl, dreaming up names, fantasizing about which features will be from Dash and which ones will be from me. Most importantly, I plan.

My baby will not be in foster care. It simply can't happen. My child must be in a nurturing, supportive, safe environment until I'm able to take care of it myself.

Not Dash. He won't see me again, and he won't see the baby. I wouldn't let him even if he wanted to. It would create more of a mess for him than he's already in, and I can't have that. I love him too much for that.

There's no way in hell I would let my mother near my child. Besides, I don't know what sort of state she's in. For all I know, she could be in a mental hospital.

Definitely not my father. He probably would do it, but there's no way I'm asking him after all I've put him through.

Not Madeline. She's only seventeen. Besides, I can't trust her with my child's life if I can't even trust her with one secret.

That leaves Jenavieve. And Max, Max with his kind eyes and love for my sister. They would be good parents. Good temporary parents, that is.

I don't have phone privileges or any form of communication. So that means I just have to wait, hoping for Jenavieve to show up again.

Somehow, I know she will. If she visited once, she'll visit again, and I think she's doing it for Elizabeth.

Entirely ironic, that.

Or maybe it's not so ironic at all. And maybe that's the point.

58
MADELINE
∽

The tenacity of my grief surprises me a little.

I thought there were neat, structured stages to the grieving process—stages that could be memorized and tested on, stages that I *was* tested on at some point in my academic career.

Turns out, it's not true. There is no formula for grief, or at least no formula that works for me.

Some days I wake up feeling crushed, like a weight is pressing unbearably on my chest. No emotions, on these days, just a persistent heaviness.

Other days, I wake up numb. I walk around the house trying to find something to do until I eventually collapse and cry. When that happens, I find a corner somewhere and wait out all the emotion. Then I get tired and sleep.

On still other days, I wake up and momentarily think the world is right. I feel the way I would on any other regular day. Well, any other day in which all my sisters are alive and well.

Then it hits me that it's not that way anymore. My adopted sister, who's actually my biological sister, is dead.

No matter how the day starts out, it always ends the same way, with me curled up on my bed in the dark, arms wrapped around myself for some form of comfort.

Noah would be comforting if I wanted him to be. He would come over every day to hold me and wait out all the emotions. He would be the wonderfully supportive person he is.

But he can't do that. I know that it will never be the same with him. Besides, this is something I need to do alone. I can no longer rely on him, and it's not his fault. It's no one's fault.

He texted me almost immediately after the accident and simply said: I'm so sorry. Whatever you need, whenever you need it, I'm here.

It was the kind, reliable thing to do. And so, because I love him, I replied: Thank you, Noah. I appreciate it more than you know.

I knew he wasn't sorry about what he said that day on the beach. He wasn't sorry about leaving me in the midst of my supposed money obsession. If he wasn't sorry about that, it's not fair to need him now.

So I endure the grief quietly, feeling the full weight of it and not speaking about it. I'm not speaking at all, to anyone.

My mother passes the days in bed, door closed, collapsed and completely unreachable. I can't bring myself to ask her about planning a funeral. It's ironic—planning events has always been everything for my mother.

This is the one event that she can't handle.

That leaves my dad. He passes his days working, trying to avoid the emotions or bury them—I don't know which. One night, after I hear that he's home and eating his takeout in the kitchen, I pad quietly down the stairs and sit across from him.

The house is dark, empty. So is he. There are hollows under his eyes, a vacant look on his face. I can't even imagine what I must look like. I haven't bothered looking into a mirror since she died.

"Dad," I say. I'm surprised at the croaky quality of my voice, then

I realize I haven't spoken out loud in about a month. "We need to plan a funeral."

He looks down, sighs, rubs his face in his hands. Looks up. Nods.

"Jenavieve and I can do most of the work," I tell him, because I can tell he can't manage this any more than my mom can. "It just needs to happen."

I don't need to say anything else. He gets it. It's not just that she deserves the respect of the event—which she does. But we have spent a month mourning Elizabeth, a month of horrible pain and vast disconnection from each other.

Elizabeth would want us to move forward. She would want us to heal. The only thing I can think of to help start this process is planning her funeral.

***

Jenavieve and I spend the next few weeks planning, and while Jen is genuinely helpful, it's me who does most of the work. I throw myself into it as if my life depends on it. In a way, it feels like it does.

Throughout it all, I speak to almost no one other than Jenavieve. I can't bring myself to visit Ashley. I tell myself that she doesn't want to see me. I may be right, but I also know it's a lame attempt at justification.

I know deep down that Elizabeth and Noah, the two best people who were ever in my life, would both want me to go see her. But knowing it doesn't change anything because they are not here. So I don't go see Ashley, and there's no one telling me to change my mind.

On the day of the funeral, I put effort into my appearance for the first time in over two months. I have to look nice. Everything must be as perfect as I can possibly make it.

I practically have to force my mother to go. It takes hours of begging, crying, raising my voice, whispering, telling her angrily that this is something she has to do.

Eventually, I help get her dressed and ready to leave the house. It's something my father should be doing, I know, but my parents are as disconnected from each other as ever.

You hear that death breaks some people apart and brings others together. All it seems to be doing to us is breaking us apart.

I suppose we've always been a broken family, in a sense, but this time it's different. This time I know the brokenness is irreversible because the only one who would try to fix it is already gone.

***

The service goes without a hitch. It is a warm and pleasant day, and there are about a hundred people at the cemetery to honor her. Not nearly as many people as my mother would invite to a standard social gathering, but I wanted to give Elizabeth the respect of not treating her funeral as social hour. The people here are the people who love her: family, friends from school, teachers.

I feel a little dazed through it all, but I keep my emotions intact. Put on your public face, is what my mother would say if she were still my mother.

There is some strange inhabitant in her now, a dark entity that was lurking outside her or living inside her all along. Either way, it makes her despondent, zombie-like, unable and unwilling to speak to anybody who comes near her. She's here, though, and that's enough for me.

My father says a few words to a few people, being as polite and sociable as he can make himself.

Jenavieve is perhaps the most put-together of everyone. She speaks to guests almost the entire time, accepting their condolences on behalf of all of us.

As for me, I ensure everything runs smoothly. I speak only to the people who are helping me make that happen. This includes Elizabeth's best friend from school, who's giving a eulogy. I thought about trying to speak myself, but I couldn't escape the fact that Elizabeth won't be able to hear it. For some reason, it bothered me too much.

When I feel my work here is done, I slip off, walking aimlessly about the cemetery. I don't like walking around all of the graves, but I find a place that's more open and only contains a couple of headstones. It's actually a very pretty spot, with trees framing the expanse of vibrant green lawn.

I stand there for a little while, until I decide to just leave altogether and go lie down at home. Just as I'm about to turn around, I feel a light hand on my shoulder.

I turn around and there he is. Noah.

"Hey," he says softly, and I can see how sad he is. His eyes look sad and tired instead of bright and happy, and I don't like it. Other than that, though, he is still Noah Smith. Still tall, toned and tanned. Same dark hair, although it's a little messier than he would usually wear it at public events.

I wonder what the grief has been like for him.

And his eyes. Still that unique, piercing gray. Despite it all, his eyes are still kind. They always will be.

"Hi," I say, still watching him, and I wonder what I look like to him. I wonder how different I am in his eyes.

"How are you?" he asks gently, and I have to remind myself it's over. I can't cry because then he will touch me and I will collapse in his arms. That will only make things more complicated.

"Not good," I tell him, because there's no lying to him. "But getting better, I think."

That is true, or at least I like to think it is. I had hoped that the funeral would steer me in the right direction, and maybe it is.

"How are you?" I reciprocate, and he looks down at the ground.

"I'm okay," he nods, as if assuring himself the truth of that statement. "I miss her. Obviously."

His gaze flits to me, and I think she's not the only one he misses. She's not the only one I miss, either. But the pain of it all has to be handled with care, treated carefully and without risk of collateral damage.

"You must be getting excited to go to Stanford soon." I break the silence and realize that I'm smiling a little. It's the first time I've worn any form of joy, on the outside or inside, since Elizabeth's death.

"I am, yeah." He grins a little, and for a moment I catch a flash of brightness in his eyes, an excited sort of hope. It makes me feel content, knowing that he has the vision of Stanford to add automatic goodness to his days.

"It'll be weird to leave Malibu, but it's nice to know that I can come back, you know?" He tries to say it nonchalantly, but I can sense the point he's embedding in, because I know him. He's trying to say that he can come back to me. And I can't let him do that, because it's too late.

"Yeah," I look up at him, forcing myself to smile. "You shouldn't worry about things here, though. You should worry about college things."

It's all I can say on that, because the look in his eyes makes me feel like I can't say more without my voice breaking.

He looks hurt. Not the sort of hurt I felt when he turned his back on me at the beach, but the sort of hurt that comes with realizing you've hit the end of something.

"It's okay, Noah," I say, surprising myself when I reach out and take his hand. "It'll be okay."

He has been my rock, my main source of comfort about everything as long as I've known him. The least I can do is try to provide some comfort for him now. Ease the pain a little bit, let him know that it's okay for him to be happy elsewhere.

There are tears in his eyes, but he blinks them away, and I know it's time to go.

"I should probably head back," I say softly, but I don't pull my hand away from his. I think it's because I know very well that this is probably the last time I will ever feel his soft fingers in mine.

He nods and looks at me like he's trying to memorize every last detail of my face. I could do the same, but I know I don't need to. I will always know his face, and I will be reminded of it every time I catch a half-smile, dimples, gray eyes.

I give his hand a last squeeze. He leans in and kisses my cheek, so gently. Then he pulls back and finally lets go.

"I'll see you, Madeline," he says, voice shaking. Madeline. He always called me Maddy.

"Okay," I whisper, and even though I don't know that it's true, I also don't see the harm in going along with the idea.

With that, Noah gives me a small nod with what I think is a ghost of a half-smile, and walks away.

I watch him retreating slowly, and the scared, desperate part of me wants to yell frantically after him. Tell him that it really is okay, that we can get through this because we're Noah and Maddy.

Elizabeth would want that. She would hate watching Noah and me leave each other for good.

Would. That's the point. Elizabeth is not here anymore. She will never know that Noah and I broke up, as she will never know anything again.

So he continues to recede, and I extend the distance, heading in the opposite direction toward my family.

Because in the end, that's what happens. We leave, and life goes on.

59
JENAVIEVE

The aftermath of Elizabeth's death would be unbearable, I am sure of it, if I didn't have Max. It's not about dependency on another person—it's about the love and support another person can give.

I found almost immediately that the best way I could get through it was by doing what she would have wanted me to do. Despite being almost five years younger than me, Elizabeth was always a sort of moral compass for me, showing me how to live and perceive the world in a way no one else will ever be able to.

So I made it my mission to live the way she would encourage me to live. I make sure my mother eats something every day, even if that means sitting with her for hours while she picks away dully at her food. I put dinner in the fridge for my father to warm up when he comes home from work. I make sure the house is clean. Madeline is very self-sufficient, but I help her plan Elizabeth's funeral and I ensure that it goes smoothly.

And I go to visit Ashley.

If I think about what she did for too long, it's almost impossible to will myself to treat her like my fifteen-year-old sister who made a horrible mistake. But if I concentrate hard enough, I can almost hear

Elizabeth telling me that that's exactly what Ashley is: our fifteen-year-old sister who made a horrible mistake.

So I go to see her once a week. I don't need to say much to her; it means enough to just be there, to provide her the company of another human. I don't push Madeline to go, not yet. Although I know deep down that one of these days, she will slip in the car and join me.

Ashley doesn't ask about home, so I don't tell her about it. I suppose it's better for her to not know that our mother passes her days staring at the wall, that Madeline barely speaks, that our father goes to work from six in the morning to ten at night.

Without Elizabeth, there is no one linking us all together. I try to do what I can to fill in the gaps, but I know I will never have the gift Elizabeth had, the gift of pure empathy and understanding. She understood all of us. She understood me when nobody else could.

I try to embody the way Elizabeth lived to the best of my abilities. It's now more clear to me than ever that psychology is what I need to do. It's what I can do to help make things right in the best way I know how. So I shadow Jacob's doctor, go to my classes, study for exams and ace them. It's set in my mind to be the best psychologist I can be for Malibu. God knows people here need help.

Max works as well, and in this way our life together continues as it always has. We work, and when we're not working, we're together.

Sometimes we walk the beach, and other times we rewatch our favorite movies. Sometimes we visit Jacob, and other times we visit my family. Sometimes we talk about Elizabeth, and other times we don't.

Two months turns into three, which turns into four, and then five, and life goes on. It's not the way it once was, and there is a sad evolution to the way things are. But, as usual, Earth doesn't stop spinning for anyone. I live my life with Max, and there is a steady sort of routine.

That is, until I visit Ashley on an evening in mid-November, an evening when the air is a little crisp and summer has finally passed.

I immediately know it's not going to be our usual visit. There is an anxious look in her eyes, as if she's been building up the courage to speak to me about something.

"What's going on, Ashley?" I ask her, watching her in what I hope is a steady way. She's always gotten easily aggravated at even the most mundane things, so I know it's best to keep my face as neutral as possible if I want to get anything out of her.

"Please don't freak out," she says anxiously, clasping her hands together.

I've never seen her this anxious, but there is something resembling determination in her eyes, too.

"Okay," I nod encouragingly. "Tell me what's going on."

"Okay," she sighs, looking up at the ceiling before looking back at me. "I'm pregnant. About five months along."

Pregnant. My little sister, my sister who should be beginning her junior year of high school, is pregnant. *Do not look judgmental*, I tell myself fiercely, because then she will surely lose it.

"Okay," I say slowly, carefully. "It's okay, Ashley. It'll be alright."

"Not if she's in foster care," Ashley blurts fiercely. "Yeah, it's a girl. I just found out," she adds with a wan smile. "And she cannot be in foster care," she continues firmly.

"Does Dashton know?" I mutter.

"No, and he won't know." Ashley shakes her head. "I mean, he might figure it out at some point, but he's not getting involved in this. He already got too involved with me, and his career is destroyed because of it. A baby in the mix won't help him."

"So what are you going to do?"

"Well, I'll be out by the time she's, like, three," Ashley says, and there's a hint of hope in her voice. "But obviously, I can't take care of her here ..." she trails off, watching my face.

I stare back at her, waiting blankly for her to finish her train of thought.

"Can you please take care of her?" Ashley asks, almost whispering. "You and Max? Just until I'm out," she adds hurriedly. "I know it's a lot to ask, but there's no one else I know who can take care of her."

This is one of those times I have to bring Elizabeth to mind and ask myself what she would do.

I look at my sister, really look at her. Scraggly hair, wide eyes, nails worn to stubs. Orange jumpsuit. And yes, a round stomach, something I hadn't noticed under the baggy clothes until now.

And then I picture my niece. My tiny niece, born in prison, helpless. She is innocent, so innocent. Just like Elizabeth was when her mother gave her up, and just like she was when she died.

I know I have my answer, then. Elizabeth's innocence couldn't be protected, but I have the opportunity to ensure my niece's is.

"I have to talk to Max," I say slowly, "but I *will* talk to him."

Ashley's eyes fill with tears, and I watch as her hand drifts to her stomach.

"Thank you," she whispers, tears streaming down her face. "Thank you, Jen. Thank you."

I nod.

As I drive home to talk to Max, I feel something I haven't felt since telling him about my eating disorder: Hope. Not the standard form of hope, the type that instills in you the feeling that life can be brighter again. Instead, I feel the sort of hope that allows you to believe that something can be *right* again.

***

Stunned. This is the only word I can think of to describe Max's initial reaction.

256

We sit together on our couch, and he simply stares at me.

"Jen," he stammers, "you really want to raise a *baby* right now?"

"I mean, we were going to eventually, right?" I note earnestly. "I know it's not ideal, but it's not this baby's fault. And she is family."

Max nods, considering. "I understand, I do," he says quietly, "but we're not even married, Jen."

"What if we were?" I blurt, almost involuntarily.

Max's head whips up, and his eyes are on mine, and there is a new sort of stunned on his face now. "What?" he asks, but it's not rejection I see in his eyes.

"I love you," I tell him, eyes tearing, "with or without this baby. I want to be with you for the rest of my life. We don't have to make it a big wedding—I don't need that. I just need you. We can even have Harper take the test online or whatever so that she can marry us, and that can be it. Just the three of us."

"You're sure this isn't about being, like, a proper family for the baby?" Max asks me carefully, but there is hope in his eyes.

"I'm sure, Max," I tell him, and I have never been more sincere about anything in my life.

He nods, and a smile stretches across his face. Then he is on his knee. "I may not have a ring quite yet," he says, and I laugh through my tears. "But no diamond can express how much I love you, anyways. You are everything. I love everything about you, and I always will. Jenavieve Blair," he says with so much love in his voice, "will you marry me? Make me the luckiest man alive?"

"Yes," I cry, pulling him to me. "Yes."

And as I kiss him—my fiancé!—it occurs to me that, almost instantaneously, the two forms of hope have converged, unifying into the wonderful notion that there is indeed some sort of balance to it all.

***

We are married on December 6, at a small church in Cambridge, near where we first met. Harper has been ordained for us, and it is simply the three of us.

Given other circumstances, I would want my family there, but it's not the sort of thing they can handle right now. And as selfish as it may be, I must soak in all the good of this moment, which can only be done with Max.

I wear the white dress and sparkly ring. I go through the entire traditional process, and while every last bit of it is lovely and memorable, what provides all the meaning is Max. Max Grayson, my husband, in all of the wonder that makes up him—in all of the wonder that makes up us.

***

One evening in late February, when Max and I are visiting Ashley, she asks us something.

"I know you'll be taking care of her, and I don't want to impose on any of that," Ashley says sincerely. It strikes me how much more mature all this has made her.

"But," she continues with trepidation, "would you mind naming her Grace?"

Grace. I suspect Ashley has chosen it for more than the sound of the word. I glance at Max, and he nods solemnly.

"Sure, Ashley." I give her a small smile. "Grace it is."

***

Grace arrives on March 9, a small, sweet baby with blue eyes, rosy cheeks and hints of golden hair.

We take her home to the nursery we meticulously designed. And just like that, she becomes our world.

Our days are consumed with her, consumed with watching her grow a little more each day.

I try to remind myself that Grace is Ashley's baby, but I can't escape the fact that Ashley is not raising her. Max and I are.

At first, I bring Grace to visit Ashley regularly, and I can see how much joy and hope it brings to Ashley's days. I try to grasp the importance of that, and I try to not get too attached to Grace. But it inevitably becomes impossible.

Max and I quickly grow to love her like she is our own, and in a way, she is. We've held her, talked to her, sang to her, loved her since the day of her birth. And so it is that, eventually, she is no longer our niece. In our eyes she is our daughter.

And I cannot let my daughter go.

60
JAMES

Each day that passes is a reminder of the time, all the goddamn time, I will miss with Elizabeth.

Just as I was about to finally be her father, it was all ripped away from me. And there is no healing from that.

Occupying my mind with something else helps to dull the pain, so I throw myself into work. It's a good thing, too, for Evelyn won't touch Detail. Ironic, considering the role Detail played in all of this.

Luckily, there are lots of employees working to keep the precious company up and running, and it is thriving more than ever with our family as the headline.

Evelyn is so severely depressed that she is unreachable. She doesn't even speak. Madeline barely spoke either for months. But she finally displayed some evidence of normalcy when school started up again.

Jenavieve holds things together, stepping up for Evelyn and me. Not only does she visit consistently to maintain our home, but she also maintains her own marriage and raises Ashley's baby.

That's right. I am a grandfather. There is a part of me that whispers that here is my chance to build a relationship before it is too late.

But a much bigger part of me says I don't deserve it. I lost Elizabeth. No—I let her go. I don't deserve to have a relationship with my granddaughter when I couldn't even be there for my daughter.

So I don't see Grace. Jenavieve tries to show me pictures and videos of her occasionally, but I force myself to be detached from all of them so that I feel nothing.

As the months pass, I find myself questioning the point of my existence more and more. It became increasingly difficult to find a reason to get up in the morning, to wake up next to my wife who may as well be dead.

She started drinking soon after Elizabeth's death. I wouldn't have known if it weren't for the fact that I drink myself. I've become a little more dependent on the bottle than I likely should be. It's when the stash ran out and I smelled the alcohol on her that I knew Evelyn's mental state was at an all-time low.

It's horrible, but at least my wife's deterioration gives me something helpful to do, something of worth. I thought about looking into rehab, but I decided that what Evelyn needed was different from that. She doesn't speak, mutters incoherent sentences when she isn't even drunk. Sometimes she disappears for hours at a time and returns in clothes that she bought in a thrift store. Since when in the hell has Evelyn Blair visited a thrift store? So I search for the best inpatient mental hospitals until I find one I like in San Francisco. In fact, I like it enough to consider having my wife admitted against her will.

But turns out, I don't have to check her in against her will. I tell her about the hospital I found, and there is something close to light in her eyes. The next day, she is gone. One phone call later, and I confirm that my wife admitted herself to the San Francisco mental hospital.

***

With my wife in the hands of psychiatric professionals, Madeline in school, Ashley in prison, and Jenavieve raising Grace, there is once again nothing more for me to do other than work.

One day, I force myself to call Sarah and speak to her for the first time in eighteen years.

I don't know if she reads Detail, but even if she does, she wouldn't know. I ensured Elizabeth's death wasn't published anywhere, especially Detail.

I stare at the contact on my phone for several minutes, and I don't even know if it's her number anymore, so I almost don't do it.

But she deserves to know. The least I can do is start giving people what they deserve.

With shaking hands, I press the call button and put the phone to my ear.

It takes four rings for her to pick up.

"Hello?" she says, and I can tell by the tone of her voice that she doesn't know it's me. She has erased my contact, has erased me, has likely tried to erase Elizabeth, too. Then again, it is impossible to erase your own child. I would know.

Deep breath. "Sarah, it's James Blair," I say slowly, and I can feel her breath catch on the other end.

"James, what ... Thomas, I'm on the phone!" I hear her snap suddenly, to the faint sounds of a boy's yelling.

"Sorry, that was my son," she says. Her son.

"Sarah, I think you should sit down. I'm sorry," I whisper, and my hands are shaking so badly that I feel like I'm going to drop the phone.

"James, what the hell is going on?" Sarah says wearily, but there is a trace of fear in her voice.

"Just sit down, please." I shake my head, press my fingers against my forehead.

"Okay, I'm sitting down," she tells me on the other end.

"I don't know how to say this, so I just need to say it," I say, forcing my voice not to shake. "In June, Elizabeth was in a horrible accident. Car accident. It wasn't her fault, but she … she died. Elizabeth died."

Silence.

"I know I should've told you sooner," I fill the void automatically, "but I couldn't bring myself to. And I'm so sorry. I will always be so sorry."

The silence continues, but she doesn't hang up, so neither do I. After what feels like an eternity, she finally speaks.

"Was it fast," she whispers, and now I can hear her crying. "I mean, was she in a lot of pain?"

"No," I say quietly. "It was so fast that she didn't feel anything at all."

I don't know if this is true. No one knows if it's true except Elizabeth, and she certainly can't tell us. But if this can ease any of Sarah's pain, it means something. Elizabeth would want all of us to think it was painless.

I can only pray that it actually was.

"Okay," she whispers. She is still crying, and I let her cry, waiting it out until she takes a breath.

"Okay," she repeats. "Thank you, James. Thank you for telling me."

"For what it's worth," I tell her before she can hang up, "Elizabeth found out about you right before the accident. I think she would've loved to know you."

"I have to go, James," Sarah says quickly, and I know that she can't hear any more, not right now.

"Okay. I understand," I say softly. "If you ever want to know anything about her, or want pictures, or anything, you know how to reach me. I know it's eighteen years too late, but—"

"Thank you, I appreciate it," Sarah says. I can tell she is trying so hard to keep it together.

263

"Of course. I hope you're doing well. You and your son and … whoever else."

"You take care of yourself, James," Sarah says, and there is a warm sort of pity in her voice. And just as fast as Elizabeth disappeared, Sarah is gone.

***

I feel I have officially hit the end of my worth.

I have made enough money to get Madeline through college and I've told Sarah that her daughter, the one I forced her to give up, is dead.

There is nothing else for me to do.

I pass the days working, going to the bar—frequenting the one I met Sarah in for nostalgia's sake—going home, eating a reheated meal and going to sleep.

There isn't much color to it, but it's not color I'm after.

On a particularly melancholy day in late July, over two years after Elizabeth's death, Jenavieve rings the doorbell.

I let her and Max, who is holding Grace, inside. As always, I don't pay much attention to the baby. I know her first birthday was in March though.

Madeline, who is home for the summer from her first year in college, comes downstairs. Grace squeals happily when she sees her.

"Hi, baby girl!" Madeline coos, taking Grace in her arms and taking her outside to play on the patio.

"How are you, Dad?" Jenavieve asks, lines of concern etched on her face.

"I'm alright." I try to smile, gesturing for her and Max to come sit on the couch with me.

"Listen, Dad," Jenavieve says, glancing at Max, "I'm wondering if you can help us."

Help? What the hell I can do to help Jen and Max is beyond me. But I figure whatever it is, it will at least give me something to do.

"What can I do for you?"

"We want permanent custody of Grace," Jenavieve says, "and I'm not sure Ashley will be eager to grant us that."

I nod slowly, considering. This is something I could help them with, and it's probably a good thing.

I glance out the window and watch my granddaughter giggling as Madeline bounces her on her lap. She's well-fed, well-clothed and taken care of by a budding psychologist and a businessman. A tad better than being parented by a seventeen-year-old in prison.

The last big custody case I won granted a baby to a drug-addict. Maybe this case can make up for the atrocity of that.

"Okay," I nod. "I'll represent you."

The look in their eyes affirms that what I am doing is most definitely a good thing.

"Thank you, thank you so much," Max gushes. "We love Grace more than anything, and we just …"

"We just don't think Ashley can raise her the way she deserves to be raised," Jenavieve finishes for him. Her voice is apologetic.

"Sure, I understand," I nod. And I do understand. But part of this morality act means I have to do something first.

***

It has been just over two years that Ashley has lived in prison, and it is my third time coming to see her.

The first was on Christmas. The second was on her seventeenth birthday.

She looks confused to see me. Obviously, I don't blame her, but she also looks a little hopeful.

"Hi, Dad, how are you?"

She looks well, at least for someone living in prison. Her blonde hair looks healthy, and her eyes are bright.

"I'm alright." I give her the same answer I gave Jen and Max.

"Listen," I say wearily, cutting right to the chase, "I wanted you to hear this from me before you hear it from anyone else. Jenavieve and Max are seeking permanent custody of Grace, and I'm going to represent them."

Betrayal. That is the first emotion I see on Ashley's face. Then rage, the old, familiar, angsty-Ashley rage.

But she can't act on it here. I suspect she would never let herself act on her rage again, after everything.

"I don't want you to not know your daughter," I continue calmly, after giving her a moment to process. "However, I do want what's best, and her living with you doesn't seem like that. I can help you get visitation rights though, good ones, if you comply now. If you just follow my lead and do what I say, you'll get the best possible relationship with Grace, minus all the responsibility that goes along with it."

"I *want* the responsibility," Ashley snaps irritably. "Don't you get it? The only reason I've survived here with my sanity for this long is because I've had something to live for. My daughter. That's it. That's all I have."

"Do you honestly think you would make a good parent for her? Better than Jenavieve and Max?" I ask, trying not to sound judgmental or rude.

"I may not have a fancy job and fancy condo right now, but that's the only difference between them and me," Ashley says firmly.

That, and the fact that you're in prison and they're not, I think but don't say.

"Look, my position isn't changing," I tell her, "and my offer to you isn't, either. If you want the best possible relationship with your daughter, you'll follow my lead."

"Yeah," Ashley grunts, "because you're the best person to give parenting advice."

My eyes flash to hers. "Excuse me?" I try to sound harsh, but my voice catches.

"I just think it's funny," she shrugs, "that you're over here endorsing the 'best possible relationship' with my daughter when you never even had a good relationship with me. Or a relationship at all, really. With any of us."

If I let her convince me this is true, I will surely stop being of any use to anyone, because I will finally give up.

Besides, she's in prison. What the hell does she know about living an independently stable life?

"So I guess you don't want my help, then," I say dryly.

"No, thank you," her voice drips with disdain. "I think I'll get my baby back on my own."

I take that as my cue to leave. I find myself wondering when I will see my daughter next, and when she will see her daughter.

***

Because I have the obnoxious tendency to win, and more so than ever since Elizabeth's death, I do just that: win.

In truth, it doesn't take much to build a case for my oldest daughter and one against my youngest.

I know I have officially destroyed my relationship with Ashley, but I tell myself it doesn't matter. Besides, I don't feel much these days. Any feelings I have go into providing money for my wife's treatment. Other than that, I bury everything in work. Oh, and I drink a lot of alcohol.

The flip side to my broken relationship with Ashley, though, is my strengthened relationship with Jenavieve and Max.

I grow to appreciate my son-in-law more than I ever have. We talk about sports, which is something I never did with the girls or Evelyn. It brings me some enjoyment. I also see the way he loves my daughter, and it confirms the possibility that there are good relationships out there, good relationships that support truly good things.

Jenavieve continues to be like a rock for me, as she has been for all of us. She checks in, makes sure I'm eating and sleeping enough. I don't know why she cares, but maybe she doesn't quite know either.

God knows how she got it, but maybe there is something in her that just *knows* the right thing to do in the grand scheme of it all.

It takes me a long time to strengthen my relationship with Grace. I simply still feel too undeserving.

But one day I decide that I will always feel undeserving, and I ask Jen if I can hold my granddaughter.

She tries to hide her shock, but it's okay—I'd be shocked, too. Two years Grace has been alive, and I have never held her.

Until now.

She sits on my lap and beams up at me like she's used to me holding her, and I want to laugh at how perfect her name is for her.

I hold her while I talk to Max about sports. I hold her throughout dinner. And I hold her while I read a book to her on the patio and Jen and Max sip wine inside.

And when my granddaughter rests her little head on my chest and falls asleep, it is then that I finally begin to cry for the first time in a long time.

I cry not out of sadness or regret. I cry because here before me is something I have done right, someone I have done right by.

The bottle stays in the cupboard that night.

268

Three Years Later

61
MADELINE

"Yes, that sounds correct." I force myself to smile, even though I'm impatient. I may be on the phone, but I want my employees to think I'm a reasonable, responsible and warm person.

"Yes, Lauren, I've reviewed the numbers, and it all looks very good. Okay, yep, talk to you later. You too." Smile. Hang up. Back to work.

My Columbia graduation gift was my mother's company.

In truth, it wasn't a gift so much as an obligation. Someone needed to step in for my mother's long absence, and someone in the family was preferable. That left me.

My years at Columbia prepared me very well for running a business. I was more than ready to leave Malibu, and the best escape I could find was New York City.

I quickly came to love the fast pace, the vibrant diversity influencing every facet of life, the freedom that came with living amidst so many strangers.

Even though I loved all of it, at the end of the four years I wanted to come back to Malibu.

There was so much sadness surrounding my home when I left it, and the sadness still exists; I don't think it will ever go away. But not everything about home is sad. There is the beach, glorious sunsets, the smell of salt outside my bedroom window, shorts and summer dresses. Peace.

New York was good for me during college, but it offered none of the things I loved most about where I grew up. So back to Malibu I came. Back to my own home, actually.

My dad is the only one who lives here, and the place certainly has enough room for one more. I assume my mom will come back here once she's discharged, but none of us really knows for sure. She hasn't been in contact with any of us for so long.

I immediately renovated my mother's office and made it my own, replacing the gray walls with light blue, trimming the room with coral.

I must do these little things, add these little splashes of color, to remind myself of the goodness of Malibu and my life here.

While I was a little afraid to take over Detail, I just kept reminding myself that no matter what I did, it would be better than my mom's recent work on it. The recent work that was nonexistent.

I homed in on my inner New York businesswoman, and sure enough, my mom's company is better than ever.

I check my calendar quickly on my phone: Work for the rest of the afternoon, then appetizers at Nobu Malibu, and then maybe I'll visit my nieces if there's time.

The busyness of my life fulfills me, makes me feel active and worthwhile.

It's now lunchtime, and I ponder my options for a moment. Sometimes I go out, other times I order in and work through lunch, and still other times I just skip it altogether.

Today, though, it's particularly warm and beautiful outside. The perfect sort of day to go and visit Elizabeth.

I do this every so often, and it always brings me a warm comfort.

I'm not sure where Liz is or what she knows and doesn't know, but I do know that if she is aware, she's happy when I come to see her.

I grab a packaged salad from the fridge and toss it in my Louis, slinging the bag over my arm and locking up the house behind me.

The drive is quiet—I usually don't like to listen to music when I drive. It's beautifully serene that way.

When I get to Liz's grave, I sit delicately on the little stone bench I installed over the summer, when I knew I'd be visiting frequently for years to come.

The stone is warm from baking in the sun all afternoon, and it feels oddly comforting.

I don't often speak out loud when I come to visit. My mind usually wanders to whatever is taking my attention at the time—likely something work-related.

There are times, though, when I force my brain to use the time here to think about Elizabeth, which is often painful but necessary.

Because as the years have passed, it has become increasingly difficult to remember her.

It's more difficult to remember exactly what her laugh sounded like because I haven't heard it in almost six years. Remembering the exact features of her face is difficult, and it aggravates me when I can't bring it perfectly to mind. Luckily, there are still the photos to look at, which help.

Today, I think fondly about the time Liz and I put on a fashion show for my mother.

I must've been around seven years old, making her eight, and I remember the scene so well because it was one of the few times my mom was home from work during the daytime.

We dressed up and paraded proudly around the living room, striking the poses we had instructed each other to use.

I wore Elizabeth's clothes and she wore mine. We paired different articles together to make up the most eccentric pieces, trying to mirror the sorts of outfits we had seen that winter during our family Paris Fashion Week trip.

I remember my mother laughing so genuinely, leaning back and clapping, shouting her praise at everything we modeled. She must've had a particularly good day at work to be that unreservedly joyous.

For our grand finale, Liz and I dressed in our matching gowns from Disneyland, skipping onto our makeshift walkway hand in hand and taking our dramatic bows.

We were greeted by the loudest of applause, and we giggled at our success.

"For a while there, Lissie, we were going to study at Parsons together to become fashion designers." I laugh quietly, talking to her tombstone as if it's her face. I guess it is the next best thing, given the circumstances.

As always, I place a daisy on the grass, which was her favorite flower and what I think is the gift she would most like.

I sit there for a while longer, trying to enjoy the peace and quiet while I eat my salad, but eventually I find myself tearing up. This happens occasionally, mostly out of aggravation that I can't have just one more conversation with my sister.

Luckily, my phone rings, shaking me from my reverie. I quickly blot my tears away and sit up a little straighter, not even bothering to check who's calling before pressing the phone to my ear.

"Hello?" I try to sound chipper.

"Hey, beautiful."

I smile without even thinking about it, and just like that, I feel good again. He has that effect on me.

"Where are you right now?" he continues. "I was thinking we

could walk the beach, get some ice cream or something if you're not too busy. It's just such a beautiful day out."

Walk the beach. I have to consider it a moment, but of course I want to walk the beach with him.

"That sounds good." I smile, a real smile this time. "I just have to get a bit more work done first. Then I'll meet you?"

"Sounds great!" I can feel him beaming through the phone. He's so supportive of all that I do, and I love him for it.

"See you in a bit. Love you," I tell him.

"I love you too. See you soon."

***

As I sit in my office now, it is one of those times when I have to remind myself why I do what I do. Since I took over the company, I have tried to use it for good. Rather than exploiting people's biggest secrets and insecurities, I have tried to focus more on people's accomplishments, all of the good things they have done for themselves and the world.

I've been at it for only six months, but I think it's gone well.

There are times, though, times like right now, when it's very hard to keep up the morality act.

Annie Anderson, who has reportedly been clean for the past five years, is apparently off the wagon again.

The source is good; the photo clearly depicts Annie snorting coke at some decrepit old bar in Los Angeles.

I scrutinize the image for a while, thinking about how sad it is. So much talent going to waste. Motherhood going to waste, too. When I have kids someday, I vow to myself, I will never jeopardize my ability to care for them.

Once again, the phone rings, awakening me from my thoughts.

I hope it's him, because then I will be automatically made happier, but it's not. It's my assistant, Natalie.

"Did you see it?" she asks before I can even say anything. Natalie has the sort of consumingly obsessive energy that makes her a great worker, and her organizational skills make her a top-notch assistant.

"Yeah, I'm looking at it right now," I say hesitantly. She's clearly excited, but I don't know if I am.

"It's golden," she gushes. "I mean, that's front-page shit right there. Give me the word and I'll put in the order right now."

I sigh involuntarily, the struggle between good and bad coming to a standoff like it so frequently does.

"Oh, come on," Natalie senses my hesitation right away. "It's not your fault she's high again."

True. But it would be my fault for the headline to be broadcast for everybody to see.

Then again, if I don't put it out there, somebody else will. This way, I'll gain from it, which means my employees will gain from it. And that's good. Right?

Maybe it is, maybe it's not. I'll never know for sure, and no one will. We all just go through life making decisions, with varying degrees of self-gratification and morality, until it all blows up in our faces.

"Okay. Yes, Natalie, go ahead and send it," I tell her firmly, because I'm the boss and I make the decisions.

Maybe my mother isn't so insane, after all. It's certainly getting easier to see how she got the way she did.

With that, the decision has been made. Time to go back to my work, to see if it is dream-fulfilling or destruction-foreseeing.

And then we start again.

62
JAMES

I don't even know if I'm married anymore.

In the legal sense, yes. The paperwork still exists, so according to the government, I am still married to Evelyn Blair.

But marriage, to me, involves being actively involved with the person you are married to, and I am definitely not that.

Since Evelyn left for the mental hospital five years ago, I have not seen her.

I've called and emailed, infrequently and fleetingly reaching her. Evelyn has had just enough contact with me to assure I know she's alive and stable, but anything beyond that is a mystery. I should probably try harder to track the progress of her treatment, but I don't know if that's something I'm even allowed to do. I don't know how it all works.

What I do know is that my wife may as well be gone, and she has been gone for years. Whatever it was that held her together shattered upon Elizabeth's death. It's a little ironic—I thought I would be the one broken beyond repair, considering it was my daughter who died.

But maybe I am broken beyond repair, at least in my own eyes. To society, being broken entails being catatonic and staring at walls, which gets you sent to a sterile institution to be taught how to function again.

I still function. I'm still a lawyer, and I'm still very good at my job. I still make quite a bit of money because of it.

But I'm not the same James. A part of me has been dead for the past six years, numb to anything else going on around me.

I only further the numbness by drinking, but I'm very good at hiding it from the five people who still love me. At least I think they still love me.

Sometimes I wonder what it would be like to get help for the drinking, but I invariably shut the idea down each time it comes to mind. The help wouldn't help anything. Alcohol *is* what helps me, and it can't be taken away.

So I keep up the same routine I have followed for all these years: Work, bar, home. Eat reheated dinner, sometimes with Madeline. Visit Jenavieve, Max, and my granddaughters.

That's right: Jen has two children now. After allowing Grace into my heart, there was no going back. I now dote on both the girls, buying them all of the dresses and dolls that I should've bought my own kids when I had the chance.

It brings me solace, though, to know that I am a good grandfather. The girls love to see me, and they love it when I read stories to them and give them gifts.

Family dinners are my favorite way to pass the time. They're always at my house, and I am always the host.

On these days—usually Sundays—I get up early and spend the day cooking and making quick trips to the store for the ingredients I need. I cook elaborate courses and fill the kitchen with the heavenly scents of caprese salad, Mediterranean pasta, chicken pad thai.

At around four o'clock in the afternoon, Madeline comes into the kitchen from wherever she's been. Then Max, Jen and the kids come over, and they all enjoy appetizers together while I continue cooking.

277

We eat at around six thirty, and after we're finished, I always make sure there's dessert for the little ones to enjoy while the rest of us clean the kitchen.

After that, we usually end up on the patio, watching the ocean, talking until everyone is sleepy.

These nights make me feel like I am a part of something, actively involved in what remains of my family.

Despite the joy it brings me, though, I never forget who I am and the irreversible mistakes I have made. The reparations now make my life worth living, but only just.

I wish someone had told me when I was young that the mistakes you make last indefinitely. That the past really does travel with you.

So, after my family leaves and Madeline is asleep upstairs, I drink. If I'm not too drunk to drive, I take myself to a bar. Usually the one I met Sarah at, for the past really does travel with you.

I can still remember the exact stool I was sitting on when I met her. To humor myself, that's usually where I sit. The bartender knows me well by now, and he looks at me like I am a sad old man whenever I walk through the door.

I suppose he's not wrong.

On these nights in the bar, I think about how this is where I went wrong. The conversation with Sarah Jenkins led to kissing her in the bathroom, which led to getting her number, which led to going to her house, which led to forcing her to give up her child. The child, who is now dead. True, Elizabeth would never have existed if it hadn't been for me. But she also wouldn't have died if not for me, and the rest of my family wouldn't be so beyond broken.

Maybe my life went wrong somewhere else. Maybe it was when I married Evelyn, or when I beat out Ben Hatching for the presidency, or maybe it was something else entirely.

Somewhere along the way, something went wrong and set off a domino effect of other wrongdoings. And while I don't know if I will ever pinpoint it, I do know that I am at fault.

And yet I am still here, and I do have something to contribute now. I can be a good grandfather, and a decent father, and a semi-decent man. I may detest myself, but that doesn't mean I can't still contribute to this world in a positive way.

I'll drink to that.

63
JENAVIEVE

Leah Elizabeth was born when Grace was three, completing the Grayson family. Maybe Madeline will finally give us a boy someday, for I have evidently ensured that the long lineage of girls will be continued.

Leah instantly became Grace's biggest project; Grace is attentive to her every need and desire, and the two are inseparable.

Today is Grace's fifth birthday, and Max is cooking his mother's delicious mac-and-cheese recipe, which is Grace's favorite meal.

Since Leah is only two, I still have to supervise the girls when they're playing together. Luckily, it is one of my favorite pastimes.

I watch them now playing in the big playroom on the lower level of our new home. With two kids, we decided we needed something bigger than a condo; we now live in a beautiful gray house with white trim, in a nice neighborhood only about fifteen minutes away from my dad and Madeline.

Leah starts to whimper a little, and Grace immediately leaps to her feet, bounding over to the bin filled with all their dolls and rummaging around for Leah's favorite. I'm proud of how caring she is and how much she loves her little sister.

Grace grows more beautiful by the day, her golden curls getting longer and her blue eyes becoming more piercing. She is the perfect mixture of Ashley and Dashton, but that's not what I see when I look at her.

I mostly see Elizabeth in the sparkle in her eyes and her bottomless love of others.

I feel a little pang whenever I think about Grace's complicated circumstances. I don't know how I'm ever going to be able to explain the events surrounding her birth, but she's only five. I have years before she'll be ready to hear everything.

But I need her to know someday about her Aunt Elizabeth, who her little sister is named after. That alone is important enough to make me ignore my reservations and tell Grace the truth when she's ready to hear it.

She does know that she wasn't born from Max and me, which was pretty easy for her to figure out when she noticed Leah's light-brown skin in contrast to her paleness.

She doesn't have any memories of Ashley. The last time they saw each other was when Grace wasn't even two years old, shortly before the court date.

My father told me that he tried to help Ashley gain visitation rights, and Max and I were both very open to settling those agreements with her. But she didn't want that. Ashley fought for full custody of Grace. It was all or nothing to her, and she lost.

I don't know where she has been since she got out of prison two years ago. I call her on important dates—her birthday, Christmas—but she never picks up. She never responds to any text messages. For all I know, she may not even have a phone anymore—she is that absent from my life.

It makes me sad that our relationship had to be lost. But I always remind myself that Grace and her secure childhood were, and continue to be, far more important.

Leah claps her little hands together upon the appearance of her favorite doll, and Grace smiles.

"Grace, you are such a sweet sister." I smile proudly at her. I don't compliment every little thing she does because I want her to continue doing the good things she does simply because that's what she wants to do.

But times like these, she deserves to hear what a great kid she is.

"Thank you, Mommy!" Grace chirps, focused on dressing her doll in one of the fancy dresses Madeline bought for her.

I turn around to see Max standing in the doorway, watching us contentedly. I wonder how long he has been there.

"Alright, my lovely ladies. Dinner awaits!" Max bellows dramatically, and Grace shrieks excitedly, dropping her doll and running to the kitchen.

"Wash your hands first, missy," I reprimand her playfully, and she dutifully washes up in the bathroom sink before bounding to her seat.

The table is already set: water poured, rolls on the table, and a heaping bowl of mac-and-cheese in the center.

I push Grace's chair in for her and put her hair up in a ponytail to keep it out of her food. Meanwhile, Max carries Leah over to her high chair, wrapping her bib around her before dishing some food onto her plate.

We have it down to a science, my husband and me. We balance ourselves perfectly between both our daughters and each other, ensuring everyone feels loved and supported and heard at all times.

My dad particularly enjoys spending time with Grace and Leah; he didn't used to, but over time, he's developed a soft spot for them. The girls love Grandpa James, as well as Auntie Madeline, both of whom they see just about every Sunday for dinner.

We feel more like a family than we have in a long time, if ever. There may be three people missing, but there have also been two people added. An almost perfect balance.

My husband sits across from me, my girls on either side of me. My life has turned out exactly the way I had always wanted it to, and I wish I could go back and tell my younger self how beautifully everything becomes.

Just as we're about to dig in, my phone chimes. Normally I wouldn't check it at the table, but something compels me to anyway.

I frown at the unfamiliar number, opening the message to read: Please tell my daughter happy birthday from me.

Ashley. I can feel my heart pounding, some automatically unnerved reaction to hearing from my sister after, what? Four years?

Deep down, though, I know that the unnerving feeling is not because I am hearing from Ashley. It's because it is a reminder of what I *did* to Ashley.

I tore her from the only person she had left: her daughter. And I promised I would just take care of Grace until Ashley was capable of doing it herself.

I broke that promise.

My eyes flit to Grace for a moment, and I feel a sudden pang when I see how much her face resembles Ashley's.

"Mommy, what's wrong?" Grace asks, cocking her little head to the side in concern.

Time to make a split decision. In the moment, I know that I should give her Ashley's message, because it is her birthday and she deserves to know that Ashley is thinking of her.

But how do you explain that to a five-year-old? *Ashley. You don't remember her, but she killed your aunt six years ago, then went to prison and had you. Oh, and your dad was a famous movie star who illegally dated Ashley. Anyway, she says happy birthday.*

There is no fair way to explain it, at least not on my daughter's fifth birthday. MY daughter. She is not Ashley's daughter, and she has no right to act like Grace is hers. Grace is my little girl—mine and Max's. And that is how it's supposed to be.

"Oh, nothing, sweetie," I say to her, smiling. Seemingly satisfied with my response, Grace takes a huge bite of her meal.

I continue to eat with my family, and as I do so, I feel better and more reassured.

This, right here, is how I always dreamed my life would go.

There's no reason to find fault with that. Why would there be?

So I go on with my dinner, living with the content awareness that my life has turned out perfectly, and everything is right with the world.

64
ASHLEY

The night air is brisk, a little more brisk than usual for Malibu.

It's a miracle I'm even able to live here still. After I got out of prison, I quickly noticed that I'd been locked out of not only my trust fund, but any source of family money. They'd all be mortified to carry any association with me at this point, so I guess they just cut me the hell off completely.

It's funny; I used to hate all my childhood luxuries with a burning passion, but now I find myself missing them desperately.

Fresh out of a prison sentence for killing somebody isn't exactly the best résumé, so at first I was hopeless, thinking there would be nothing for me to do to make the money I needed.

But of course, there's always a way, and it didn't take long for me to find it. All it took, in fact, was one night in a bar and one lonely man who was a little drunk and very rich for me to discover a simple way to make bank.

I've kept at it since I got out, so it's been about two years now. It pays for my hotel rooms and meals, and it provides a more self-sufficient life than I thought possible.

It's a pretty decent job, and in essence requires very little from me. All I have to do is look pretty, flirt with rich men at expensive bars, and spend the night with them. Maybe more than one night if they're particularly good business.

My "virtue," or whatever, doesn't concern me. It's not like I've had no experience with men. Besides, love stopped being meaningful to me when I lost my sister, my family, my boyfriend, my daughter.

My daughter. That is the reason I'm still in Malibu.

She may not live with me, and that may depress me to no end, but I'm still a mother. So wherever she is, I am.

I continue my walk, enjoying the fresh crispness of the air. Sometimes I order a Lyft, when I've budgeted well for the week, but other times I simply prefer to walk to the bar. Tonight is one of those nights.

It's also one of those nights for my shortcut.

Instead of walking down the busier roads, which provide the quicker route to the bars, I slip into the little trail that leads me through the residential part of town.

I walk past pretty houses—idyllic, charming structures lined with flower bushes and white trim.

I know these particular houses, in this particular neighborhood, very well, because this is the neighborhood where my daughter lives.

I found the house one night when I was walking to the bar like usual. I'd adopted the habit of looking into the windows of houses, which sounds creepy but really wasn't. I guess that a part of me just yearned to catch a little glimpse of the stability I never had. I saw all of these families eating and laughing together, and I hoped that my daughter was living that sort of life. One day I was shocked to catch a glimpse of Jenavieve through the window. It was unmistakably my sister, though, and I knew at that moment that I had just received my golden ticket.

Most parents cherish reading books with their kids, taking them out for ice cream, surprising them with trips to Disneyland.

As for me? I cherish catching glimpses of my child through a window.

It is her fifth birthday tonight. I wonder if she knows that I am thinking of her, then I realize what a foolish thought that is. Jen ripped her away from me. Why would she let me be any part of Grace's thoughts?

Deep breath, Ashley, deep breath.

I get these spurts of rage still, and now I am afraid of what they might do. They have already killed somebody, after all.

There's probably—no, definitely—something wrong with me, but the wrong is simply who I am. Anyway, I suspect that "something wrong" is all too often used as an excuse for people's fucked-up actions. If there's one moral thing I'll do in my life, it'll be not jumping on that bandwagon.

Hopefully, I have timed it right so that I can see Grace through the window eating dinner.

Pretty creepy, I know, but I have to do what I have to do to see her. I don't bother anybody. I stand across the street to ensure they never know I'm there.

I stand still now, eyes on the house. It's a nice, two-story Craftsman-style place, gray exterior with white trim.

The light is on in the kitchen, as I can see through the window, but no one is in there. Damn it! All I want is to see her, to know that she is having a good birthday.

I wait for five minutes, which turns into ten, which turns into fifteen, and they're not coming. Time to go.

Just as I'm turning on my heel, I catch something out of the periphery of my vision. I turn, and there they are. Jenavieve and Grace.

I watch my sister scoot in Grace's chair and carefully pull her hair back in a ponytail. I can see my daughter's profile, and from what I can tell, she looks well. Plump cheeks that aren't too plump, rosy red lips, long lashes, beautiful golden hair. Beaming smile.

Jen looks well, too. Long, ice-blonde hair pulled back. Designer jeans and a blouse that looks like it's from some fancy boutique. Diamond ring so massive and glittering I can see it from here.

Max ambles into the room, carrying a toddler in a purple dress. They had a second child. Leah, I think her name is. At least Grace has a sibling to play with.

I watch as Max places her carefully into her high chair and fastens her bib. The kid is cute, I must admit. Rosy cheeks, little dark curls. She hits her spoon against her tray, and I can see Max laughing as he dishes some pasta onto her plate.

He looks just as good as Jenavieve. He's wearing a t-shirt that clearly shows his muscles, and he just looks happy, like my sister. They all look happy. Anybody passing by would think to themselves, *What a charming little family. So sweet, so innocent.*

If only they fucking knew.

What would happen if I went and rang the doorbell right now? Granted, I look a little slutty in my low-cut top and stilettos, but Grace wouldn't notice any of that. She'd just be happy to see me.

If it weren't for the stupid restraining order, I would do it right now. Demand to be let in, let into my daughter's life like I deserve.

But I can't jeopardize what I have, which is a way to see her whenever I desire. As long as I don't make a scene, that won't be taken away from me.

There has to be *something* I can do, though, just to let Grace know that I care. After all, it's her fifth birthday.

I consider my options for a moment, coming up with only one: Text Jenavieve.

I would rather not, considering I want nothing to do with Jen or

Madeline for as long as we're all alive.

But it's the only way I can get to Grace. And mothers must make sacrifices for their children.

Sighing, I reach into my Louis Vuitton satchel—a gift from a generous stockbroker—and pull out my new phone (a gift from a generous computer scientist). I hope Jenavieve still has the same number she had years ago, or else this won't work.

I send her the message, and my phone shows it going through. Now, I wait.

Almost immediately, I can see her checking her phone. Even though her back is to me, I can see her hand holding the phone underneath the table, surely reading my message.

Nothing. Grace is right next to her and is watching her with a look of concern on her face. I must've freaked my sister out a little.

I am completely still, watching the scene carefully to see if Jen passes along the message.

"Tell her," I mutter, even though she obviously can't hear me; she doesn't even know I'm here.

There is a moment of hesitation, in which Grace still wears her look of concern, and then it is over. My daughter smiles and takes a huge bite of her food, and there they all go, back to being the charmingly innocent Grayson family.

Unbelievable. Well, not really unbelievable, come to think of it. I am completely isolated, the family outcast. Always have been, always will be. That will never change, which means my nonexistent relationship with my daughter will also never change.

But there's always something good to focus on, despite it all. When I was really little, I had my sisters. We were happy and innocent, and we loved to make up games to play during the parties.

Then, when I didn't have my sisters, I had Dash. My love, my forever favorite person, even though I know I can never see or speak to him again.

And now I have Grace. Maybe not the way I want, but she is still my little girl, and that means enough to keep me functioning.

So it's okay, really. I think about how lucky I am to have what I have, as I walk my lonely self toward a lonely bar to be with lonely men. I wish I knew how lucky I was when I was young, but I know now.

Have grace.

Have grace.

Have grace.

65
DISCHARGE

~~~

D ischarge day. The implications of this day fill me with a sense of finality, a sense that this is the last of something.

This is it. All the years of therapy, crippling depression and mood-lifting medications have led to now. Now, seated in my familiar chair, in this familiar office, across from my familiar therapist.

I always thought she would be thrilled to see the last of me, but since our last conversation, I believe that we have forged a new connection.

In any case, this will be the last meeting I will ever have with her, and this time I know it's true. There was a sense of incompletion last time I left, but this time is different.

This is it.

I have given my all for this meeting. I'm wearing jeans and a cardigan in place of my usual baggy sweatpants and t-shirt. The jeans are a little loose because I've kind of become a rail in here, but they make me look more like someone who cares about others' opinions. I've brushed out my hair, too, adding hairspray to make my blonde waves look more glossy than frizzy. And I'm forcing myself to sit up straight and not fidget for the duration of the meeting. This is as good as I'll get.

"Well, Evelyn, today's the big day," my therapist smiles warmly at me over her glasses. I find myself looking around her office a little more thoughtfully than usual, because this is really the last time I'll be seeing it. I always registered her big oak desk and light-gray walls, but I never noticed the framed Harvard diploma on the wall, or the tall bookshelf lined with American classics and self-help books. I wonder if the books are meant for her patients or herself.

"You've been through the drill before," she continues, "but as a refresher, I like to meet with patients one more time before discharge. It's a nice way to finish up any last conversations, reflect, or simply just chat."

Last time, I was a sorry participant in this final meeting. I forced myself to say a few cheerful things, then stared at the wall while my therapist recited words of encouragement.

Now, though, things are different. I'm not coming back.

I watch her across the table and am struck, like I was during our last meeting, by the sudden realization that she is just a human. She, too, has insecurities and questions about the world, figments of darkness surrounding her thoughts.

If I have to have one last session with her after all of the years she has stuck by me, the least I can do is speak with her candidly.

This time I won't let pessimism and my distaste for the world cloud what I have to say about what I find to be true.

"Okay," I nod. "Okay, what would you like to know?" I watch her intently. After all these years of her asking the questions, it's my turn.

She's a little taken aback but speaks quickly. "How do you feel?" she asks. "And I mean *really* feel."

Well, she asked for honesty, so honesty she'll get. Besides, she can see right through me at this point. She'll know if I'm answering truthfully or not.

"I feel ready," I tell her confidently. "Ready to go. Ready to see what's next out there. There's something to be said about this strange universe of ours offering an unlimited bounty of beauty, and I hope to find it.

"If I'm being honest with you, though, I don't know if I'll find it. I'm not really sure how it's all delegated, or if there's any system at all, but if there is, I'm certainly not deserving of the unlimited bounty."

I pause, look up at the ceiling for a second, thinking of how to articulate it.

"But," I shrug simply, "maybe I am deserving of the beauty. That's the thing: I don't know. You don't know, although you probably have a better grasp of it all than I do. But even then, none of us knows a damn thing!"

I laugh, because it's funny to say it out loud. Here I am, in a mental hospital, telling my therapist that no one knows anything about how this world operates.

"If there's one thing I've learned here," I continue, "it's that we all perceive things a different way. I feel guilty for Elizabeth's death, but you don't think I should. And so on, and so on.

"So if we all perceive the things that happen to us and each other in different ways, what's the right answer?"

I'm waiting for her to respond, but she doesn't. She simply continues to watch me intently, seemingly absorbed in what I'm saying.

"And I think it aggravates us when we realize that there isn't an answer, because we like to know how things are supposed to go. We like to know what's right and what's wrong with every little detail of our lives, and we set some pretty good parameters for those things.

"But all of those parameters, they're constructed by us. We are the creators of everything we perceive life to be. And that is the ultimate irony of being: Our standards of success and failure, sanity and madness control our lives, but we control the standards long before they have a hold on us.

"It's a cycle. It's all a cycle, and it never ends. We know the Earth is spherical, but I don't think the circle is simply physical. I think it's everything. The balance you speak of? It all circles back around."

"Full circle," she murmurs, "it all comes full circle, is what you're saying."

"Exactly." I smile, and I am satisfied that she actually seems to understand it. These are the things I wish everyone could know, but at least one person does now. Maybe there is hope for her to make things better.

"So," my therapist says slowly, thoughtfully, "it appears you have reached a point of genuine acceptance. Acceptance of your life, and your actions, and everything, because you realize that there isn't a way to define what's right and wrong, if your actions were good or bad, or ... anything."

"Yes," I respond simply, and she looks a little disturbed.

"But don't you think ... I want you to have standards, Evelyn," she says, and there's a little bit of exasperation in her voice. "Standards about how life should be lived, now that you're about to do it on your own again."

"Oh, don't worry." I wave my hand nonchalantly. "I'll follow the rules. I'll do the accepted things, created by the accepted people, because that's what we do.

"Let me tell you, I've met some socially accepted people who have gotten up to some questionable antics, myself included," I grunt, "but I won't go off breaking the rules. I simply understand that there's not a logical explanation for them, at least an explanation that serves as one answer for everybody."

My therapist is looking at me like she can't tell if I'm a genius or completely insane, and to her credit, I may be completely and utterly insane.

But it doesn't bother me anymore. My definition of insane is different from hers, which is different from the therapist next door. There is such a weightless feeling to really grasping these things.

I don't think my therapist has quite grasped it yet, but that's okay. She's being a helpful, contributing citizen of the world because of it. She's doing just fine. I simply hope she doesn't break like I did.

"Alright," she nods carefully, eyes still focused on me. "And your plan? You said the Uber will be taking you to the airport so you can go back to your home in Malibu, correct?"

"Yep," I tell her confidently, although I don't know if it's true. I don't know what's left for me there. I don't know what's left for me anywhere.

"You have to call me as soon as you get there, so I know you arrived safely. Okay?" She furrows her brows, peering at me through her glasses.

She's concerned, then. Not concerned enough to stop me from leaving, because she sees that I am the most stable version of myself that I've been since I first walked through these doors.

But she doesn't know what's going through my head. As much as these people try to understand, the only way you can know everything about a person is to be the person themself. And even then, you may not know everything.

"Of course," I say warmly. "I'll check in, just as we talked about."

There is a pause during which my therapist is considering me, maybe considering if she's making the right decision in letting me out.

But everyone agreed it's time for me to go, including the lead psychiatrist. My therapist is going along with the standards. Being a good citizen. And I know that alone will be enough for her.

Sure enough: "Okay, Evelyn. I'm going to go grab your final discharge papers for you to sign, and then you're all set to go."

***

My therapist insists on walking me out to the Uber. She walks with me out of her office, down the hall, out of the ward, down the stairs, and out into the crisp San Francisco air.

The sun is shining, and everything has a fresh, new tint to it. I breathe it all in deeply, savoring it.

And then it is time.

The Uber driver pulls up, and he places all my belongings in the trunk, and then watches me expectantly.

"Sir, can you please give me a moment?" I smile at him, pulling back some of my old social graces to get what I want. I still have it in me, I guess, for he nods gruffly and settles into the front seat.

I turn around and face her. "There's one more thing," I tell her.

"What's that?" she asks, and I know she'll be hanging on my every word.

"I wish things turned out better for my family." I shake my head. "I mean, I guess I don't know exactly how it's been for them, these past years, but somehow I know it didn't turn out well. And I wish they could've figured it out. I wish the standards could be made better."

Before she can say anything in response, I say, "Anyway, thank you. Thank you so much, for all that you've done for me. You're really great at what you do, and I know I was ... difficult. Thank you for not giving up."

She looks touched at that, a little surprised to see me showing emotion, probably. "Of course," she says softly. "It was my pleasure."

I turn away and duck into the cab. Just as I am halfway seated and about to close the door behind me, she says a little urgently, "Evelyn. Don't give up. Remember that there's still so much beauty out there."

I look at her one last time and smile, chuckling a little. "Ah, but that's the irony of being, remember? We think the beauty is 'out there,' otherworldly, but we're the ones who create it in the first place. There's no beauty—there's nothing at all—unless we say there is."

I shut the door behind me, but I still hear her call out, "So make new standards, Evelyn."

That's a nice thing for her to say. I decide I like the sound of that, creating new standards, and so I configure it into something worth holding on to in my mind.

"Where to?" the driver asks me, shaking me from my trance.

I only pause a moment before saying, "Anywhere is fine. Wherever you're headed, just drop me off somewhere along the way."

He looks at me like I'm straight out of a mental hospital, but off we go, and I am finally on my way home.

66

Ten years later, and I still find myself thinking sometimes about Evelyn Blair.

She was a complex patient, and I have yet to meet anyone even closely resembling her in all the years I have been a therapist.

On days like today, I find myself remembering our meetings, remembering the years we spent trying to get her out of the dark space in her head.

We got her out, eventually, but I don't know what she was steered into. She was very self-assured when she left, but there was something so unnerving about it all.

I never did hear from her. I never found out if she went to Malibu, and I don't know where she is or what she's doing now. Despite my attempts to make contact with her, she never responded.

It made me want to do something. I wanted to find her at first, but then I realized that Evelyn no longer has any obligation to us. If she ever wants help again, she'll have to walk through those doors on her own.

I used to think she would make her way back. I would walk out of work half expecting to see her coming up the walkway with something more to tell me about life and the irony of being.

But that never happened, and I think it's clear now that it never will. She's gone.

I find myself thinking about her family, too. After so many years of treating Evelyn, I got to know her family almost as much as I got to know her.

Evelyn was so worried about them when she left. I remember her telling me so, how she was so upset that their lives hadn't turned out well.

It's the thing that bothers me the most: That Evelyn thinks life didn't work out for any of them.

I wish I could tell her that it's not true, because I know things about her family that she doesn't, things I wish I could tell her now.

I know that James retired early because he had the financial means to, and created a foundation at Pepperdine in Elizabeth's name. I know that he is healthy and happy, a loving father and an even more loving grandfather.

I know that Jenavieve has a beautiful life with Max and their daughters, a life filled with joy. I know that she passes her days feeling that she is living her life the best way she knows how, and I know that her family is just as joyous as she.

I know that Madeline continues running her mother's company and does a good job with it. I know that she uses the site for good, making it a celebration of life. She found her way back to Noah, and the two fell even more in love than they were when they were kids.

And I know that Ashley met a good man, a kind and intelligent man her own age, with whom she became very happy. I know that she settled down with him in a nice home, and that the restraining order is altered so that she can see Grace from time to time.

These are the things I wish I could tell Evelyn, because they are so important for her to know. The Blair family turned out okay, more than okay, in the face of everything they went through. They created the beauty, and because they did so, they reaped the benefits of that beauty. They live beautiful lives. Each and every one of them.

***

I don't know if any of this is true, but it's true to me. After all, Evelyn said that the irony of it all is that we control what controls our lives in the first place.

And so I make this my reality. It is my reality that the Blairs turn out the way I want them to—comfortable, happy and satisfied with the outcomes of their actions. And because I know only my own reality, I am correct.

At least, this is what I tell myself.

For if I didn't, I truly would lose all the sanity I have left.

ACKNOWLEDGEMENTS

To my parents—Thank you for your unwavering belief in my abilities as both a writer and a person. You raised me to have big dreams and an even bigger work ethic. Without your support for this project, it never would have been published. Thank you, and I love you.

To my sisters—Thank you for your enthusiasm and support. I am lucky to be able to call my sisters my friends, and I love you both very much.

To my editor, Kristy—This book reads the way it does because of you. Your meticulous editing, open creativity, and complete kindness made this project a wonderful experience from start to finish. Thank you for treating me like a true writer and for propelling this project forward at all times. I truly would not have been able to do this without you.